THE BEAST OF ROSE VALLEY

To René,

enjoy the beast!

J.P. Barnett

LORESTALKER - Book 1

J.P. BARNETT

THE BEAST OF ROSE VALLEY
Lorestalker - 1

FIRST EDITION SOFTCOVER
ISBN: 1622530713
ISBN-13: 978-1-62253-071-7

Editor: Mike Robinson
Interior Designer: Lane Diamond

EVOLVED PUBLISHING™
www.EvolvedPub.com
Butler, Wisconsin, USA

Printed in Book Antiqua font.

BOOKS BY J.P. BARNETT

The LORESTALKER Series
The Beast of Rose Valley
The Kraken of Cape Madre (Coming Fall 2019)

CHAPTER 1

Jake Rollins had never seen an animal turned inside-out. A lifetime of horror movies had led him to expect a heaping mass of fake, syrupy goo. He swallowed hard, took a deep breath through his mouth to avoid the rotten stench, and knelt by the carcass, surprised at the sadness the lamb's horror-frozen face provoked in him. A gruesome reminder—not like he needed one—of life's fragility.

He expected to vomit, but nothing came up. He just stood there, staring with morbid curiosity at the lamb's two meaty red halves. It didn't seem possible or natural.

Surely, this was just a terrible prank.

Tall and lean, Steve Witmer stood beside Jake, easily exuding physical strength without the unnecessary bulk of large muscles. He wore Wrangler Jeans, an old t-shirt, and well-loved, scuffed-up cowboy boots. His maroon Texas A&M baseball cap tilted low. The colors and the logos changed sometimes, but Steve looked pretty much the same every day. Keeping up a ranch left no time for fancy fashion.

"You boys do this for publicity, did ya?" Sheriff Cam Donner asked, circling the carcass.

Strangely stocky for a tall man, the sheriff stood six-foot-three and barrel-chested. He wore a mustache in the customary way of small-town law enforcement, with his face shaded by a straw cowboy hat, and his eyes shielded by those large, dark aviator glasses sold exclusively at some secret cop store.

Though all three men were born the same year, Sheriff Donner still called them boys. Twenty years ago, they'd walked the same stage to receive their high school diplomas, and before that they had been an inseparable trio of friends. Somewhere along the way, Cam became a bully and never grew out of it, though Jake had to admit that it had served him well as the town sheriff.

"No, sir," Steve said. "Ralph just found it this morning. Just making the rounds like always. Seemed odd to find an animal ripped in half like this, so I thought I should call it in."

The sheriff looked at the remains one more time. "Looks like a coyote got to it to me."

Utterly preposterous, and everyone knew it—even Jake, who had spent a career in the air-conditioned peace of a cubicle. For all the predators roaming the Rose Valley countryside, none of them could have perpetrated this horror. This was something new and vicious.

Jake wiped his brow. The sun barely peeked across the horizon, but that didn't stop the heat from permeating his clothes. Dying brown grass carpeted the fields, and even the small hills the locals liked to call "mountains" had long ago given up their greenery, serving as a reminder that this particular Texas summer threatened to break all records.

While Steve and Cam squabbled about the likelihood of a coyote, Jake pulled out his cell phone and re-read the text message he'd sent to Shandi Mason earlier that morning. The message indicator showed *Read* instead of *Sent*. Good. If Shandi had gotten his message, then she'd be here soon. A person could get anywhere in Rose Valley in just a matter of minutes.

"Ain't no reason to get everybody's panties in a bunch over this," Cam said. "Maybe it was a coyote. Maybe it wasn't. But if you make a stink over this, every rancher in town'll be up my ass about it."

"Not for nothin', Sheriff," Steve retorted. "but if we *don't* tell the other ranchers about this, it's just going to cost us all a lot of money. We need to let people know so they can take proper precautions. Keep an eye out."

Cam pulled his sunglasses off and moved aggressively towards Steve. "Just clean it up and keep it to yourself, y'hear me?"

Steve didn't answer. He headed back towards a nearby four-wheeler and fetched a pair of gloves from the bed of the trailer. Though strong and self-assured, Steve tended to avoid fights. Like Jake, Steve knew the politics of Rose Valley. Though Cam didn't hold the highest seat of power, crossing him promised to be a dangerous proposition, even for the mayor.

The sheriff put his sunglasses back on and headed back towards his brand-new suburban, its frame sitting high off the ground on comically large tires, its windows tinted darker than legally allowed. It must have cost the tax-payers a fortune. Cam stood as near royalty in Rose Valley, though. He could have anything he wanted. The title of Sheriff carried a lot of weight.

For his plan to work, Jake needed the sheriff to be there when Shandi arrived. He needed to make sure that Shandi would see the scene before Steve cleaned it up, that she could confront Cam directly—on record—about why this lamb had become the star of its own horror movie.

"Cam!" Jake hollered after the sheriff.

Cam turned, an irritated scowl on his face. "It's Sheriff Donner, son."

Jake fought hard to not roll his eyes. "Sorry, sir. Sheriff Donner, sir. Won't happen again, sir."

Jake saluted haphazardly, caring very little about the accuracy of the gesture. Cam had never been in the military. He held an elected position in a town of just over two-thousand people, which he wielded with reckless abandon, but godhood still barely escaped his grasp. Jake and Cam had shared a friendship once. To Jake, they would always be equals, regardless of Cam's asinine arrogance.

Cam looked at Jake for a few seconds, clearly considering unholstering his gun. "What do you want?"

"How similar is this to the goat over at Serendipity?" Jake popped off.

Cam's nostrils flared as he stomped back towards Jake. "Ain't nothin' the same. Just a dead goat. For pete's sake, this is a ranching community. Animals die all the damn time. Why do you boys gotta go make a mountain out of a mole hill?"

Technically true. Animals *did* die all the time. Of heat exhaustion. Of predation. Of old age. Of various veterinary ailments. But not from bifurcation. Such a cause of death wholly defied the natural order of things in Rose Valley—or anywhere else, for that matter.

Jake did his best to meet the sheriff's gaze. Jake loved Rose Valley. He'd spent his youth frolicking through town, building cherished memories. But even paradise suffered from the tarnish of politics, and Jake had no interest in playing them.

The sound of gravel crunching under tires interrupted the conversation. Jake glanced over and grinned. Success! Yes, he could fumble through a fight with the sheriff, but Shandi Mason practically owed her career to it.

Her green Toyota Camry pulled up behind the sheriff's Suburban, blocking his exit route. The door of the car flew open and Shandi shot out like a cannonball, a Nikon camera on her hip and her cell phone out in front of her, serving as a voice recorder. Unbridled purpose burdened her every step, displaying her full intent on taking down—or, at the very least, embarrassing—the sheriff.

She walked towards Cam. "Sheriff Donner. There have been reports of livestock mutilations across Rose Valley. Care to comment?"

Shandi was short— certainly compared to Cam—but somehow, she made the sheriff seem small and weak.

Cam bristled. "Dammit, Shandi. How the hell did you find out about this?"

"Anonymous tip," she shot back.

Cam looked directly at Jake. "Anonymous, my ass."

Shandi's bright, piercing green eyes dared the sheriff to press the issue. She'd pulled her fiery red hair back into a pony tail, unveiling in full her striking, determined features. Jake knew she hated exercise, but apparently good genetics, an active job, and the burdens of being a single mother kept her fit and attractive.

While certainly qualified for bigger and better things, she'd remained in Rose Valley, and worked now for the Rose Valley Reporter, writing rote articles about the drudgery of small-town life. A rare story like this excited her inner investigative journalist.

"Come on, Shandi," the sheriff pleaded. "You've got more important things to do. It's just a dead lamb."

In high school, Shandi had run in the same circle as these three men, even though her parents tried to keep her away from the older boys. She had been particularly close to Jake, but their friendship had evaporated when Jake left town for nearly two decades. Since his return, they'd begun to reconnect, and Jake hoped this lead would further strengthen their bond.

"A lamb *and* a goat, Sheriff. Both torn in half. Neither one eaten. You don't find that strange?"

The sheriff sighed, his broad shoulders slumping down. He marched back to his Suburban in a juvenile huff with no more words, and in an act of minor defiance, drove through the field to escape Shandi's blockade and what had become hostile territory.

Shandi grinned as she turned towards Steve and Jake, entirely too pleased with herself. "Mornin', boys!"

She pulled the Nikon from her hip and, without permission, started taking pictures of the bloody pieces of the lamb. Steve didn't object, but he did throw an exasperated look to Jake, one full of unspoken memories of the endless mischief Jake and Shandi heaped on him over the years.

"So, whadyathink, guys? What did this? I mean, ripped in two? That's insane. Nothing could do that, right?" She talked with a fevered clip, unlike most in Rose Valley.

Steve shrugged. "Who knows. I'm going to have to hire some extra help to keep an eye out, though. I can't afford to be losing my sheep to whatever did this."

"I really appreciate the text," Shandi said, flashing a quick wink Jake's way. "The sheriff made Bill over at Serendipity clean it all up before I could get there. A picture is worth a thousand words, they say."

"It's a pretty gruesome picture." Jake said.

"Do you think cheetahs could do this?" she said. "They've got some over at Relics Wildlife Reserve. Maybe they got out."

"No idea. Seems like it would take two cheetahs to rip it in half like this. And then why wouldn't they eat it?"

Shandi dropped the Nikon back to her hip. "Yeah. Good point. Why kill anything if you're not going to eat it?"

With Shandi done with her pictures, Steve walked in, picked up the back half of the lamb and tossed it into the four-wheeler's trailer. Jake could tell he just wanted to move on with his day. Steve had a lot of work to do and speculating about wild animals didn't feed the chickens or move the sheep.

"Sheriff says it was a coyote." Jake rolled his eyes, making it clear that he didn't buy into the theory.

Shandi laughed. "Right. I think it's more believable that aliens did this."

Steve picked up the front half of the lamb. "Probably just some prank. School's starting up again soon. The kids get crazy towards the end of the summer."

Shandi replied, "Pretty macabre prank."

She glanced over the scene one more time. Satisfied that she had gotten what she needed, she approached Jake and embraced him in a quick, light hug.

"Thanks again for the tip, Jake. You should get out more. You're good people." She flashed him a wistful smile before turning to Steve. "Have a good one, Steve."

Steve nodded and touched the brim of his ball cap. "You too, Shandi."

She walked over to her Camry and climbed in. Within moments, Shandi tore away from Watermelon Ranch, returning things to the quiet bleating of sheep and the laid-back unflappability of the ranch-hands. The ranch felt empty without Shandi's energy.

She would write one hell of a story. Perhaps about the Sheriff's Department trying to hide grisly livestock mutilations from the masses. Or maybe a piece about how the sheriff failed to provide protection for the citizens of Rose Valley from a dangerous creature.

Whatever her angle, Jake knew that Shandi would take any opportunity she could to crucify her ex-husband.

What kind of creature could, or would want to, wreak this much havoc? Jake imagined a predator lurking in the shadows of Rose Valley, unknown to science and poised to shock the world with its existence. He imagined Bigfoot, or chupacabras, or something else newer and more dangerous. After a year of rehabilitation from a car accident that nearly killed him, the mystery of an unknown creature stoked a fire within him that had been dormant for far too long.

He had a mystery to solve, even if it meant embracing his place in the world once again.

CHAPTER 2

Shandi slammed the paper down on the desk of her editor, Dan Carter. His slow, measured demeanor brought into question his fitness to run the paper now, but he had shepherded the Rose Valley Reporter through decades of news.

"What the hell, Dan?" Shandi yelled, her flushed complexion matching her hair.

Shandi reached over and flipped the paper to page seven, tearing multiple pages along the fold as she went. There, a meager headline flatly stated: "Coyotes Attack Local Ranches." Shandi's name graced the byline, but one would be hard pressed to find any remnants of her original article.

Dan remained calm. Dan was always calm, maddeningly so.

"I know, I know," Dan said, throwing up his hands as if to physically defend himself. "Look. The sheriff called and had some concerns about what you might print. It's the same story, Shandi. It's just less editorialized."

He had a point. She couldn't think clearly when it came to Cam, and her writing betrayed her attempted professionalism. Her original article focused as much on character assassination as the incident. She wouldn't admit that out loud, though, especially to Dan.

"The headline is misleading," she said. "There's no proof that coyotes did this."

Dan peered over the bifocals that clung to the tip of his nose. "The article is clear on the fact that the Sheriff's Department *says* that coyotes did it."

"That's a load of crap, Dan. You've seen the photos. You know a coyote didn't do that. You also know that most of our readers don't even read the articles unless the headline is salacious. That headline pretty much guarantees no one will even read it. What happened to journalistic integrity?"

Dan sighed. "If you want journalistic integrity, go to the big city. In Rose Valley, we have to play by different rules. One of those is to not piss off the most powerful person in town."

She couldn't imagine leaving her job with the Rose Valley Reporter. Rose Valley was her home, along with all of its annoyances and idiosyncrasies. Dan knew that. He'd encouraged her to leave more than once if she couldn't adapt to the ideals of a small-town paper. He'd tried so hard to mentor her into mastering the politics of Rose Valley, but it seemed to have been the one lesson she deftly evaded. Ironically, her refusal to learn that lesson made her one of the best journalists in the Reporter's history.

"Will you at least admit that it wasn't a coyote that killed that lamb?" Shandi pleaded, "Let me keep investigating. Find more evidence. Let me find something to refute the claims of the sheriff."

"Of course. Just remember that it's the news we're after, not the sheriff," Dan said, shifting his gaze back to his computer.

Shandi skulked back to her office. As she approached her desk, she noticed a piece of paper on her chair; an expense report she needed to sign. She plopped down, grabbed the nearest pen, and quickly scribbled her signature over her typed name, *Shandi M. Donner.*

Just looking at her legal name filled her with rage. Though she used her maiden name on her work, she avoided going through the bother of changing it back legally.

Every document she signed and piece of mail that she sorted, made her angry with Cam all over again. She should have gotten over it long ago, she told herself, but his arrogance and aloofness always got to her. Glimpsing something real in him, she'd given him the benefit of the doubt, exposed all of herself to him even as others had warned her at the beginning of their marriage.

Cam Donner worked hard to suppress the genuine, caring part of himself, burying it deeply under layers of machismo. She'd pried it up for a time, but she didn't have the strength to win the war of emotional attrition. Once he became the Sheriff, all hope was lost.

He'd protested when she left, at least. She liked to believe that it meant that some part of him did love her at one point, though it might've just been fear about how a divorce would reflect on him as a public figure in Rose Valley. It didn't seem to have affected him too much. He'd won re-election after his first term in a landslide.

Shandi switched her monitor back on. As she began typing in her password, a sudden knock brought her attention to the door. She looked up and saw Geneva, the paper's secretary. Her genuine kindness lit up any room, but she didn't have many skills. Shandi always imagined secretaries at real papers as upstart young journalists out to make a name for themselves, but the Rose Valley Reporter sadly lacked any upstart.

"We got a call from an employee over at Relics Wildlife Reserve," Geneva said. "Something about the cheetahs escaping? I'm not sure. Thought you might want to cover it."

Shandi immediately grabbed her Nikon and headed out the door. Cheetahs? That was hardly any fun at all. She'd hoped for a more exotic ending to the mystery of the livestock mutilations. It seemed strange that the reserve wouldn't have reported the missing cheetahs earlier. If they'd escaped early enough to have mutilated the goat out at Serendipity Ranch, that would mean that Relics had sat on the news for almost a week before calling anyone. That didn't make sense.

Her drive to the Relics Wildlife Reserve took less than ten minutes. Having visited the park numerous times for various stories over the years, she knew exactly how to navigate the winding roads to the cheetah exhibit. Pulling up and finding no sign of Cam's suburban, she felt the release of previously-hidden anxiety.

She slipped out of her car and surveyed the scene. A number of Relics jeeps circled around, as well as one police car. A quick inventory of the personnel told her that she'd be dealing with Deputy Dub Higgins. Dub represented someone she could work with—and manipulate—to get the story she wanted.

Deputy Higgins and a Relics Wildlife Reserve Ranger stood near a large hole in the fence. The title of "ranger" only meant something in the context of the corporation that ran the park. They shared nothing in common with the famed Texas Rangers or the National Parks & Wildlife Service.

As she walked up to the group, Dub's face lit up in a huge smile. The ranger, however, winced at her approach.

"Mornin', Shandi!" Deputy Higgins hollered, grinning.

Dub carried naive sweetness in abundant supply. After being elected Sheriff, Cam had avoided even the simplest request from Shandi. So if she needed an errand to be run or a multi-person chore completed, Dub valiantly filled the void. Shandi suspected that Dub acted of his own accord, not out of duty to Cam.

"Hey Dub. What's going on here?"

Before Dub could answer, the ranger spoke up. "Ms. Mason. I'm not sure how you were notified of this, but we have it under control. No need to make a scene. We don't need any bad publicity, you understand."

Shandi vaguely recognized him from school, though she was more familiar with his popular sister. Shandi couldn't quite place his name. "I'm not here to cause trouble. Just trying to report the news."

Immediately the ranger seemed to loosen up. "Someone broke the fence here and some of our cheetahs escaped. This pen held our new mother, Adalina, and her two cubs."

Shandi pulled her phone out and popped open the voice memo app. "Do you mind if I record this?"

The ranger looked slightly uncomfortable, but gave a curt nod. Shandi requested he repeat his last statement so she could record it. A name like Adalina stood little chance of sticking in her brain otherwise.

"Thanks," Shandi said, being sure to flash him her best smile. "So, have you recovered the three escaped cheetahs yet?"

Even from her peripheral vision, Shandi noticed Dub shift nervously next to her. The ranger glanced across the cage almost imperceptibly, causing Shandi to follow his gaze to an area of the cage littered with tufts of cheetah fur.

The ranger cleared his throat. "We're actively searching for only, uh, two of the cheetahs."

A second glance revealed bits of cheetah carcass mixed with the fur; one of the cubs, no doubt. The poor thing had been ripped to pieces. Blood and entrails were strewn about.

"And why did you wait so long to report this?"

The ranger seemed confused by the question. "It happened last night. We reported it first thing this morning."

Last night? That seemed impossible. If the cheetahs had escaped last night, then they couldn't have possibly perpetrated the livestock mutilations.

It hit her all at once. Whatever had mutilated the goat at Serendipity, and the lamb at Watermelon, had likely killed this cub. She looked at the fence again. She assumed earlier that it had been cut open, but the jagged, uneven points of the metal suggested otherwise, each link stretched to the breaking point.

Her mind raced as she turned towards Dub. "Are there any suspects yet? And don't say coyotes."

Dub pulled his straw cowboy hat from his head and wiped his brow with the back of his hand. He stalled for time while he thought about his answer. Shandi recognized his discomfort about talking to her—Cam would surely disapprove—but he liked her too much to take a hard stance with her.

"Well, it obviously wasn't coyotes, no. Maybe some kids thought it would be funny or something. Or maybe some of those hippies from Austin drove up. Some of 'em don't care for Relics keeping these wild animals all caged up like this."

"Thanks, deputy. Seems pretty cruel for anyone to do that to a cheetah cub. Surely the mother would have defended her cub from that."

"Yes, Ms. Mason," the ranger interjected. "We would expect so. We can only assume that whoever did this took the other two. Maybe to sell. Cheetahs could fetch a hefty sum to the right buyer."

Dub shifted his weight and glanced sheepishly at Shandi. He hid some tasty nugget of information, she could tell, something that might run counter to the ranger's theory, perhaps. If neither Dub nor the Ranger could be persuaded to tell her, she would just have to find something herself.

"Thanks," Shandi said. "Mind if I take a look around, take a few pictures? No bad publicity—I promise. Getting this in the paper might help you find the perpetrator."

The ranger assented with a nod, clearly unhappy with the situation. No doubt, he didn't have full jurisdiction in this case, and would have to answer for his cooperation to his superiors later. The cold-hearted journalist in Shandi didn't care much if the ranger got in trouble.

She walked around the scene and took some pictures. Between the fence and the dismembered cub, Shandi became increasingly intrigued with each new piece of evidence. The slaughter of the cub certainly seemed like it could be related to the livestock mutilations, but tearing a fence in half required even more strength.

As she snapped macro shots of the fence, she glanced down and noticed blood on the ground outside of the enclosure. She walked back to the cub. Her skills lacked much in the way of zoology training, but all the pieces of the cub seemed to be accounted for, so where did the blood outside of the cage come from?

She took note of where the ranger and deputy had gone. The ranger sat in his jeep, frantically barking into his cell phone. Deputy Higgins leaned over the hood of his squad car, filling out paperwork. They were separated. Perfect.

Shandi walked over to Dub and lightly brushed her hand across his back to get his attention. His damp uniform practically dripped with sweat. By the time Dub looked up from his paperwork, Shandi greeted him with a fixed stare and a wide smile.

"Off the record here, Dub. Are the other cheetahs even alive?"

Dub looked her up and down, possibly to figure out whether she hid a recording device, or possibly because her tank top revealed a little too much cleavage and his height gave him a good view.

"Dunno. Maybe. Maybe not."

"What about that extra blood over there? Is that from one of the other cheetahs?"

Dub glanced over at it. "Oh that. No. That's from a gazelle. They found it dead there at the opening to the fence. All in one piece and everything. Something managed to snap its neck and then ate through its belly. The ranger thinks maybe they used it to lure the cheetahs into submission or something. He thinks it's the cheetahs that ate out the belly."

"Seems strange that someone would kill a gazelle by snapping its neck, right?" Shandi said. "Why not just rope it and lead it over here while it was still alive? Or shoot it."

Dub shrugged. "I don't know. The fence is the most suspicious thing to me. I'm not sure how they opened it that way. I would have expected the links to be cut, not broken. And I'd think that dismantling the door would be far easier than going through the middle of the fence."

Dub offered a good point. Certainly, even in an adrenaline-fueled rage, Shandi would have no hope of breaking the chain link like that, and she suspected few humans on earth could manage it.

Shandi nodded. "Thanks, Dub. I appreciate it. Tell Marie I said hi."

Dub smiled back. "No problem, Shandi. She keeps saying how we ought to have y'all over for dinner. I'm just always working, ya know."

Shandi laughed. "Oh, I know. Cam runs a tight ship. Let me know if you hear anything more that you think we should release to the public. You have my number."

"Will do. Have a good one."

Shandi returned to her car. Clearly, there had to be some relationship between this and the other mutilations. She would need to compare photos, maybe talk to Steve or Bill again, then cross-reference all the information to get closer to the truth.

Finally, after years of reporting on school lunches, there was something *real* to report in Rose Valley.

CHAPTER 3

The lithe, bedraggled cat carried her kitten into the brush and Jake followed, squatting down to fit himself into the tiny burrow she'd made. He sat cross-legged across from them as the mother ran her tongue over the shivering kitten. The little hollow was filled with sadness. They didn't know he was there. He was invisible. He shifted in discomfort, until finally he couldn't stand it and squeezed back out into the cool night air.

A splash came from his left and he turned to see his ex-wife, Liz, standing in a creek, fully dressed but soaking wet. She reached down and splashed some droplets his way, but when they reached him, they instantly evaporated.

She ran from him, rounded a corner and disappeared. Jake rushed to catch up and found only the mouth of a cave. A wave of frigid air washed over him as he stepped inside.

A campfire sat in the middle of the cave, but he couldn't feel the warmth of the flames. Around the fire sat various animals, all of them eerily personified, sitting cross-legged as a human would. He moved to join their circle and they vanished, leaving only him and the dying fire. He sank to the ground, desperately trying to feel warm again.

Suddenly, Liz appeared beside him, still drenched in water though she now wore a one-piece bathing suit, her hair flat and stringy against her shoulders. He stood up as she put her arms out in front of her as if to hug him, but instead she pushed hard against his chest, sending him stumbling backwards into the fire.

The flames licked at his skin, sending sharp pain through his body. He swatted vainly at the flames and, screamed, but the screams only came out in piercing growls. His bones rattled, he gritted his teeth and then his head struck the ground with an agonizing thud –

***

Jake snapped awake, his chest heaving from the nightmare. He tried to hold on to the particulars, but as usual they'd slipped away into darkness. Memories and thoughts flooded his mind, and he felt an almost electric alertness that would surely keep him awake for hours.

This dance of dreams and wakefulness had become all too frequent in the last year. Usually, his nightly litany of regrets involved his divorce, but, lately, unknown images of vicious predators had been coming to him. Memories of Liz intermingled with ominous, threatening creatures; riffs on scary cryptids that had frightened him as a child but fascinated him as an adult.

Before the divorce, Jake and Liz had visited Scotland. Liz wanted to experience the history and the people, but Jake insisted that they squeeze in a visit to Loch Ness. For him, it represented a pilgrimage of sorts. When he thought about that day, he could still feel the sharp Scottish air whip against his face, while he prayed for some vestige of his childhood fantasies to pop up from the serene waters of the lake. Unsurprisingly, they saw nothing out of the ordinary.

A memory randomly popped into his mind of a woman who had commented on his abandoned blog. He couldn't remember her name, but she'd left a comment on a post about chupacabras, chiding him for getting some of the facts wrong, and going out of her way to document his inaccuracies in excruciating detail.

At the time, he reacted only in annoyance. What kind of troll scours the internet to correct facts about non-existent creatures? He wondered now, though, if that same person could be helpful. Perhaps there existed previous reports of animals being mutilated in the way the lamb had been. This lady could maybe help him solve the mystery.

Without turning on any lights, he felt his way into the other room to his laptop, the bright light of the screen blinding him as it came on.

Jake popped open a web browser and went to his blog. He hadn't updated it in years, and no one visited it any longer. Blogs had largely fallen out of fashion once long-form posts gave way to tweets of 140 characters or fewer. He clicked *cryptids* in the category list on the right, which navigated him to a list of articles that he'd posted under the heading *Cryptid Corner*.

He scanned the list until he found the article about chupacabras and clicked through to the comments section, which contained only one from someone named "Skylar Brooks."

With a lead to go on, Jake searched for the name and got a number of hits. He scanned through the results and quickly got a picture: Skylar Brooks was a grizzled old man with a handlebar mustache. He owned a museum in Missouri, had written multiple books, and—most importantly of all—had a Wikipedia page documenting his career as a cryptozoologist.

Maybe the lamb had been killed by a wild animal. Or perhaps it had been a high school prank. However unlikely, Jake still entertained the idea that something else entirely lurked in the shadows of Rose Valley. Something unknown. And maybe Mr. Brooks could help him classify this thing.

He messaged Shandi:

Jake Rollins: Hey. Weird request. Could you send me the pictures you took of the lamb out here?

While waiting for a response, Jake passed the time by looking through Skylar Brooks' biography. The man boasted various degrees in biology and zoology. His father had served as a cryptozoologist before Skylar and garnered some renown within the community for his nationwide investigations. Skylar had even consulted on a number of History Channel specials, though Jake always struggled to connect history and cryptids.

Shandi Mason: Something is wrong with you, Jake Rollins. Check your email.

The animated ellipsis came up again, followed by another message.

Shandi Mason: Please don't hang these on your walls. I'd hate to think you were a psychopath. :P

Jake smiled, sent a thumbs-up emoji, and a then a proper response.

Jake Rollins: No promises. This place could use some decorating. Thanks for the quick response.

He downloaded the pictures and started a new email to Skylar Brooks. He typed up a brief description of the mutilations, asked for any information that Mr. Brooks could provide, and attached the photos.

Re-reading the email, he questioned whether he should send it. Then, with one hasty tap, the email was off.

With that out of the way, Jake leaned back in his chair. With any luck, Mr. Brooks would write back with some information. Even information that ruled out an unknown predator would be helpful. It would be another piece for the puzzle, and something he could forward on to Shandi.

Another ding from his chat app.

Shandi Mason: Why are you up so late?

Jake Rollins: I could ask the same of you.

Shandi Mason: Working. Papers don't write themselves, ya know.

Jake Rollins: Fair enough. What ya workin' on?

Shandi Mason: Story about Relics. Some of their cheetahs were kidnapped. Catnapped? Cheetahnapped, I guess. lol

Jake Rollins: Really? That's crazy. We were just talking about those cheetahs. Do they know who did it?

Shandi Mason: No. The park seems to want to say they were stolen for money, but it doesn't really add up. One of the cheetah cubs was torn to shreds like that sheep out there. I'll send you the pics for your blood & gore psychopath collection. :P

Jake laughed softly. Amazing. Well, amazing as something involving grisly mutilations could be. The kill count tallied up to a goat, a sheep, and now a cheetah cub. Jake took the fact that the rampage continued as a promising sign. More evidence meant a greater chance to actually get to the bottom of whatever roamed through Rose Valley.

Jake Rollins: Maybe it was coyotes :P

Shandi Mason: haha maybe so.

Jake Rollins: What does His Majesty Sheriff Cam Donner think about it?

Shandi Mason: Dunno. Haven't talked to him about it. Dub was on the scene.

Jake Rollins: Ah. Lucky you. That boy will do anything for you.

Shandi Mason: Yeah. Unfortunately, it comes at the cost of him ogling me like a piece of meat.

Jake Rollins: Can you blame him? Marie is such a dog. :P

Shandi Mason: lol. Right? I hear men don't go for that exotic, sexy foreigner vibe. Not when they can have a short, be-freckled redhead.

Shandi's appearance didn't warrant self-criticism. Her height seemed about right to Jake—not too short—and he liked the dusting of freckles over her face. Any man would agree that Shandi Mason possessed an abundance of eye-pleasing qualities. With their long-rooted friendship, though, thinking of her that way almost felt like betrayal.

Jake Rollins: Some guys like freckles and red hair.

Shandi Mason: Let me know when you find him.

Jake Rollins: Yes, ma'am. I'll put my feelers out and check with all my guy friends.

Shandi Mason: Oh. So... Steve, then? I'm fairly certain he's not interested.

Jake Rollins: lol. Yeah... I suppose you're right.

The conversation hit a dead end, but Jake wanted it to continue. Since his return to Rose Valley, he had become a hermit, but Shandi had gone out of her way to talk to him, to make him feel welcome again. People who abandoned Rose Valley straight out of high school did not always receive a warm reception. Shandi represented a neutral zone. Safe harbor. Talking with her provided peace and sanity in a town that largely rejected him.

Jake Rollins: How do you do it?

Shandi Mason: Do what?

Jake Rollins: Work all the time like you do.

She didn't respond right away. Jake waited, worried that she had gotten distracted with other things. To kill the time, he absent-mindedly clicked back over to his email to check for new messages, disappointed to find none.

Another ding. He clicked back to the chat app. A picture was loading. As it came in, he saw Shandi, holding a glass of red wine towards the camera. She pointed at it with her other hand, her mouth turned up in a goofy grin. Her red mane was tied back in the usually messy ponytail, adorable wisps of hair framing her face. The old t-shirt she wore looked comfortable and relaxing, sending a chill up Jake's spine as he suddenly remembered that he wore no shirt.

Shandi Mason: That's my secret.

Jake Rollins: I thought wine made people sleepy.

Shandi Mason: Nah. It turns me into a Pulitzer prize winning journalist. :P

Jake Rollins: In your head, I guess.

Shandi Mason: Ouch! You'll see someday. The only thing holding me back is that nobody actually reads the Rose Valley Reporter.

Jake Rollins: That's not true. There are at least 10 solid readers.

Shandi Mason: lol. I stand corrected.

Jake Rollins: I always read your stuff.

Shandi Mason: You don't even subscribe to the paper.

Jake Rollins. Well, yeah. But Steve does.

Shandi Mason: How sweet. You steal someone's trash for me. What a devoted fan! :P

Jake Rollins: Aww. Be nice. We're only thinking of the environment by sharing.

Shandi Mason: I'm just teasing you. I'm excited about all of this. I just gotta get Dan to stop censoring it.

Jake Rollins: Meh. It's not really his fault. Cam's got his nuts in a vice.

Shandi Mason: LOL. Cam has this whole town's nuts in a vice.

Another break in conversation. Jake yawned. Finally, his mind seemed to be winding down.

Shandi Mason: Anyway. I think this wine may actually be making me sleepy. Who knew?

Jake Rollins: Um. Me? I knew.

Shandi Mason: Oh, shut up, smartass. :P

Jake Rollins: =X

Shandi Mason: :) Get some sleep. You need it.

Jake Rollins: Okay. Good luck on the article

Shandi Mason: Thanks, Jake. G'night xoxoxo

Jake Rollins: night, Shandi

He fumbled through the dark and threw himself back into the bed. He felt sleepy and safe now, his mind wandering around aimlessly as he drifted off. He thought of Shandi's green eyes, twinkling as she pointed at her wine. And then of Liz; the divorce. And then of the mutilations. And back to Shandi, who morphed into Liz...

Cheetahs...

Goats...

Sheep...

Cryptids...

The accident...

Sleep.

CHAPTER 4

The morning sun crept through the blinds. Jake vaguely knew he needed to wake up, but his mind was caught in a loop of terror. He saw the Arrowhead Research truck coming out of nowhere, slamming into his car and exploding in a shower of sparks and glass. Fire surged through his body, the same excruciating pain from that night. He fought to escape it, some part of him insisting that only the memory haunted him...

...until the sunlight caught his eyes, and he jolted awake.

Jake sat straight up, heart pounding, his right leg throbbing in pain. Most days came with minimal aching, but occasionally some part of his body would inexplicably betray him. No doubt the pain had summoned the memory to his subconscious.

He glanced at the clock. 9:16am. Later than he usually slept.

The pain from the accident waxed and waned these days, enough that he no longer kept his painkillers next to his bed, so he hobbled towards the bathroom to fetch them. On his way, he grabbed his phone from the nightstand and pulled up his email. He sighed.

Nothing from Skylar Brooks.

Jake washed down two hydrocodone and looked at himself in the mirror. Despite having overslept, he looked haggard, worn out. A shower would do him good, but the clock demanded that he get on the road. If he missed his game with Bernard, he'd never hear the end of it.

As he studied himself in the mirror, he inspected his scars, some of them finally losing distinction against his healthier skin. They would never go away, but maybe before long he could pass them off as the remnants of a badass story instead of the painful memories of months of rehab and surgeries. His arms looked pretty good, muscle definition peeking out from scarred skin, conjuring the briefest glimpse of Jake from a previous era.

He stumbled back to the bedroom and opened the tiny closet door. He'd meant to stay in Steve's guest house for only a few months, but almost a year had now ticked away.

He slipped on an old t-shirt that had once fit him snugly, but now hung loosely on his frame. Putting on his jeans proved a bit more of a struggle with the throbbing in his leg, but he finally managed to get them on. He opted for flip flops, both because of the weather and the fact that bending over to tie his sneakers would invite too much pain.

He grabbed his keys and wallet and walked out into the burning sun. Steve's kindness knew no bounds, having provided even an old ranch truck for Jake to use. The truck started with a deep rumble. The air conditioning on the old Ford had given up years ago, but Jake didn't mind. Driving this rusty monstrosity enlivened him, reminding him of their high school days when this very same truck served as Steve's ride. It had been brand new back then. Now it was edging toward being an antique.

Jake took off down the gravel road to the main highway, waving at Steve who tended to horses. Jake had no interest in becoming a rancher. If Steve cared that Jake didn't help out around the ranch, he never let on.

After a few minutes of driving, Jake pulled into Mikey's Burger Shack. The perfectly rectangular building sagged under years of trying to survive its shoddy workmanship, first as a bank, then a Burger King, and now the new home of Mikey's. Burger King learned the hard way—just one in a long line of chain restaurants—that there existed little room for a corporate presence in Rose Valley.

Jake jerked open the door. Before he had time to even register the crowd, he heard Bernard's voice: "You're late, Rollins."

"Yeah, yeah. Sorry, Bernard. Overslept."

"Sit down. It's your turn," Bernard said, motioning to the chess board in front of him.

Jake slid into the booth. That last game had ended in Jake's defeat, and today was his chance to reclaim his honor. Jake studied the board briefly, quickly realizing that Bernard waited for him to make a move. Bernard had started without him with the classic white opening. The first few moves of their games was always the same.

The waitress quietly slipped in and placed a styrofoam cup of coffee next to Jake. He took a big gulp—the coffee at Mikey's rarely exceeded the temperature of a pleasantly warm bath.

"I s'pose you heard about the killing out at Watermelon Ranch, being that you're a permanent guest there and all," Bernard said nonchalantly as he moved his knight out.

"Yeah, of course. I saw it with my own eyes. It was some gruesome stuff. Sheriff says it was coyotes, but there's no way."

Bernard took a sip of his own coffee. "Mmmhmm. Weren't no coyote. It was the beast."

Jake stopped looking at the board and looked up at Bernard, who sat there expressionless. "The beast?"

"Sure 'nuff. I ain't never seen it. It's been a long time since anyone has. But my pops used to talk about him all the time. Went around killing all the animals back in '42. You gonna move?"

Jake moved his knight out in response before continuing, "Did they catch it?"

Bernard laughed. "You cain't catch the beast. He just does what he pleases and then goes back into hiding. He shows up every now and again. It ain't no wonder that he's showing back up now. It's been a long while."

Jake went through the motions of continuing the chess game, but his mind raced to process the intrigue of Bernard's tale. Was it possible that Rose Valley had its own cryptid that he had never heard about? It seemed unlikely, given his obsession with such things.

"Anybody ever see it?" Jake asked.

"Pops said he saw it once. Used to tell us the story when we'd go out campin'. Scared the bejesus out of my sister. I wasn't ever scared, though. He ain't never hurt nobody intentionally." Bernard leaned back in the booth and took another sip of his coffee. Both men had silently agreed to put the game on hold.

Jake tilted forward, propped up on his elbows. "What did it look like?"

"Pops reckoned that it was a man gone mad. Looked like a man, but feral. No recognizing in his eyes. He was big and strong and he ripped up animals like they was made of paper. Pops said others claimed that he was hairy. Had glowing eyes. Sharp teeth, too.

But Pops never saw none of that. Ol' Pops tried to chase him. Fired at him a couple of times. Swore to us that he hit him, but the beast just kept runnin'. Faster than Pops could keep up."

Bernard took another sip of coffee before continuing. "Pops lost half his sheep that year. Took a big hit. I was in mama's belly at the time, so I came into the world when Pops didn't have no money. When he was sore with me, Pops would say that he wished the beast had killed the rest of his sheep so that he could have had an excuse to orphan me."

Jake's head spun with these new puzzle pieces. Though probably just Rose Valley folklore, he thrilled at the possibility that there was a kernel of truth inside this story.

"Why didn't they hunt it down?" Jake prodded.

"There weren't a lot of men 'round back then on account of the war. Pops had a bad case of the gout, so they let him be. I reckon Pops didn't think he could take the beast down all by hisself."

"Come on, Bernard. Are you serious? Is this for real?"

Bernard put three fingers up. "I swear, Jake. Scout's honor. And you can believe me on that, too. I'm an honest-to-god Eagle Scout. Ain't got no reason to lie about it."

Bernard leaned forward and made his next belated move. Jake obliged and began playing on autopilot, already resigned to the fact that he'd lose today's game as well.

Years of amateur research had told him that any cryptid that stood a chance of being real required a big enough area and enough resources to support a breeding population. This thing couldn't have been alive since 1942, but it may have birthed offspring. He didn't know the exact numbers, but there would have to be dozens, if not hundreds, of these creatures for them to stick around that long.

The rural areas of Rose Valley remained largely uninhabited, but it seemed impossible that such a violent creature could remain undetected for more than seventy-five years.

But maybe it hadn't. Maybe there *had* been sightings and mutilations misattributed to things like coyote attacks. He would need to check old copies of the Rose Valley Reporter, but how? Had they digitized their catalog?

Jake exposed his King without noticing.

Bernard squealed, "Checkmate!"

CHAPTER 5

Macy held her knees together as tightly as she could as the fields *whooshed* by on either side of the road. She never dreamed that Wes would force himself on her, but then again, she didn't want to give him the wrong idea, which was also why she wore jeans on dates even in the summer.

His right hand rested on her thigh now, furthering a journey that had started at her knee.

Wes' left hand gripped tightly to the steering wheel of his Ford Mustang, the whine of the engine protesting its speed. Macy knew he wanted to impress her, but she didn't quite know how to tell him that this wasn't the way. After all, she liked Wes—a lot.

Despite being cautious of his roving hands, Macy felt this summer with Wes had exceeded all other summers. She maintained that Wes had the cutest dimples in town. Also, he acted like a gentleman around her more often than not, and—most importantly of all—he captained the town football team as the starting quarterback for the Rose Valley Jaguars.

Macy worried about where their relationship would go after the school year started. Wes would be busy with football, and she would return her focus to academics. Wes might change his mind about her when he reunited with his jock friends and the allure of the Jaguar cheerleaders.

Her friends told her that she should lock it down by sleeping with him, but Macy was cautious. She'd experienced firsthand what happened when a relationship moved too fast, and now she dealt with the aftermath every day, constantly bouncing back and forth between living with her mom and her dad. As great as Wes treated her and as desperately as she wanted their relationship to last forever, the more mature part of her knew that the long game meant getting out of Rose Valley.

She glanced over at Wes and he looked back at her, melting her with his beautiful smile. Macy had worked so hard to look pretty for him tonight. She lacked basic knowledge for putting on make-up correctly, but she'd worked on her face for hours. And despite genetics fighting very strongly against it, she even managed to tame her wild red mane into something resembling straight hair.

Macy played with her hair now, as she watched the road, and felt her heart jump in her chest when she saw something crossing in front of them. Too close for Wes to have any hope of stopping. She gasped.

"What the..." Wes exclaimed as he jerked a hard left. Macy held her breath and put her hands on the dashboard to brace herself.

The Mustang hit the rumble strip in the shoulder and then careened off the road into the grassy ditch. Wes fought with the wheel to try to get it back on the road, but the speed—not to mention his inexperience—proved too much. The Mustang slammed into a fence post, and stopped. He threw the gear shifter into park and jumped out of the car.

Macy took stock of the situation. She had rope burn from her seatbelt, but otherwise felt fine. The airbags remained neatly tucked into the dashboard. Wes must have slowed them down enough before they hit the fence.

She unbuckled her seatbelt and stepped out of the car. Wes stood in the middle of the highway, peering into the distance. She followed his gaze and could only vaguely make out the shape of something disappearing into the tree line. Macy took some solace in the fact that Wes also saw whatever they almost hit.

"What was that thing?" Wes said, finally turning back to Macy.

Macy didn't know the answer. "I... I don't know. A... a man... maybe?"

Wes shook his head. "Maybe, I guess. But bigger, right? And running weird. Like a gorilla or something."

Macy rolled her eyes. "Have you ever even seen a gorilla, Wes?"

He looked briefly toward the ground. "Well, no. I mean. On TV, yeah. But not in real life."

"Exactly," Macy said as she pulled her cell phone from her back pocket. "I'm calling my dad."

Wes rushed towards her. "Oh man. Don't call your dad! He's gonna be so pissed. Call your mom. She's cool. She'll understand. We can just get the car towed. There's no reason to involve your dad with this."

Macy shook her head and clicked *Dad - Work* in her contacts. "He'll find out one way or another anyway, and my mom isn't going to be able to help that guy that we almost hit."

The phone rang a few times, then a voice came on the line: "Sheriff Donner here."

CHAPTER 6

Macy melted into Shandi's arms the moment the deputy opened the door to the interrogation room. Tears streamed down Macy's face, her smeared makeup like that of a sad clown's. Shandi immediately wrapped her arms around her daughter, desperate to take away the fear and pain.

"What happened?" she asked. "Did Wes hurt you? Are you okay?"

Macy didn't lift her head from Shandi's chest, but Shandi could still make out her muffled words. "I'm okay. It was just an accident. There was a thing in the road. Some animal or man or something. Wes swerved to miss it and hit a fence post, and then..."

Macy went from tears to sobbing as she related the story. "I called Daddy and he came and... and... he handcuffed Wes and Dad won't believe me. Wes is going to be so mad at me. He told me not to call Daddy, and I did and now I messed everything up."

Shandi's heart hurt for Macy. Though Shandi certainly had her issues with Cam, the relationship between Macy and Cam tended towards the healthier side. Macy had always been daddy's little girl, and Shandi respected that relationship. Macy rarely experienced Cam in full-on sheriff mode.

While wearing the mom hat, Shandi's journalist side started creeping in. What had Macy seen? Some animal or man? Which was it? Between Macy and Wes, they would know what they had seen. Both grew up in Rose Valley. They knew the local fauna just like any kid would.

Shandi pried Macy off her and looked into her eyes, a brilliant green against her porcelain skin and fiery red hair. Shandi secretly loved that Macy looked far more like Shandi than Cam. "Listen. I'm gonna talk to your dad and get this sorted out. It's going to be okay. He's just being protective. Are you okay in here?"

Macy attempted to compose herself, nodding her head and sniffling. Shandi glanced over to the interrogation table and noticed a bag of Reese's Pieces, a Coke, and Macy's cell phone. Obviously, Cam didn't suspect her of any criminal activity, so it must have just been someplace to keep her while Cam did something else. But why keep her isolated like this?

"Okay. Good. You just hang out here and I'll figure this out. Text me if you need something." Shandi reached around to her back pocket to ensure she had her cell phone with her. She did.

She stepped out of the unlocked interrogation room and walked down the hall to the other one. The fact that Rose Valley even had two interrogation rooms made it the envy of many a small-town sheriff.

She looked through the one-way mirror where Cam sat menacingly across from Wes. Unlike Macy, Wes' hands sat awkwardly tethered to the table by his handcuffs. At the moment, Cam watched Wes try to write something on a piece of paper. It seemed a bit heavy-handed to make him do that handcuffed.

She considered barging into the room to lay into Cam, but thought better of it. He would only fight fire with fire, and it behooved her to keep things calm, for Macy's sake. She opted to gently knock on the door.

Cam stood up and pointed a finger at Wes. Without the intercom on, Shandi couldn't make out what he said, but it most assuredly came with a stern warning.

The door opened just enough for Cam to slip through. He gently closed it behind himself. "Shandi."

"Hi, Sheriff." Shandi made a special point of calling him by his title. She liked to imagine that it stung just a little to have her address him so formally, but she realized deep down that he probably didn't care. He had placed that title above their marriage, after all.

Cam rubbed his eyes, which were bloodshot and sagging.

"Why in the world do you have Wes Morris in handcuffs?" Shandi asked.

Embarrassment flashed briefly across Cam's face. "He damaged private property. I thought Bill might want to press charges."

None of that really explained how Cam could justify handcuffing Wes, but Shandi supposed Cam's actions sprouted from something more primal and fatherly. Macy could have been hurt, and Wes would have been to blame, intentionally or not, and that angered Cam. Shandi didn't like an angry Cam, but she could handle papa-bear angry much better than former-husband angry.

"Macy says Wes swerved to avoid a collision and ran into the fence. Could've happened to anyone. You can't arrest the quarterback just because he accidentally put your daughter in danger. Hell, you couldn't arrest the quarterback if he murdered your daughter in cold blood."

That rang true. As much power as Sheriff Cam Donner had in Rose Valley, Wes Morris wielded even more. The Jaguars would have a legitimate chance at

State this year, which meant the townsfolk cared only about winning, ready to defend Wes with their dying breaths. They would riot before letting the sheriff keep Wes off the field.

Cam remained surprisingly calm and patient with her. "I know. I just... I'll let him go, of course. He just wouldn't stop going on about seeing a gorilla in the road. I thought he was drunk or high or something at first. He's not, though. He just saw something that he can't explain."

"A coyote?" Shandi blurted out.

Cam closed his eyes and took a deep breath. Shandi searched his face. It had never been easy for Cam to admit that he might be wrong.

Cam motioned to Wes through the mirror. "I expect that Wes knows what a coyote looks like. I don't know what he saw. That's why I'm having him draw it."

Wes' tongue hung halfway out, his eyes heavily focused on the piece of paper. Despite the age gap, Shandi found him endearing. She wished Macy would choose someone more upwardly mobile, but in thinking back to her teenage years, she couldn't begrudge Macy for being smitten with him.

Cam reached into his shirt pocket and pulled out a piece of paper. He unfolded it and handed it to Shandi. "This is what Macy drew."

Shandi took the paper and tilted it towards the brighter light coming through the mirror-window. Macy excelled in the sciences, not the arts, but the intent of her drawing shone through the rough, unsteady pencil lines.

The sketch depicted what looked like a man, though Macy had guessed he was maybe seven feet tall. She drew him in profile, hunched over, his arms slightly longer than one would expect for a normally proportioned person. He wore no clothes. Macy had a drawn a star over his genitalia.

Under the drawing was a series of Macy-scribbled bullet points:

> *Walked funny, with a limp or something*
> *Ran really fast away from us when we got out of the car*
> *Normal hairy man body hair*
> *Shaggy haircut & beard*
> *Weird face*
> *Eyes glowed in the headlights like a deer*

Shandi shivered as she studied the drawing. Everything suddenly felt otherworldly, as if she floated outside of her own body. How could her own daughter have run into such a creature?

"I know," said Cam. "It seems impossible. It may be exaggerated, but even if we just have a streaker loose in Rose Valley, we need to catch that sonofabitch."

While Shandi wanted to process and think about the situation, Cam bristled with the anticipation of a fight. She recognized that that's why he *did* make a good Sheriff, despite being a genuine asshole.

Likely, this strange man-beast mutilated the goat, the sheep, and maybe even sprung the cheetahs out of Relics Park. Shandi suppressed the urge to smile at this huge lead.

Cam put his hand on the door handle. "Looks like Romeo is done. Time to compare."

He left Macy's drawing with Shandi and went back into the interrogation room with Wes. Within a few seconds, he returned with Wes' drawing. Cam studied it for what seemed like an eternity before letting Shandi see it. Time ticked by slowly.

When Cam finally handed over the new sketch, Shandi immediately took it in. Wes clearly spent more effort on his drawing, imbuing it with incredible detail, every hair meticulously drawn into place.

Wes had drawn the creature mostly in profile. His incarnation had more than a beard, the entire face obscured with graphite-colored curly hair and snake-like eyes. The arms bulged with massive muscles and weren't as long as they were in Macy's rendition.

Like Macy, Wes attached a written description:

Walked like a tiny armed gorilla
Super hairy
Glowing eyes, like a serpant
Ran really fast
Moved with a weird gate

Shandi chuckled when she interpreted his description as a miniature gorilla carrying a machine gun and an old, unpainted gate. Wes wouldn't be winning any spelling bees in his future, but the earnestness of his idiocy was charming.

"This is insane," Shandi finally said. "I don't understand what this is. Is it a man?"

Cam shrugged. "I don't know. Maybe. They did go through some trauma, so it wouldn't be out of the question for them to incorrectly remember what they saw. I talked to them both about whether they had discussed the creature with one another and both said they hadn't. That's why I wanted them to draw it."

"It seems pretty clear that they saw the same thing."

"Yeah. Seems like." Cam gently tugged both pictures out of her hands.

"Wait. Can I have copies of those? To put in the paper? It might help us find others who have seen it."

Cam shook his head. "No. You can't do that. I need to keep this secret so that I can use them to corroborate any other sightings. If you put 'em in the paper, we'll have everyone in town claiming they saw this exact thing."

Shandi hated to yield authority to Cam. For her, getting the information out there took top priority, so she wanted to protest, but the voice of Dan Carter haunted her mind. *Play nice with the local law enforcement.*

In this particular case, it seemed a reasonable request.

"Also, it might not be possible," Cam continued. "but if you can convince Macy to keep it quiet, that would help too. We don't need all her friends making things up."

Shandi laughed out loud. "You left her cell phone in there with her. All her friends already know. That ship has sailed."

Cam actually smiled as he rubbed his neck. "I guess you're right. I shoulda thought of that. I forget that she's so old sometimes."

"You and me both, Cam. You and me both."

CHAPTER 7

Jake quickly undressed down to his boxers, shivering in the shock of cold air on his skin. The woman with him had seen him like this many times. She appeared taller than a tape measure would read, lean and wiry. Some might describe her as emaciated now, but Jake's memories of her painted a different picture. Her blonde hair sat atop her head in a messy bun, her makeup applied with practiced precision. She looked tired, but appropriately alert for this particular meeting.

Her name was Deirdre Valentine, but her friends—those she had left, anyway—sometimes called her Dee. She had graduated as the valedictorian of her class and now boasted perhaps the most impressive resume of any graduate in the history of Rose Valley.

Jake didn't know the exact path that she'd taken after graduation, but he knew it involved several Ivy League schools, illustrious internships, and distinguished awards. That she'd wound up back in Rose Valley was still hard to believe.

Deirdre lightly ran her hands over one of the scars snaking up Jake's torso. He shivered. Her fingers sent jolts down his body. He watched her blue eyes study him, though she was focused on his every scar.

Occasionally she would stop, take notes on a clipboard, then resume her work. The first time Jake had endured her studying his nearly-naked body to check his healing, it caused him extreme discomfort. It felt invasive—inappropriately intimate. He struggled to separate the vivacious girl he knew in high school from the highly accomplished woman before him. Over time, however, the memory of Dee evaporated and left only Dr. Deirdre Valentine.

Deirdre stood up and finally met Jake's gaze. "Okay. Things look good. The scars are healing nicely. You can get dressed now."

She picked up and stared at the clipboard, as if enraptured by its contents. Many months ago, Jake had figured out that she did this to give him some private space in this clinic that hardly had any.

After the accident, Jake had taken a settlement offer from Arrowhead Research. It had stipulated that, in addition to financial compensation, he would receive all his medical treatments directly from Arrowhead Research—free of charge, of course. Deirdre Valentine served as the lead researcher of biomedical development. Why she agreed to personally take on his case was a bit of a mystery.

The one room outbuilding in which they now sat had once functioned as a research facility, and had since been repurposed into this small, makeshift clinic solely for the Jake's rehabilitation. Truthfully, he would have been perfectly happy with them covering his medical bills, but Arrowhead had seemed all too eager for some other arrangement. Arrowhead Research had been operating in Rose Valley for almost a hundred years. It had grown from a couple of doctors in a barn to a huge facility, employing some of the best minds in the country. In Rose Valley, Arrowhead Research employed more people than any other company; indeed, it was the financial lifeblood of the town. Probably their "generosity" to Jake came from a desire to preserve their public image.

Visiting this clinic always reminded him of the accident. Arrowhead Research medical personnel had been the first on the scene. Rose Valley existed in a blackhole of civilization; the nearest fully functional hospital was at least twenty minutes away by car. Waiting for traditional medical help may have left him dead on the side of the road. Accepting their settlement meant that he received care by some of the best doctors in the world, and that he would save on gas money and travel time for his appointments. Not a shabby deal, really.

Deirdre looked up once Jake was covered. "Before the injection, I want to ask you a few questions."

Jake had received an injection of an experimental drug on every visit; one she insisted would speed along his recovery. The side-effects had been minimal, and the speed of his healing had exceeded all expectations. Once it went on the market, it would surely cost a fortune. Jake felt privileged to receive it for free.

"Go for it," Jake replied.

"How's your sleeping?"

"Mostly good. I have nightmares sometimes. Usually about the accident. Sometimes about things that I can't remember when I wake up."

Deirdre wrote something down before continuing, "What about pain?"

"Pretty minimal at this point. Sometimes I'm stiff when I wake up. Occasionally there's pain in my knee. The hydrocodone usually knocks it right out, though."

"Good. We need to get you off that, though, so try not to take it any more than you have to. I'd like you to switch to over-the-counter pain medication. Ibuprofen will probably work best, but you can try Aleve or Tylenol as well."

Deirdre got up and went to the small mini-fridge at the back of the room. Jake took the opportunity to throw out some small talk.

"So, have you heard about the livestock mutilation stuff in town?"

She carefully filled a syringe with a translucent golden liquid. "No, I haven't. I don't hang out in town much. Honestly, I feel like I'm always here."

Jake filled her in on the pressing town news, hoping to pique her interest, and regaling her with his theories of a new, unknown animal. Though she was clearly a doctor now above all, a small part of him still hoped the younger "Dee" rattled around in there somewhere. Jake had crushed on Deirdre for years in high school, and nothing had come of it. She seemed cold and distant now, making it hard to remember what had once so fascinated him about her—other than the fact that she was gorgeous, of course.

Her brow furrowed at what he told her. She looked worried. As he finished the story, she picked up her clipboard. Jake followed her eyes. They seemed to stare blankly.

"That's pretty crazy," she said, smiling. "Maybe Rose Valley has its very own Bigfoot."

Dr. Deirdre Valentine did not smile often, and this smile seemed forced and uncomfortable. While hoping to draw her out, his talk appeared to have had the opposite effect. Jake felt foolish.

"You know what?" she said. "You've done really well. You won't need to see me at all for much longer. I don't think there's any reason to keep you on this." She picked up the syringe and emptied it back into the bottle, before placing it in the refrigerator.

He *had* been doing really well. Jake had felt more like his old self in the past few weeks than he had for the entire year. Nonetheless, the prospect of ending these injections was almost melancholic. They had made him feel better. Would his recovery come to a halt without them? Maybe he'd also miss seeing Deirdre so regularly.

Deirdre crossed the room back to Jake and extended her hand. "Unless something comes up, I would plan for next week's appointment being your last. The guys over in epigenetics will be happy to get their lab back."

Jake instinctively took her hand as he stood up from the examination table. Her frigid touch sent tingles up Jake's arm, but she had a practiced, solid grip. Deirdre gave him a professional smile this time. One of the many faces of Deirdre. As Jake attempted to decipher Deirdre's facial expression yet again, he recognized the thrill of trying to understand her, the possibility of reconnecting with the woman inside. He would miss her. Like the beast, she represented an enigma that he desperately wanted to solve.

CHAPTER 8

The click-clack of her heels on the concrete floors might have been deafening to those in the offices she passed, but Deirdre didn't notice. Nor did she notice her pace very nearly qualified as a jog. She tried to remain expressionless, to keep the panic at bay.

Reaching her office, she shut the door and sank into the chair behind her desk. Immediately she rose again, began pacing the room and then stopped to slip off her high heels, throwing them haphazardly into the corner of the room. Minutes later, she removed her lab coat as well.

Deirdre rethought the situation from the beginning multiple times. She had to solve this.

She needed more information.

Sitting down at her desk, she logged onto her computer and pulled up the research that had been digitized upon her request, clicking through old photographs and reading through reports her staff had painstakingly typed-up from handwritten manuscripts. Yes, all the information appeared to drive her toward one conclusion.

Her heart pounded. Her face flushed. Her hands shook. A lifetime of achievement stood on the brink of extinction. She had no friends, a string of failed relationships, and never got enough sleep. There was nothing in her life worth anything except her career. How could she get out of this mess without losing it?

It was a stupid careless mistake, driven by hubris and the shadow of loyalty. She hadn't taken the time to consider the possibilities. If she had, she would have seen this coming. It was entirely her mistake, though, and despite the ramifications, she could still fix it.

She pushed back from her desk, spinning her chair towards her file cabinet. Leaning over to reach the bottom-most drawer, she put in the combination, popped it open, and peered inside. Her breath caught in her chest. She had only used it a couple of times, all in the same week of training, and now, as she scooped it up in her hand, she worried that she wouldn't remember how to use it.

How hard could it be, though? Point it. Pull the trigger, right?

The gun felt heavier than she remembered, but the longer she held it, the more natural it began to feel. She vaguely remembered something about a safety, so she checked it to be sure she wouldn't accidentally shoot herself.

Gingerly, Deirdre put the gun in her purse. She blinked away tears. Was this fear? Maybe, but she could conquer it just like every other challenge in her life.

CHAPTER 9

Shandi and Jake had shared most of their childhood but standing before her in the archive room of the Rose Valley Reporter, she saw him for the first time.

Though she'd always pictured Jake as a generously-framed individual, he'd lost a lot of mass during his recovery. Still, though, he easily hulked over her. After the accident, he'd grown a beard to help hide some of the scars, which to Shandi made him more distinguished. His deep, dark brown eyes danced with wild excitement as he relayed Bernard's story about the beast.

In high school, Shandi had fallen in love with this part of Jake's personality. His passion was contagious. Jake might say the two of them had a lot in common, and Shandi might have agreed at one time. In hindsight, though, she'd just been reflecting Jake's enthusiasm. Her confidence had concealed from her more impressionable side. She loved all her friends dearly, of course, but Jake had made a bigger impression on her than most, something she only realized years after he'd left Rose Valley. Jake finished his retelling of Bernard's tale. In this instant, Shandi realized her enthusiasm was real and her own.

"There has to be a link," she said thoughtfully.

Jake smiled. "Exactly. There has to be, right? You really should convince Dan to digitize this stuff. I was bummed when I couldn't get this online. How am I going to find anything without a search engine?"

"Oh, we do have a search engine. We call it 'your eyes'. It's not quite as fast, but it gets the job done." Shandi smiled. "It actually shouldn't be that bad. Bernard said it was 1942?"

Shandi walked to the left of the room and gently ran her fingers along the spines of the volumes. On this side of the paper's archive room, each dusty spine displayed a single golden year.

"You're in luck," she said. "Back in '42, the paper was only published once a week. We've only got 52 papers to look through. Shouldn't be too bad." She happened upon the volume she was looking for and stretched up to snag it.

As she reached, Jake appeared behind her, almost too close. He grabbed the book with ease, and for a brief moment they brought it down in tandem. Shandi let go and Jake carried it to the lectern in the middle of the room, which Dan had commissioned specifically for perusing old issues of yellowing newspapers.

Jake sat the book down and stepped aside. "I don't want to get in trouble with Dan. Maybe you should do the honors."

Shandi lifted the cover and placed it against the surface of the lectern. The first paper read *Volume 1508, Wednesday, January 7, 1942*. They both scanned the cover. Only smiling faces and minor accomplishments stared back at them. No mutilated livestock or terrified townsfolk. She flipped the page. Each paper in 1942 boasted only two pages, each printed on the front and the back. Every waxy page crackled with fragility, requiring Shandi to use both hands to turn each one.

As they read and searched, silence filled the room. Shandi presumed to know how quickly Jake read, and so turned the page at a consistent pace. He didn't complain. After a few minutes of page-turning, doubt started creeping in. Perhaps Bernard made it all up: the gleeful rantings of a mischievous old man.

Then she came to *Volume 1549, Wednesday, October 21, 1942.*

She stopped. The clear, bold headline overtook the front page. Under the catchy words stretched a tall, solemn-faced man in a lab coat, standing next to a mass of something indistinguishable, obscured by the shadows of cruder photography. Shandi shivered at the thought of what it might be.

The caption read: "Dr. William Cordova, with one of the affected animals."

While Jake could see over her, Shandi moved to the side so he could get closer. He quickly did so, putting them side by side, her shoulder touching his bicep. To her surprise, she didn't mind him in her personal space. Without any words, they both leaned in to read the article.

***

LIVESTOCK MUTILATIONS DESTROYING ECONOMY

A rash of animal mutilations has ravaged local ranches. Timothy Jones of the Big J ranch has lost half of his sheep this year. Many other ranchers in the area have reported similar losses.

Dr. William Cordova of Arrowhead Research has been studying the phenomenon with the cooperation of local ranchers.

The animals are often torn to pieces according to Mr. Jones, with only minor evidence of being eaten. Mr. Jones has theorized to this reporter that such cases were likely the work of scavengers.

Mr. Jones described the culprit as a man-like beast with supernatural speed and strength.

Dr. Cordova disputed Mr. Jones description. "There is no evidence that an animal as described by Mr. Jones exists. It was likely a trick of the light."

Mr. Jones refuted Dr. Cordova's assessment, insisting that he saw a feral man attacking his sheep. He claims to have shot this creature at short range, but that it was not injured and quickly ran back into the trees near his property.

Regardless of the culprit behind these mutilations, the economic impact on Rose Valley is significant. Though Dr. Cordova has assured us that this event will soon stop, ranchers are understandably very concerned.

***

As she read, her heart-rate quickened. This article definitely described whatever Macy saw on the road. Shandi attempted to collect herself, wondering if she should just blurt this out to Jake.

Once Jake finished, Shandi spoke first.

"Why was Arrowhead Research even involved in this? Seems odd that they would have been interested."

"I dunno." Jake shrugged. "They were probably the closest thing to experts in town. It doesn't seem that strange that they would have been consulted. It's wild that Arrowhead's been around that long."

Jake reached into his pocket to get his phone, slightly dragging his shirt up as he did so, revealing the scars along his side. Shandi tried not to wince.

"Mind if I take a picture?" Jake asked.

"Of course not. Go right ahead. There's probably some rule about no flash or something? I dunno. This isn't a museum." Shandi moved away from the lectern to sit in a chair along the wall.

She had promised Cam she wouldn't tell anyone about the incident with Macy and Wes, but she wouldn't be able to keep that promise. It pleaded to be shared. Too important. Too vital to this line of research. It also didn't hurt that Jake would find it valuable, and that somehow satisfied her.

"So, uh. I have something I want to tell you," Shandi finally said, before she had even fully given her mouth permission.

Jake dropped his phone back into his pocket. As he crossed over to her, she realized she was sitting in the room's only chair and that he would be towering over her. She didn't like that feeling, and immediately stood up.

"Oh yeah? What's up?"

"So, last night, Macy got into an accident, and—"

"Oh my God," Jake cut in. "Is she okay? Why didn't you tell me? We didn't have to do this today."

Shandi shook her head. "No, no. She's fine. Everything's fine."

He seemed to calm down. He had only met Macy once or twice. The two of them certainly had no relationship. Why would he care so deeply for Macy?

"Anyway. Her boyfriend. He swerved to keep from hitting something. Ran into a fence post. No harm done."

Jake eyed her. "Okay. I'm glad she's okay. I assume there's more?"

Shandi nodded and took a deep breath. "The thing he almost hit. I think it was this thing. That Tim Jones describes in the paper."

She watched as his face shifted from confusion to excitement. Jake absent-mindedly stroked his beard as she recounted the entire story. His excitement grew when she described the drawings, and then visibly fell when he learned that the sheriff had taken them.

Jake seemed excited. "This is amazing. This should be on the front page of the paper. How is it not on the front page of the paper? This should be national news. This is a big deal, Shandi. A big deal!"

She agreed, but still felt helpless. "It's something, all right. I want to get this in the paper, too, but my hands are tied. I promised Cam I wouldn't. He needs to keep it a secret in case others see it. I need something else to go on. A photo or some more eyewitnesses. Something that doesn't get funneled through the Sheriff's Department."

Jake's eyes dropped briefly, imperceptibly. Did the mention of Cam annoy him? Whatever his reaction, it disappeared quickly and without lasting signs of emotional baggage. They each shared a rocky past with Cam, and she worried that Jake might see her acquiescence to the sheriff as a betrayal.

He moved on with his thoughts. "Others might have seen it. There might be more in the paper after October 21. We should see if we can find something. And then maybe..."

Jake trailed off before resuming. "Can you look through this? I've gotta go talk to Steve. Maybe we can bait this thing out."

Shandi felt Jake's exhilaration flow through her like electricity. They built off each other's energy, it seemed, and, in that moment, she felt more alive than she had in years.

In that moment, Shandi Mason may well have done anything for Jake Rollins.

But for now, she only nodded.

CHAPTER 10

"You know these things ain't free, right?" Steve said, expertly coaxing one sheep out of the herd.

Jake looked on, happy to let Steve do the work. "I'll reimburse you? How much does a sheep cost? Like $50?"

Steve laughed. "Try more like $300. These are premium sheep, man."

"Seriously? Three-hundred for a smelly animal that you then have to feed and take care of? Are you sure you're in the right line of work?"

"It's a living," Steve shrugged.

Though sheep-wrangling was not part of Jake's array of skills, he did have his part to play. He'd spent the bulk of the day playing around with motion detectors he'd gotten at the hardware store. If he managed to rig everything up correctly, they would trigger his phone to take live video at the detection of the slightest motion, whether from the sheep or the beast.

When he'd come home with all the equipment, Steve rightfully pointed out that Jake could have just bought a game camera instead. Jake acted as if he wanted the challenge of figuring it all out, but it had really just never occurred to him to buy one.

"Okay," Steve said. "She's not going to be happy about this. They don't like being away from the herd. She'll probably bleat all night long. It's going to be annoying." He put a collar around the sheep's neck, then attached a leash that was bound to a stake in the ground.

"With any luck, the beast will come for her and shut her up," Jake teased.

Steve gave Jake a stern look, then shook his head.

"Don't get my sheep killed, man. Scare away whatever comes for it. I'm going to the opening game tonight, so you're on your own if the 'beast' comes calling." Steve put the word *beast* in air quotes.

Tonight's celebration of catching pigskin and helmet-knocking precluded any hope that Jake would have back up. The entire town would flock to the stadium, but Jake couldn't stomach the thought of so much socializing just yet. In fact, he had been bedridden the previous football season, so he hadn't been to a single football game since his return to Rose Valley. It was not unthinkable that this could make him the town pariah.

"Oh, hey," Steve said. "Assuming you don't get eaten by the 'beast' tonight, wanna come over for dinner tomorrow? Cory's coming over."

He weighed his options. He didn't relish the thought of being a third wheel, but he would be within walking distance to the guest house, so he would have an easy out.

"Are you sure? I hate to intrude."

"Nah. Don't worry about it. Cory wants to get to know you better anyway. You are living on my property, after all."

Jake's feelings on Cory constantly flipped back and forth. Steve had been single for a long time, and Jake wanted to be happy to see him in a relationship, but he worried that Steve had taken the only choice available to him. Steve deserved better than to settle, but the dating pool of Rose Valley was not very deep.

"Yeah, okay, sure," Jake finally relented.

"Great. It'll be fun." Steve started his walk back to his house. "Speaking of which, enjoy your monster hunting tonight."

"Later."

As Steve walked away, Jake immediately went to work setting up the equipment. He preferred to stay outside and try to see the creature firsthand, but he thought better of it once he started reflecting on those gory bits of bifurcated lamb. Keeping his limbs intact seemed like the more important goal. And getting it on video would be a crucial start to getting the word out.

There'd been no word from Skylar Brooks since Jake had sent the email, and this nagged at him. Maybe Mr. Brooks would take him and the situation more seriously if there was footage. At the very least, it would provide the third-party evidence that Shandi would need to take this thing public.

As Jake fumbled with the setup, the sheep made a terrible racket. Steve hadn't been lying about that. Jake had carefully chosen the location of his bait so he could watch from the window of the guest house. Hopefully the beast wouldn't see fit to go farther and barge into his space.

After he finished up, Jake returned to his guest house, rolled the rickety computer chair to the window and sat down.

Now he would wait.

Jake had a primal instinct to want to see this thing for himself. He had spent a lifetime fascinated with cryptids, always wondering in the back of his mind if it was all merely fantasy and folklore. Tonight, everything would change. Tonight, he would prove something no one ever had.

He found it easy to keep watch at first, the adrenaline of excitement surging through him, but boredom pushed its way in before long. He got up and made some coffee, guzzling it down as fast as he could. The minutes and hours ticked by, and he fought hard to remain vigilant, pushing back against the sleep that threatened to overtake him.

He tried to think about things. About Deirdre. And Shandi. The football game. Perhaps next week, he'd work up the courage to go. It would be a good excuse to hang out with his friends, and there had been a time when he legitimately enjoyed the sport. Yes. He would go next week.

Somewhere lost in thoughts, he lost track of his surroundings as his eyelids betrayed him, and he drifted off to sleep.

CHAPTER 11

Shandi gave the attendant five dollars and entered Jaguar Stadium. It was a paltry sum of money, but it irked her that press didn't get in for free, even if the paper footed the bill. Sports reporting barely elevated itself above the weather.

Shandi's understanding of football had grown mightily over the years, especially when Macy had started crushing on Wes Morris. Her daughter, who had previously spent entire football games beneath the bleachers with her friends, had transformed into an avid football fan. Their courtship only existed in Macy's dreams the previous football season, but her crush became an obsession and she insisted that learning about football would endear her to Wes. Clearly, it had worked.

As Shandi walked up the stairs into the bleachers, she took note of Cam standing along the fence. The fence acted as a shrine for the true football fans of Rose Valley. Mostly peopled with old men, all those armchair coaches who viewed the players as little more than figures and stats.

Ironically, Cam had despised football when they were married. Once he'd seriously committed to running for sheriff, though, he became an overnight expert, as one did not get elected as sheriff in Rose Valley without credentials as an enthusiastic Jaguars fan. The fact that Macy had also quickly learned the game for her own selfish reasons bothered Shandi.

The game hadn't even started, and the fencers were already yelling to some of the players and at the coaches.

"Oh come on! That play will never work!" one guy yelled.

"Seriously, you're warming up Campbell?" another man's voice echoed.

The litany of critiques filled the air, in such great volume that Shandi lost track of it all. Listening to the complaints on the fence, one might think that the Jaguars had no hope, despite a mountain of statistical evidence to the contrary.

Macy had ridden to the game with friends and was probably out there somewhere in the crowd, maybe blowing kisses to Wes. Shandi tried to remember what it was like to be young and in love.

"Shandi! Sit by us!"

The voice came from Dub Higgins, still in his deputy's uniform. Sitting beside him was a short, beautiful woman with long dark hair and chocolatey eyes. Unlike Shandi's pale, freckled skin, Marie seemed to sport a smooth, permanent tan.

Shandi really didn't want to sit with the Higgins family, so she quickly looked around for some other seat—for some other person she could use as an excuse. She needed someone who would play along. Her eyes searched the crowd before finally landing on her mark—Steve and Cory.

"You know, I would love to," said Shandi. "but I promised Steve I'd sit with him and Cory. Raincheck?"

"Of course, dear," Marie said, with a faint accent.

Shandi bounded up the stairs towards Steve. As she approached, she realized that he and Cory were sitting with someone else, an old schoolmate named Deirdre Valentine. Despite Deirdre having moved back to Rose Valley years ago, the two of them had strangely never run into each other. Certainly, the good doctor heretofore lacked the time to attend a Rose Valley football game.

Though still very much Deirdre, she looked underweight and extremely tired, and all of Shandi's instincts told her that something more pressing than football now drained Deirdre's energy.

Shandi muttered so only they could hear. "Play along."

Steve immediately smiled. Cory stood up and hugged her. Deirdre looked confused.

"Thanks for coming. It's so great to see you!" Cory oversold it, talking a bit too loudly.

"Hey, Shandi," Steve said, playing it much cooler. "Have a seat. You remember Dee, right?"

Steve called her Dee, but Shandi had only ever called her Deirdre. Deirdre held out her hand and Shandi shook it. In high school, Deirdre had always managed to steal away Jake's attention. But that had been years ago. Shandi felt silly for her lingering jealousy.

"Hey, Deirdre," Shandi said, coolly. "Good to see you."

"Likewise. I've been back for years now, and I realized what a shame it is that I don't get out and spend time with old friends. It seemed like a football game was a great way to remedy that." Deirdre's initial grin grew into a wide, friendly smile.

No matter how the years had treated her, Deirdre still possessed Aphrodite-level beauty. It wasn't fair that she also got an Einstein-level brain.

"I didn't realize you and Steve were so close," Shandi said, trying to bait out why Deirdre had chosen to reunite with this particular set of friends. Shandi didn't remember Steve and Deirdre running in the same circles. Some of Deirdre's closer friends had, in fact, never left. Had she fallen out with them? Why not sit with one of them?

Deirdre responded, "Well, you know time changes our perspective on things. I had hoped Jake would be here, but Steve says he stayed behind."

Of course, Jake stayed behind. He hadn't been to a football game since he'd been back, and if Deirdre were really any kind of friend, she'd know that. What angle was she playing here? Shandi decided she didn't care—or rather, didn't want to care.

Rather than fixate on the reappearance of Deirdre Valentine, Shandi chose to sink herself into her job. She took a seat beside Cory, fished out her notepad and took in the crowd, jotting down colorful notes that she could use for her coverage.

After a moment, she heard Steve say, "You should come over for dinner tomorrow. Jake will be there."

Shandi looked up, excited at the chance to see Jake. Yet Steve's eyes weren't addressing her. They were on Deirdre.

Steve continued, "Might be good for you guys to see each other outside the clinic."

Deirdre nodded and smiled. "That sounds awesome! I'd love to!"

To Shandi, that reply sounded exaggerated. Forced, even. But it was probably her own petty high school hangovers talking.

Cory chimed in. "Good idea. Now we don't have to worry about Jake being awkward all night."

Shandi chuckled. "Yeah. He can awkwardly fawn over Deirdre instead."

The group fell quiet. Deirdre looked at Steve. Steve looked at Cory. Deirdre broke the unease with an uncharacteristic and forced waifish giggle. Shandi took refuge in her notepad.

A strange hush suddenly fell over the crowd. Faint screams and sharp gasps echoed across the stadium. Then a loud crash as a bench flew into the bleachers. Frantic murmurs and screams filled the air again as people scurried in different directions, pushing, yelling.

Chaos erupted. Shandi stood up, but her height prevented her from being able to see past the people in front of her. She jockeyed for a better view before putting her hand on Cory's shoulder and stepping up on the bleachers. There was something going on down on the field.

Shandi glanced frantically down to the track around the football field and saw ... something.

Saw *it*.

Here before her stood the monster that Bernard conjured in his stories. The weird creature that slaughtered their livestock. The mysterious man-thing that had caused Wes to crash his car. Shandi scrambled for her camera, brought it up to her face and, after minor fiddling, flipped it to video mode.

From what she could see, the creature looked much as Macy and Wes had described. It looked like a humanoid male of enormous bulk. Its long hair obscured most of its face and it was smeared in dirt. Its movement seemed foreign, though; hunched over like a gorilla, but never using its shorter front arms for support.

Shandi's breath sped up as she forced herself to remain calm enough to get it all on film. If she were closer, she might have felt a stronger urge to run, but from this distance she felt safe. She would need all the details later, and she couldn't afford to give in to the fear that threatened to take over. Macy had guessed it was about seven feet tall, but Shandi's mind put it closer to six-foot-three or four, at most.

It hadn't thrown anything else into the bleachers, but it waded through the equipment on the field like it were walking through a field of wheat, ripping shoulderpads in half, and shoving benches out of its way. It seemed aimless, with no intent or purpose other than destruction. It picked up a five-gallon cooler and smashed it between its hands as if it were an egg. Gatorade exploded in all directions.

The display strength jolted Shandi back into the presence, needling her to take stock of the things that mattered. She needed to find Macy. Shame rushed through Shandi's blood—why hadn't she connected with her daughter earlier? Any person with good sense would run from the stadium, but Macy had the common sense of a teenager.

Shandi shoved the Nikon into Steve's hands. "Whatever you do, don't stop filming. Ok?"

Steve nodded. His eyes were wide and his face white. Deirdre had run. Cory stood next to Steve, seemingly frozen in fear. Maybe Steve wouldn't keep the film rolling, but Shandi had a more urgent task now. She sprinted forward, pushing through the crowd and shoving the people who had stayed out of the way. Most seemed mesmerized, unable to move or react. Shandi hoped that they wouldn't regret it.

When she reached the bottom of the bleachers, frantically searching for any sign of Macy, Shandi glanced back to the beast as it turned towards Dub, who slowly crept out onto the black spongy track, his gun raised towards the creature. A gun wouldn't be enough. Shandi feared this might be the last time she saw Dub Higgins alive.

CHAPTER 12

The screams of the crowd faded into the background. Dub's chest tightened with fear, but he'd signed up for this when he put on the uniform. It's what the badge meant, and he had to protect Rose Valley from this hairy agent of chaos. Having Cam at his side would not have gone unappreciated, though.

"Stop! Put your hands up or I'll shoot!"

He had never fired his weapon at a person before, but then, this sinewy creature barely qualified as a person.

The football team retreated across the field, trying to put as much distance between them and the beast as possible. The cheerleaders tripped over themselves as they crowded into the stands. There were still too many people in the bleachers, standing like zombies, even though he was distracting the beast. They were paralyzed.

Or they were idiots.

The crowd had quietened a little now, but murmurs could still be heard, as some tried to verbalize what they were witnessing. At least everyone on the field had been smart enough to give him room, but now he felt vulnerable and alone, facing off one-on-one against a force that he couldn't possibly hope to stop.

Marie's voice pierced through the crowd noise. The fear in her screams broke his heart. He wanted to go to her, hug her, assure her that he would be fine, but this would not end easily. The standoff had begun.

"Stand down," he shouted again. "Now!"

The beast paused briefly, and slowly turned towards him. Its eyes followed him, full of hunger and rage. Instantly Dub regretted the attention. Suddenly even his gun felt powerless.

The beast emitted a low growl. It moved towards him, as Dub shouted and warned and cussed, trying desperately to persuade it to disengage. His finger tensed on the trigger. He was the last line of defense between this... thing... this man? It had to be a man, right? Dammit. Where the hell was Cam? Dub needed backup.

He dropped one hand from his gun and glanced over the crowd. There was no way Cam would have run in a situation like this. Perhaps he hadn't brought his sidearm. Though police frequently ignored the rule, the school purported to be a gun-free zone.

As he turned back to the beast, he realized that his focus had drifted for too long. The beast rushed towards him faster than he could react and latched on the hand holding the gun, sending a blinding pain up his arm. The metal of the gun dug deep into the palm of his hand, as it crushed into his skin. He gazed down his arm, trying to stay on his feet, his eyes transitioning from his wrist to the huge monstrous hand wrapped around his own. He struggled to break free, flexing his arm and bending his elbow, but that just led to more pain. There would be no escaping this grip.

The pain coursed through his arm and down his legs and he had no choice but slump to the ground. His shoulder wrenched as it struggled to support his weight. The beast squeezed harder. Dub's fingers cracked as blood started seeping out of the beast's fist, causing Dub's vision to blur. He fought to stay conscious, trying to fight the feelings of hopelessness.

Marie's screams jolted him back. He stared at the beast and tried to gain his footing; to push through the pain and get back on his feet. He needed to save Rose Valley. He needed to save Marie. He thought of the adoption papers they would submit soon. Of the baby that Marie had wanted for so long. He would not deny her that. The beast could go to hell.

He stood again, which caused the beast to double down on its grip, and Dub to scream in pain. He reeled back his good hand and punched the beast as hard as he could, but it stood firm. He imagined pain in his left hand now but couldn't feel it through the agony of his mangled right hand. Though it had gained him no ground, Dub reared back and punched again, but the creature's face barely moved from the blow.

A shot rang out. Then another. And another. The beast blinked, as if in surprise, and let go of Dub's hand. Had Cam not scored any hits? Dub tried to stay standing but fell to his knees, using his good hand to support his weight. His gun dropped to the ground, crushed and useless. He tried to ignore the gushing blood.

Two more shots flew wildly past their target. Cam took a step towards the beast with every shot, each one causing the beast to retreat even as they appeared to miss. Cam passed Dub now and drove the creature back to the other end of the field, though the creature hadn't weakened.

Dub felt warm hands embrace him. He could smell Marie's perfume. He fell back into her arms and she struggled to keep him upright. He outweighed her by at least a hundred pounds, and he knew that her slight frame wouldn't be able to support his weight. His strength sapped away, though, and he allowed himself to melt into her, struggling to keep his eyes open. He didn't want to lose sight of the beast.

Almost impossibly through the crowd, Dub heard Macy Donner: "No, daddy! Run!"

Cam's gun clicked in vain. If anyone else had a gun, none of them were brave enough to brandish it now, leaving Cam alone without a weapon. Cam holstered his and backed slowly towards Dub, unwilling to turn his back on the beast. He looked down for Dub's gun, grunted and kicked at it. The action caused Dub to really look at the mangled remains of his hand. It didn't resemble a hand at all anymore, only a bloody mass of meat and bones.

The beast growled again and sprinted toward Cam. The speed of its bounding gait exceeded that of any person.

Dub looked in Macy's direction. Shandi held her tight, her face buried in her chest. Good.

Cam saw the beast coming in time to pull his gun back up. There were no more bullets, but he turned the gun around in his hand to use it as a club. Under the stadium lights, tensed for a fight, Cam looked heroic and powerful.

Yet it was obvious Cam stood no chance.

When it seemed Cam would be imminently ripped limb from limb, the creature stopped only a few feet from him, and stopped impossibly quickly, with little to no inertia. Cam stepped back.

The beast glanced skyward. If it were a dog, Dub would have said that it smelled something it didn't like. It let out a blood-curdling scream that echoed through the stadium, then ran off in the opposite direction. The beast kept running until it disappeared from view.

Silence filled the stadium. Cam remained tense. Adrenaline continued surging through Dub's body, his consciousness pulsing in and out.

Before passing out, Dub saw Cam nod toward Macy. Dub recognized the sentiment, the defiance in Cam's face. A father's desire to show his baby that fear could not triumph in Rose Valley.

Yet fear was all Dub felt as darkness overcame him.

CHAPTER 13

A bright white box, infinitely long. Jake ran one direction then another but couldn't find the end. He yelled into the void, heard his echo transform into a vicious growl. He sat in the middle of the white space. Then he heard a voice float by him, sweet and melodic at first, but then frantic and screaming. He couldn't make out the words.

The ground under his feet began turning red, and though he jumped there was no getting away from it. The redness spread in every direction, stopping at the base of the walls.

He ran, fast as he could. Faster than he thought possible. The red turned to green and then to black. It got so dark, he couldn't see anything anymore.

Then, out of nowhere, a sheep appeared before him, bleating in the emptiness. It eyed him.

Screaming erupted, from everywhere at once. People were crying in fear. Tons of them. He put his hands over his ears but it did nothing—as though the noise came from within him.

Then it stopped, and there was only silence. The sheep walked towards him, growing larger with every step until its eyes were level with his own. Its mouth opened, issuing strange noises. Rattling and banging. It wasn't a noise an animal could make.

The noise continued as the sheep shut its mouth and turned to run away from him, shrinking back down to size. A deep hatred welled inside Jake and he gave chase. As fast as he ran, the sheep ran faster, bounding along. The clanging continued. Jake stopped. Everything faded back to white.

***

Jake's head exploded with noise, and he awoke in a panic. He calmed his breathing, then lost focus as he realized he was sitting in bed wearing boxers, with no idea of how he'd gotten there.

The sheep's muted bleating filled his bedroom. The beast hadn't taken the bait. The sheep's incessant noise served as only background now, though, surely not the cause of his panic. He remained quiet.

There was a light clicking noise. The sound of metal turning. A soft creak.

Someone entering the house.

Nothing that even remotely resembled a weapon sat near his bed. He had put his baseball bat by the window, now too far away from him to be of any use. He stood and clenched his fists. He had only punched one person in his life, and that had been back in high school.

Footsteps. Loud ones. The intruder wore boots.

"Jake? Where the hell are you?"

Only Steve. Jake relaxed. "In here."

Steve appeared at the door as Jake turned on the lamp next to his bed. Steve looked different than normal; shaken and scared.

"I was beatin' on the door for five minutes!" Steve said, uncharacteristically frustrated.

"Sorry. I guess I was dead asleep. Are you okay?"

"No. I am not okay. That thing. That beast? It's real. I saw it. The whole town saw it. It almost killed Dub Higgins."

Jake went numb. "No, no, no. That can't be right. Bernard says it doesn't hurt people."

"I don't give a damn what Bernard says. That thing showed up at the football game and shattered Dub's hand. He'll be a gimp the rest of his life."

Steve seemed mad, which Jake found disconcerting and alarming. He imagined the scenario from Steve's point of view. Jake understood awe, fear, or excitement, but why anger?

"Did they catch it? Or kill it? Is it over?" Jake asked.

"Nah. The sheriff shot it. A bunch. It ran off. Fast. Everyone was so shocked, no one chased it. No one did anything except Dub and Cam. A bunch of goddamn cowards."

Ah. Steve's anger aimed squarely at himself. In a moment of action, Steve had failed to act.

"It's probably better that more people didn't engage it."

Steve answered slowly. "Maybe. But it's still out there. I thought you were crazy. I don't know how to process this."

They moved into the living area where Steve sat in the chair, staring out at the sheep he had placed there earlier. Jake recognized Steve's agitation, but curiosity got the better of him. "What did it look like? What was it?"

"I dunno, man. Bigfoot?" Steve shook his head and stared at the floor. "Kind of like a dude, but not. It was too strong. Too big. Too fast. I just -

"Why didn't you answer your phone?" Steve asked, abruptly changing the subject. "I tried calling, texting. I don't know what you would have done, but you're the only person I know who even has a chance at understanding."

Jake pointed out the window. "My phone's out there. It was supposed to catch video of it if it came for the sheep."

Steve stood up. "There'll be tons of video now. Hardly seems to matter."

True. Whatever video Jake might have captured would be inconsequential next to the forthcoming avalanche of evidence. Fantasy had become reality now. Steve moved towards the door, though, so Jake put on the nearest t-shirt he could find, slipped on his flip-flops, and followed Steve outside. Maybe new video wouldn't help, but it gave them both something productive to do.

The sheep's bleating intensified as they moved towards the trap. Nothing seemed amiss.

"I'm going to put her back in the pen. I'll be right back," Steve said, immediately going to work.

Jake took out his phone and looked through the app charged with capturing the video. It reported three newly captured videos, but that didn't mean there would be evidence of the beast in those files, not that anyone needed it now anyway. He largely ignored the avalanche of texts and missed calls. The ones from Steve and Shandi made sense, but when he read Deirdre's name on one, something jumped inside him, stealing his focus. Before even looking at the videos, Jake opened Deirdre's text.

Hey. Steve invited me over for dinner tomorrow. So excited! See you soon.

Every text previous to that one telegraphed professionalism, somber and to the point. Reminders of appointments. Suggestions about pain management. This text from Deirdre marked the first that strayed from her capacity as his physician. Jake found it strangely unsettling, but exciting at the same time.

To have talked to Steve, Deirdre had to have gone to the football game, which also seemed atypical.

Stranger still, the text came in tonight. Had she sent it before the incident at the football stadium? Surely, she wouldn't have sent it afterward. He checked the time of the message with the intention of asking Steve when the beast had shown up.

Jake forced himself to stop thinking about Deirdre and went back to the video app to watch the videos. He hit play on the first one. The placid image never wavered. Perhaps something had moved in and out of the detection zone before the phone started recording.

He hit play on the second video. The head of a sheep moved into frame. Could sheep jump? It appeared that it had, tripping the motion detectors with its own head. No other frames belied movement.

He hit play on the third video just as Steve returned, the faint smell of sheep wafting off him. At first, he saw only more of the still image of dying grass in the moonlight...

But then, right before the end of the video, something blurred across the screen. It moved fast, but they both saw it. The shadowed form took up the entire frame.

Without a word between them, Jake moved the video back and paused at the blur. He clicked through the video frame by frame until one of the frames came into focus. The creature on the screen could not be mistaken for anything else; the large, hairy bipedal beast.

"How the hell? It's five miles between here and the stadium. When was that video taken?" Steve asked.

Jake backed out of the video and checked the file to find a recording time of forty-five minutes ago. Steve looked at his watch: a quaint old Timex from another decade.

"Okay," said Steve. "I guess that's possible if it was moving really fast? It was at the stadium about two hours ago. I can't believe it's been that long. I must have stayed after longer than I thought."

"You said it was moving pretty fast. But why did it come here? And why didn't it kill the sheep?" Jake said.

"Beats me. I don't understand why it does anything. What's driving it? What does it want?"

Jake didn't have the answer to that question. It had mutilated livestock and at least one cheetah cub. It had killed a gazelle and broken a deputy's hand. None of it added up to the actions of a creature just trying to survive. It could have surely killed Dub, but it hadn't. This thing seemed to be driven by something other than instinct alone.

His mind nagged him into bringing Deirdre back into the forefront. "Hey. I know this may be out of left field, but was Deirdre Valentine at the football game by any chance?"

Steve cocked an eyebrow. "Yeah, she was sittin' with us. Why do you ask?"

Her message had been from one and a half hours ago. That meant she had to have witnessed the incident with the beast and *then* texted Jake. Why would she not mention something like that? How could having dinner at Steve's be her number one priority? Perhaps her seeming disinterest masked something more. Surely not.

Jake replied to Steve, "No reason. Just wondered."

CHAPTER 14

Shandi had never seen so many cars filling the parking lot of Mikey's. They almost seemed to be heaped on top of each other, double-parked and up on the curbs. Her intent to quickly grab her lunch at the drive-through was halted by the number of cars parked along the side of the building, cutting off access to the window. She considered abandoning her plan altogether, but luck soon afforded her a parking spot.

When she pulled open the door to the restaurant, the murmurs overwhelmed her. All the seats were taken. The chivalry of the cowboys had them leaning against the few empty walls, while kids played underneath the tables. Though guns were not an uncommon sight in Rose Valley, Shandi couldn't help but notice how many more of them hung on the hips of its residents today.

"We gotta find this thing," said one man. "Kill it."

Dozens of different conversations echoed in the small space, every one of them referencing the beast in one manner or another. Fear. Defiance. Confusion. Shandi could hear it all mixed in with the crowd.

Another woman lamented, "There ain't nothin' on the shelves down at the supermarket. Gonna have to eat beans and cornbread for a while."

Her friend responded, "Y'all oughta come stay with us. We got a whole deer in the freezer still. Might be safer together."

As Shandi waited in line to order her food, she tried to hold on to as many of the descriptions as she could pick up in the crowd. Someone referred to the beast having glowing eyes, while another added sharp teeth and claws. One old lady described the beast with demonic wings, covered in fire and brimstone—a demon straight from hell, the old lady guessed. Clearly, these residents preferred to gossip rather than search the internet for the dozens of videos that were already popping up online.

"Shandi!" called a voice behind her.

She turned to see Bill, his long form looking particularly haggard. A lot had happened since the mutilation of one of his goats out at Serendipity Ranch.

"I've got some pictures you might want to see," he offered, sidling up beside her.

The entire morning had been a deluge of phone calls and emails. Shandi had already seen enough photos and videos. Heard the rantings. Geneva had stopped answering the phone altogether, and Shandi had thrown together a questionnaire just to give all the people some way of feeling heard. She should have known better than to have stopped here, of all places. If the town was going to congregate anywhere, Mikey's would be it.

Still, she felt obligated to welcome all news. "Whadya got, Bill?"

He held up his cheap phone in front of her and showed her a blurry picture of the beast next to the football field. He slid through more, one by one, waiting for her to react to each. The photos were fine, Shandi supposed, but she'd already seen better. At least Bill wouldn't be spreading stupid rumors about wings and claws. Hopefully.

After the slide show had run out, Shandi smiled. "Thanks, Bill. Why don't you email those to me. Maybe we'll use'em in the paper."

They most certainly wouldn't.

The line moved forward. Only one person left before she could get the energy her body begged for.

She'd stayed up practically all night with Dan to alter what had been planned for Saturday's paper. It had gone to print late, but at least it had the proper front page story about what had happened. Ordinarily, they only made a quick edit after the game to add the score and a brief description, but ordinary no longer applied to their situation. The game had been canceled after the beast had run away; an extremely rare and blasphemous action for Texas high school football.

Shandi and Dan had brainstormed on what they should call the monster and settled on calling it "The Beast." Though simple, it hearkened back to the existing Rose Valley folklore that Bernard had shared with Jake, even if most people knew nothing of it before Friday night.

The horror now had a name.

The gruff voice of Mikey brought Shandi back to the present. "The usual?"

She nodded as Mikey scratched some indecipherable marks on a green order pad. She didn't pay attention when he read her the total, took her card, and ran it through the scanner. Business complete, she stepped over to stand among the people crowded around the pickup area.

"Do you think it's Bigfoot?" a kid asked his mother.

"No. It's just some sick man," she suggested. "Sheriff Donner will catch him right quick. Don't you worry none."

Shandi had had minimal contact from the Sheriff's Department since Friday night. She couldn't imagine how many reports they faced. Normally, she herself would be hounding the department for information, but since she experienced the scene directly and had her own video, she thought it better to leave Cam to deal with the madness.

A man beside them jumped into their conversation. "Did you see how fast that thing moved? Ain't no man."

Someone needed to bring these people down from the hysterical high they all seemed to be riding. Shandi wondered whether such anxiety could lead to a riot. Or a mob. Surely both would be more dangerous to Rose Valley than the beast.

"Shandi! Here ya go!" Mike shouted above the roar of the crowd.

Finally. Shandi took the greasy bag from Mikey, grateful for the opportunity to return to her office. To the quiet. To the normalcy.

Or the illusion of it.

Honestly, Shandi doubted that they could ever return to normalcy. In that moment, it felt entirely impossible. Shandi couldn't name all the ways in which Rose Valley would be irrevocably altered by this event. She knew that regional news outlets would descend upon the town in short order. Maybe the story would even get to the national news; a prospect that provided more fear than excitement.

She squeezed through the crowd as quickly as she could, praying that no one else would stop her. Most of them had already visited the paper earlier in the morning, thankfully, so they had no more use for her.

Her pocket buzzed as she slid down into her car. She dropped her bag of food in the passenger seat and fished out her phone to see a text from Jake.

Sorry I didn't respond last night. I didn't have my phone with me. Steve filled me in.

The animated ellipses popped up, indicating another text. Shandi had forgotten that she had even texted Jake.

Another message.

I set up a trap to catch it. I have video proving that it was here at Watermelon Ranch after the game last night.

Shandi hovered her finger over the attachment. Another video to watch. Maybe the fact that the beast had gone to Watermelon Ranch after the game meant something, but it didn't seem terribly important given the other evidence. She decided to watch it later.

Shandi tapped out a reply.

Thanks. That's at least something new. Slammed at work right now. I'll text you later.

She forwarded Jake's video to Cam and started the car, grateful that no one had blocked her in.

On the drive back to the office, she tried to focus in on the beast. To solve the problem. To even see the problem clearly. An animal would be easy to deal with, even one completely unknown to science. An animal could be hunted. Killed. It could be explained by science. Its patterns could be predicted and accounted for. The beast hinted at something else entirely, seemingly a man but with strength and fortitude that couldn't be explained.

As she drove through the deserted streets of town, Shandi briefly wondered if maybe Rose Valley *should* prepare for the prospect of a demon straight from hell.

CHAPTER 15

Steve lived in a double-wide trailer that had been there as long as Jake could remember. The tangle of steel and rubber at the bottom hid behind a layer of masterfully-laid rocks. The large porch connected to a carport, which gave way to the only entrance into the fence surrounding the house. A cattle guard kept the animals out.

An imposing satellite dish took up most of the back yard, no longer serving any purpose. In their childhood, however, Steve and Jake would stay up all hours of the night trying to catch the pre-aired shows that secretly flew across unpublished satellite links. Occasionally they would hit the motherlode and catch *Star Trek: The Next Generation* days early. Before girls, such a feat served as the epitome of excitement.

The smell of barbecue saturated the air as Jake walked towards the house. Not simply hamburgers or hotdogs on an open grill, but real, slow-cooked barbecue; likely brisket, the national meat of Texas. The people of Rose Valley heralded Steve for his skills with a smoker.

It looked like Cory had already arrived. The driveway was otherwise empty, which Jake took to mean that Deirdre had not yet arrived. Despite the craziness enveloping Rose Valley, Jake found himself anxious about tonight. He felt like a teenager again as he prepared for the evening, trying on multiple outfits, never quite being satisfied with his options. He settled for a short-sleeve button-up over an army green t-shirt and a pair of worn jeans. He had very nearly shaved off his beard, but thought better of it and settled for a close trim. He looked as respectable as he could muster.

As recently as a few days ago, Jake had written off the Deirdre he'd known in high school. A stoic and cold professional now took her place. She had led him back from injuries that could have left him maimed for life. The prospect of spending time with her outside the clinic now exhilarated but also terrified him.

Putting his post-divorce life back together served as a full-time job, giving him little time to ponder whether he wanted a relationship. A script played in his head, warning him that any attempt at something new would only be ruined by all the same mistakes. As he finally walked onto the porch to start the night, he briefly considered going back to the shanty and texting in sick.

As Jake reached up to knock, he marveled at the resiliency of the human mind. Not twenty-four hours beforehand, they had all been part of something that should have altered their perception of reality, and maybe it had in ways that hadn't yet registered. Here they gathered, worried about relationships and barbecue, pretending like the violent creature skulking in the shadows didn't really exist. Maybe as defense mechanism, but Jake welcomed the distraction.

The door opened without him having to knock. Cory emerged on the other side of the screen door wearing a blue apron with a cowboy boot on the front, his easy smile shining.

"Are you Steve's sous chef now?" Jake teased as Cory propped open the screen door for him.

"I wish. He won't let me touch anything. Every time I try to help, he takes over. I think he might have a complex. He did let me set the table, though, so I guess I'm more of a maid."

Jake laughed and stepped into the house, still surprised at the decades-old decorations that still filled the shelves and walls. When Steve had moved in after his parents' passing, he'd left things mostly the same.

A few new additions dotted the room here and there, however. Steve's high school rodeo trophies adorned some of the shelves. The number of photos increased over the years, now showing off his parents, his brother, and Cory. The television stretched larger than Steve's mom would ever allow, and the giant computer desk that had once taken up a large portion of the living room had now morphed into a small, skinny table bearing no electronics whatsoever.

"Have a seat." Cory ushered Jake into the living room. "Can I get you something to drink? Wine, beer, bourbon?"

Cory and Jake didn't know each other very well. Surprisingly, Cory hadn't gone to school with them in Rose Valley. He had grown up in an even smaller town—if that could be believed—called Pecan Pass, fifteen miles up the road.

"I'll just take some water," Jake said. "If you've got any."

Cory grinned. "I dunno. If it weren't for me, I think Steve would live on canned beans. His cupboards are pretty bare."

Cory disappeared into the kitchen, just around the corner from the living room. Jake could hear the preparations underway. The living room boasted only a couch and a loveseat, and Jake lowered himself into the latter.

Cory popped around the corner. "Heads up."

A bottle of water came hurtling through the air. Jake twisted to catch it but missed and the bottle sailed past and struck the floor. Cory laughed. Jake picked it up and took a long swallow, wishing he had been graced with better reflexes.

Steve's voice echoed from the kitchen: "Are you nervous?"

Jake figured the question was for him. "Umm... I dunno. I guess? I'm mostly confused. She never let on at the clinic."

Steve appeared from around the corner, wearing no apron. Just his typical Wranglers, t-shirt and cowboy boots. "I dunno about that, but she seemed all kinds of excited when I invited her. You must have tickled her fancy somehow."

"I bet he tickled her fancy *real* good," Cory said.

Steve turned back to the kitchen with a smile on his face. "Back to work, you."

He walked towards the door, grabbed a baseball cap from a rack full of them, and turned back to Jake, cocking his head towards the open door. Jake recognized the nod as friend code for "come outside with me so we can talk." Jake grabbed his bottle of water and followed Steve outside to the smoker. Jake's mouth began to water as they got closer to it. It smelled divine.

Steve focused on the barbecue when he spoke. "I don't know where this is leading with Dee, but I'll tell you the same thing now that I told you twenty some-odd years ago. Sometimes the best option is the one right under your nose."

Jake took a few beats to comprehend. In high school, Jake had been hopelessly devoted to Deirdre, enamored with her intelligence, wit, and beauty. She never showed an interest in dating him, but when even the mere hope presented itself, Jake would return to her side—no matter who he left behind. Steve and Jake shared the bond of brothers. Steve never got left behind.

Shandi, on the other hand...

"That's high school stuff," Jake said. "We're all adults now. Shandi's moved on. Assuming she ever even liked me to begin with."

"Oh, she definitely did. I think you were both too stupid to realize it, though. Why was everyone in high school so stupid?"

"Except you, of course."

"Naturally. Everyone should just listen to me. All the time. The world would be such a better place."

"You're the one who invited her."

"Cory made me... bastard." Steve couldn't contain the smile when he mentioned Cory. "Seriously, though. Dee's great, don't get me wrong. But she strung you along back then, and I just want to make sure you don't let her do it again."

Jake felt brotherly warmth. He had stormed back into Steve's life out of nowhere and Steve would have been well within his rights to treat Jake like a stranger, but he hadn't. He had taken Jake in. Treated him like family.

Jake squeezed Steve's shoulder. "Thanks, man. Don't worry. I got this."

Steve nodded. "Okay. At least we had 'the talk'. Now, don't go destroying my guest house with your escapades, comprende?"

"No promises," Jake replied with a wink, as the barking of multiple dogs pierced the air.

Soon after came the familiar crunching of gravel as a black Cadillac CTS pulled around the corner and parked behind Steve's truck, just barely clearing the cattle guard.

"Looks like you're up, Casanova."

Jake walked away from Steve towards the car. Two of Steve's shepherds stared expectantly at the car door. Ungrateful mutts. Where had they been when he'd walked over?

He visited Deirdre at least once a week since he'd returned to Rose Valley, but as she stepped out of the car, he saw Dee for the first time in twenty years. The dogs trailed behind her as though she carried prime rib in her pockets. Jake found her equally irresistible. She seemed otherworldly, encompassing years of fantasy and regret.

"Hey, you," she said as they drew close enough to one another. Her perfume clouded him, mingling with the smell of the barbecue.

No. Jake did not have this under control at all.

CHAPTER 16

As its name implied, rolling hills encircled Rose Valley on every side. Entering the town provided a picturesque view of ranches and small businesses, with houses sprawling out from the city center without any discernible forethought. Zoning laws barely existed. Like any town, some buildings groaned under the weight of a century of existence, while some lightly popped out over the landscape with the hope of fresh construction. But somehow, all the chaos came together to present a unified front. A town that refused to yield to the higher-populated big cities down the highway.

As she steered her yellow Jeep Cherokee over one of the hills, Miriam felt fatigue pulling on her eyelids. Years of training had taught her to ignore the slight nausea and the urge to pull over and nap. The man in the backseat practically bounced with energy; he'd had the luxury of sleeping while she'd prepared this trip. In their group of four, she was the responsible one.

A simple and terse command issued from the backseat: "Pull over."

Miriam pulled over as requested, put the Jeep in park, popped out of her seat, and opened the door for the man in the back. He stepped out into the night air with the regal grace that conveyed his stature—or, at least the stature he imagined he deserved.

Miriam spent almost every day of her life with this man. His mere presence still made her uncomfortable, though, despite her insatiable and uncontrollable need to please him. He stood six-foot tall, with a manufactured, but effectively distinguished air. The hair on his head clung closely to his skull, cropped with military precision. A day without shaving drew attention to the length of his face, but his mustache overpowered the stubble, expertly groomed in a manner generally reserved for bikers and wild west lawmen. His eyes were small, alert, and calculating, promising to diligently pick apart everything in front of him. This man commanded respect, leading a mission with energetic purpose. He always moved with purpose.

As the man peered out over the town, Miriam slinked back into the driver's seat. While the man looked out on the city, Miriam found herself studying him—really looking at him. His outfit would look comical on most, but he wore it as if he'd come into the world wearing it. Khaki shorts with more pockets than one could ever use. A matching khaki shirt with even more pockets, the sleeves rolled up and buttoned into the rest of the sleeve. He looked as if he might lead a safari.

She knew the reason they had traveled all the way to Rose Valley with very little notice. The incredible events of Friday night garnered his attention. He viewed himself as the savior of Rose Valley and undoubtedly believed that only he could deliver them from the nightmare. Miriam had accompanied him on this trip over and over. In Florida. In Oregon. Even in the wilds of the Canadian Yukon. It always ended the same way, but somehow, he continued to believe that the next one would be different. Miriam didn't know what stalked the residents of Rose Valley, but she doubted very strongly that it hailed from a mythical line of hidden creatures. Perhaps it had escaped from a zoo, or stalked the town with the anger of a spurned townsman. The odds tended towards the mundane.

She struggled for most of her life to understand why they did it, but Miriam now realized that this fruitless pursuit of the unknown only conveniently covered up his true intentions, though she wondered if even he knew why they persisted. Regardless of the outcome, they would walk away from Rose Valley with a solution to the "beast" problem. A mundane solution to a mundane problem, no doubt. But that's all he really wanted, anyway. All would hail the great and powerful Skylar Brooks. But to Miriam, he would always just be dad.

CHAPTER 17

Awkward.

That was the best word to describe this evening so far. At times, Deirdre seemed warm and present, then would revert to cold and distant. Jake felt the same tingling adrenaline rush in his gut as he did on roller coasters.

Steve and Cory managed to keep the evening from completely going off the rails. They kept it light through the awkward times. Cory proved especially good at keeping the conversation moving, having far more success than Jake at getting Deirdre to talk. The fact that Cory and Deirdre both worked in the medical industry helped.

Now they sat lazily in Steve's living room. Steve in his spot, Cory next to him, comfortably close. Jake and Deirdre sat next to each other on the loveseat, neither comfortable nor close. His sweaty palms and racing heart annoyed him. At their age, he shouldn't have to guess as to whether Deirdre wanted him to make a move. Did *he* even want to make a move?

The conversation had fallen silent. Steve gave him a subtle look that only Jake picked up on, clearly understanding its meaning. Steve needed them to wrap it up.

"The barbecue was excellent, Steve," Jake said as he stood up. "Thanks for inviting me over. And Cory, that was the best table setting I've ever seen."

Cory grinned. "Thanks. It was some of my finest work."

Jake turned towards Deirdre to tell her goodnight. Whatever grand goals he'd started the night with had surely crumbled. She looked up. Her eyes locked onto his. She smiled. His heart skipped a beat. Without him offering it, she took his hand. Not to shake it, but to use it to pull herself up off the loveseat, barely straining Jake's muscles as she floated to her feet effortlessly.

She dropped Jake's hand, her fingers lingering on his just briefly. Or had he imagined it? Warm and present Deirdre crept back into the room, and Jake's misgivings about his chances with her started to evaporate. He swallowed hard as she looked into his eyes.

Her soft voice filled with a new vulnerability when she spoke. "Walk me to my car?"

Jake nodded. Steve and Cory laughed. Deirdre didn't seem to notice. She just grabbed her purse and started walking toward the door. Jake turned towards Steve, overwhelmed with panic and confusion and hoping Steve would have an answer for him. Steve only shrugged.

His heart racing, Jake took a deep breath and followed her outside. He caught up to her as they got to the bottom of the porch steps. They walked side by side until they arrived at her car. She turned towards him and leaned against the driver's side door. Darkness consumed most of the ranch around them, but the moonlight glinted off her big blue eyes in an ethereal way.

"It was fun, right?" she said.

Jake tried to sort out his feelings on that question, but replied before he found the true answer. "Yeah. Uh. Thanks for coming."

She glanced behind her. "That's where you live?"

Jake followed her gaze to the guest house. "Yep. That's my very humble abode. Well, it's Steve's really. I'm just staying there temporarily."

She eyed him with a smirk. "Temporarily, eh?"

"Well, maybe not as temporary as I had hoped. Probably not for much longer. Time to move on and all that."

"I dunno. It doesn't look that bad. Looks quaint and comfortable."

Her eyes bored into his soul. For the first time that night, Deirdre seemed in charge of the conversation. She stalked him, intent on destroying him, eating him, or conquering him. He struggled to find a defense mechanism to protect himself and came up short, knowing that his will paled in strength compared to the allure of her feminine form.

"Yeah. It's okay. It's fine for one person, ya know. Everything I need."

"Tiny houses are all the rage now. It seems so efficient. I've considered getting one myself. I've never been inside a house that small."

"Oh. Well. It's good. Yeah. You might like it. Low upkeep. Low electric bill. All that. It's not mobile like some of them. Steve and his dad built it for Steve to live in while he went to college up the road. It's not anything special, really."

Deirdre rolled her eyes and giggled. "You are *not* very good at taking hints, Jake Rollins."

It hit him embarrassingly late. She wanted him to invite her in to his place. Foolishly unprepared for this eventuality, his mind raced. Did he want that? Emotions flooded his body as he tried to sort out the situation. A beautiful woman stood in front of him. A woman he'd pined after for years in his youth. The opportunity had arrived to finally follow through. How could the answer to this question be so difficult?

Deirdre didn't let him make the decision. She took his hand and practically pulled him across the cattle guard towards his house. Her grip tightened around his hand snuggly, not making it impossible to get away but strong enough to ensure pain if he tried. She moved with surety and intensity. The situation became surreal and impossible and far too easy, heightening his discomfort.

Jake never locked the door. Deirdre must have assumed as much because she opened it without asking and only let go of his hand when they both made it through the doorway. Jake shut the door behind them, wondering if she intended to rip his clothes off next. Normally, he would have worried about her seeing his personal space, but it happened too fast for him to be concerned with it.

She moved around the room, looking at his few cheap decorations. His diploma on the wall. A few action figures on his desk. Certainly not the things of a distinguished, grown man worthy of the affections of a world-renowned researcher. He stood motionless before the door.

Deirdre poked her head into his bedroom. Then the bathroom. Then she took a tour of his kitchenette. None of it impressive. All of it impossibly interesting to her, apparently.

She made her way back to the couch and sat down, looking up at Jake by the door. He cleared his throat. "Not much, huh?"

"I like it," she said, patting the couch next to her, as if he were a dog.

Jake went and sat down on the couch, facing forward. She turned to him, her knees touching his thighs. She smiled.

"So, what do you do all day? I mean when you're not visiting me at the clinic or going through your rehab exercises?"

She suddenly seemed less intense. It no longer seemed imminent that she would pounce on him at any second. Jake felt more comfortable this way, his confidence rising as he regained some composure.

"I play chess with Bernard down at Mikey's most mornings. Sometimes I hang out with Steve. Been doing a lot of research into the beast lately."

"Ah yes," she said. "I saw an interesting effigy to it on the way here in someone's yard. Not sure whether they mean to scare the beast away or welcome it."

When Jake didn't respond, Deirdre continued, "You always did love cryptids. Is what you think this is? A cryptid?"

"Sure. What else could it be?"

She twisted her mouth up in a strange, indiscernible way. "It could be a lot of things. Maybe it's just a crazy person? Someone who lives out in the woods. Someone insane. More often than not, things have a completely rational explanation."

"Yeah. But a man couldn't do the things this beast has done. He ripped animals into pieces. He shattered Dub's hand. Whatever this is, it's stronger than a man."

She took her eyes off him and looked around the room as she replied, suddenly distracted and disengaged. "Stronger than most men, maybe."

Before he could reply, she stood up suddenly. "Mind if I use the restroom?"

"Yeah, of course."

She went to the restroom and took her purse with her. Jake didn't think anything of it. He supposed she might need to touch up her makeup, though he didn't see any reason why she would. Concerning him more was the increasingly-difficult task of getting some kind of bead on her intentions.

He leaned back into the couch and took multiple deep breaths. Certainly, on some primal level, Jake wanted to continue with her. He wanted to feel her in his arms, feel her perfect lips pressed against his. He recognized that physical attraction and worked hard to push it aside and focus on whether he actually had an interest in Deirdre.

He could hear her in the restroom. He heard a faint click, and then a *thunk* and metal rattling as it rested on the counter. He couldn't place the sound. It seemed heavy for standard female bathroom stuff. Maybe she only meant to touch up her make-up, because she clearly didn't intend to go the bathroom.

His pocket vibrated. It was a text from Shandi.

How'd the big date go?

How did Shandi even know that Deirdre would be there? A wave of guilt washed over him. But why? He owed nothing to Shandi, nor did he need to justify potentially hooking up with Deirdre.

Talking to Shandi about Deirdre sounded horrible, but he needed to answer her. He wanted to answer her. He thought through what he might say, searching for something truthful, without seeming too scandalous.

As he thought it over, Deirdre came out of the bathroom and hovered behind the couch. Jake didn't look up.

"Something wrong?" she said behind him.

Jake panicked. "Um. No. Everything's fine. I just need to answer this text real quick."

She didn't move back to sit next to him on the couch. She stayed behind him. He thought it odd, but not odd enough to worry about it as he quickly pecked out an answer to Shandi.

Not over yet. I'll text you later.

Shandi immediately started texting back. He knew he should put down the phone, but he needed to see what she'd say for reasons that he couldn't explain. He felt Deirdre behind him, shifting her weight, possibly reading over his shoulder? He glanced at her.

She was in the same position behind the couch, her bare hand slipping something large and metal and black into her purse. A gun? No. Surely not. Well, maybe. A lot of people carried guns in Rose Valley.

She looked him square in the eyes. Unlike the Deirdre that had sat beside him just minutes before, this Deirdre looked scared, distant, and cold. Just like that, she changed again, her eyes giving no indication of violence.

He read Shandi's reply:

Ooooh. Can't wait to hear the deets.

He dropped his phone into his pocket. "Sorry about that. Where were we?"

Deirdre looked around the room. She seemed confused, lost. Maybe even a little angry? She surely read Shandi's name on the texts, and maybe that brought up some form of jealousy? Something about her seemed off now.

"Um, I don't remember," she had the grace to give a faint smile. "Ya know. It's getting late."

She glanced at her wrist, but the bare skin showed no signs that she ever wore a watch. She laughed at herself and walked around the couch to Jake, embracing him in a hug. Jake wrapped his arms around her, easily engulfing her small, bony frame. Her purse got trapped between them, and the softness of her breasts and the smell of her hair electrified him. She leaned out, his arms still around her waist, their faces hovering only inches apart from one another.

Jake wavered between confusion and lust. He didn't know what he wanted now, much less what she did.

She looked down, breaking their gaze. Her hands dropped from his shoulders. He released his hands from her waist.

"Um. I'll see you at the clinic?" She nodded as if answering the question for herself. "Yes. I will see you there. Have a good week, Jake."

Deirdre spun around and disappeared through the door in just a few steps. Jake stood there dumbfounded, trying to remember whether he had at least mumbled a good night to her. He felt sad and relieved all at once. He cursed himself for checking his phone, lamenting the years of pining and yearning that he wasted for a text with another woman. Somewhere in the many facets of Deirdre that evening there existed a small window of opportunity; she could have been his.

Trying to sort out his feelings about Deirdre, Jake collapsed onto the couch and reached into his pocket to retrieve his cell phone. Without thinking, he brought up the text app and sent a text to Shandi.

Ok. All done. No juicy details. You know Dee. She was always an odd one. What's up?

Shandi did not respond.

CHAPTER 18

Shandi shoved her phone into the drawer of her bedside table. She needed something to make her feel normal in all the chaos; something to beat back the fear and worry. She'd wanted to turn to Jake, and the fact that Deirdre had taken him from her made her angry. What right did Jake have to come back into Rose Valley and make her feel like a stupid little girl again?

The house reverberated with Macy's current favorite love song. It had played no fewer than a dozen times over the past hour. Shandi felt quite certain that music had been better in her youth, but of course Macy disagreed. Shandi was the mom. She could have forced Macy to turn it down. Shandi opted not to interfere, though. She remembered the emotional turmoil of that age. All too well, at the moment.

What she actually needed came in a bottle. That would make her feel better. Or put her to sleep. She would settle for either one.

In the kitchen, she pulled open the cabinet door to discover all the wine glasses dirty in the dishwasher. Trying to dismiss the nagging notion she might have a problem, Shandi grabbed a disposable Solo cup instead. *Classy,* she thought. *Very classy*. She filled it halfway with wine.

The song ended. Peace. Quiet. For about ten seconds until it started up again, with its upbeat lyrics and light, springy music.

Shandi decided to enjoy her wine on the back porch. The warm night air enveloped her as she turned her eyes to the beautiful clear sky. The moon cast a happy glow over the trampoline Macy hadn't used for years.

The night was hot though calm, allowing her to clear her head. It had been an insane day in Rose Valley, and she felt like she somehow sat at the center of it all. She knew that she couldn't really claim that honor. Certainly, Dub and Marie felt more directly the shock of an evil beast terrorizing their town. Cam surely had his hands full. But being regaled with the paranoid ramblings of nearly every citizen in Rose Valley took its toll on her.

It had only been one day since the football game, and things would only get worse from here.

She closed her eyes and sipped her wine, trying as hard as she could to put the beast out of her mind, but the brief serenity of the night shattered with the screams of Macy echoing into the backyard.

The music suddenly stopped.

"Mom!" Macy's frantic voice echoed into the night air, followed by her terrifying, throaty scream.

Macy sounded impossibly close, almost like she was outside. Had she opened her window? Shandi rushed towards the door, having no doubt that Macy's screams were urgent and important. Before she made it inside, something emerged from around the corner of the house.

Not something. The beast.

Shandi ran inside and latched the lock, knowing that a glass door wouldn't protect her from the force of nature on the other side. Macy stood behind her, her screams dribbling off into terrified whimpers. Tears welled up in the corner of her eyes, and she clamped a hand over her mouth.

The beast stood on the porch, looking at Shandi through the glass. Its eyes locked onto hers, barely visible through the long brown hair framing its face. Though she suspected it before, she knew for certain now, a man—not a beast—leered at her through the glass door.

His body heaved up and down, as if breathing proved more difficult than it should have. He did not advance towards Shandi. He only stared at her. His eyes did not glow. He did not have wings or horns. His fingernails were abnormally long, but not sharp. Hair coated most of his body, thickest around his scalp and beard.

He stood with a strange slouch, his biceps wide as tree trunks, his chest like steel. In his hand he held a stuffed animal. He squeezed it with such force that white clumps of stuffing oozed from the seams. Shandi recognized it as one of Macy's.

"Macy. How did he get that?"

Macy answered through her sniffling. "M-My window. It was open. Scallops was on the bench."

That explained Macy's scream.

Shandi kept her eyes locked on the beast's, seeing only the feral needs of a wild animal.

"M-Mom," Macy said from behind Shandi. "We should g-go. We should run. W-we should call daddy."

Shandi didn't have her phone with her. Macy must not have had hers either, or she would have already been calling. Neither of them could stomach letting the beast out of their sight right now. Shandi felt certain that if she turned her back to him, he would descend upon them. In truth, Shandi possessed no script for how to handle this situation. She searched for a way to deescalate, but could come up with nothing that didn't end in bloodshed.

The beast's mouth turned up into a snarl. His eyes focused. In a snap decision of pure instinct, Shandi turned and ran towards the front door, grabbing Macy along the way. Halfway there, she heard a loud thud and cracking glass. Macy screamed again.

Shandi grabbed the keys hanging on the wall and jerked Macy through the door. Neither of them wore appropriate outdoor clothes, nor did they even have shoes on.

She didn't know if the beast lurked behind them in the house or would meet them in the yard. She hoped the former.

She let go of Macy, who understood fully what she needed to do. They both fell into the car, slammed the doors, and Shandi started the engine. She saw him out of the corner of her eye, felt his wild primal eyes following her.

She threw the car into reverse and backed out of the driveway. Once she got her car aimed in the right direction, she floored it. In her rearview mirror, the beast loped behind them. She looked at the speedometer as her car groaned up to forty miles per hour. Somehow, the beast galloped impossibly fast, managing to keep pace.

"Come on, come on," Shandi cried to the car. "Go faster, you piece of crap!"

It accelerated slowly. To fifty. Then sixty. The beast started falling behind. Macy cheered. Shandi kept her foot on the pedal. The beast stopped in the road, howled, then disappeared into some trees on the side of the road. Shandi relaxed her hands on the wheel.

She should have driven to the Sheriff's Department. Or to her mom's house. Or to Cam's. But by the time her mind caught up with her actions, she realized that she headed towards none of those places. Macy either didn't notice or didn't question it. She did, however, belatedly put on her seatbelt.

Shandi's head began to clear, but she still felt her heart racing in her chest. Rather than turning around and doing the logical thing, Shandi chose to continue toward her destination.

Without thinking about why, Shandi exploded at Macy. "Why the hell was your window open? It's a hundred degrees outside and there's a homicidal monster on the loose! Are you crazy?"

"I'm sorry. I-I-I. Wes. Wes was coming over," Macy said as she started crying. "I'm so sorry mom. I didn't mean to. Please don't be mad at me."

Shandi's heart softened. Though she didn't like that Macy intended to sneak a boy into her bedroom, right now it seemed utterly unimportant. She reached over and stroked the back of Macy's head. "It's okay. I'm sorry I yelled at you. When we get to a phone, you need to call Wes and tell him not come over."

Macy's crying intensified. "Oh no. What if he goes over there and that thing gets him?"

"I'm sure Wes'll be fine. The beast chased us away from the house, remember. He probably won't go back."

She didn't really know that and shuddered to think of the beast rummaging through her house. So far, the beast had followed no discernible pattern. For all she knew, he would take up residence in her bedroom. If he did, she had no intention of being the first to find out. She would make sure someone crazier than she scouted the house before they went back.

She took a deep breath and slowed down as she approached their destination. She suddenly regretted coming here, but as soon as she passed through the gates of Watermelon Ranch, she felt safer. This ranch provided no tangible security benefit—the beast had mutilated a sheep on this very property, after all.

"Mom? Why are we here?"

As she pulled the car up beside the old truck she'd spent so much time in as a teenager, Shandi didn't know that she had a good answer. In fact, she worried greatly that she would walk into an awkward and uncomfortable situation. She briefly pictured Jake and Deirdre answering the door naked, shocked to see her.

"I don't know, baby. It's just where I thought we needed to be."

CHAPTER 19

What the hell was she thinking? If she had pulled that trigger, it would have ruined everything. Steve and Cory would have heard the gunshot. She would have had time to get away, but they would have easily pegged her for the murder. Not to mention the horrible, gruesome mess she would have left behind. Even if no one had heard the gunshot, she would have had no hope of cleaning it up. She had never shot anyone, but she knew enough to know that if she had shot Jake in the back of the head, there would have been brain matter in places that no one could ever clean.

It had occurred to her when she was confident and pulling him by the hand, that she could have slept with him. Led him into the bedroom, shimmied off her clothes, and pressed her lips against his. He wouldn't have refused her. Then, after she had worked him into a euphoric coma, she could have put a pillow over his head and held it firmly against his face until he stopped breathing.

She didn't do that, though, because she couldn't entertain the idea without feeling nauseous. It wasn't Jake. He was an attractive man. Deirdre just couldn't imagine herself naked with anyone. The very thought of it turned her stomach. She didn't fear nudity. She saw all manner of naked bodies, both living and dead, as part of her job, but the intimacy of sharing herself with someone else felt like a violation of her very being. Even for a cause as important as this, she couldn't bring herself to do it.

And so, she found herself at an impasse. Her conviction to kill Jake was as strong as it had ever been and still imminently necessary. She knew that things in Rose Valley were going to get worse if she didn't carry through. No one knew that yet except her, of course, but that didn't matter. Every death that The Beast wrought on the town would be a death that she had to feel guilty for. The Beast hadn't murdered anyone yet, but he would. It was inevitable.

She had endless drugs at her disposal, many of which would kill Jake peacefully. A less-educated person may have gone that route. An average person may have felt confident that they could choose a cocktail that would be both deadly and untraceable, easily slipped into a shared meal. She could probably get away with it. The coroner might not think to check some of the more exotic possibilities, but there were no guarantees, and Rose Valley's very own roving reporter had a habit of not letting things go. If Deirdre lost control of Jake's dead body, then she'd also lose control of the trail of evidence leading back to her. She couldn't take that risk.

She had been acting too impulsively, but now it was time to approach this problem like the scientist she was. She would see Jake again at the clinic. It would just be the two of them in a remote outbuilding, half a mile away from the main campus. Dozens of research cadavers were cremated at Arrowhead every month. With control of her environment, she could kill him and cremate the body before anyone suspected a thing.

Deirdre pushed down feelings of shame and embarrassment. She'd handled this so poorly. The voice of her dad echoed in her head: *Every mistake is an opportunity to learn.* Now she knew to look for the signs of emotional compromise and force herself to approach her next attempt more logically. Of course, she would never need to murder anyone else. She wasn't a serial killer. She just had to fix this one mistake.

CHAPTER 20

Jake sat up and stretched his arms. His back ached, and the circulation in his left leg had been cut off. The years of being able to comfortably sleep on an old, rickety couch had long passed. Such a feat proved to be an especially bad idea for someone recovering from a painful accident. He shook his leg.

"Mornin', Mr. Rollins."

Jake jumped at the sound of her voice. He knew of his houseguests, of course, but still startled to find her in the room with him. "Good morning, Macy. You can call me Jake, by the way. How'd you sleep?"

She sat at the kitchen table, playing with the ends of her fiery red hair. "Didn't. Not much, anyway. Thanks for letting us sleep here."

He rubbed his leg. "No problem. Happy to help."

"Need help up?" Macy said nonchalantly.

"Nah. I'm just an old man. I'll get there."

Macy giggled. "You're not that old, Mr. Roll—Jake. Same age as my mom, right? She's not old. She's a 'spitfire.' That's what they say around town. Everybody's scared of her."

Jake smiled. "They're not wrong. Everyone's scared of your dad, too. You have a couple of intimidating parents."

Macy looked up at Jake as he finally made it to his feet. "Daddy's not scary. He's just good at his job, so people do what he says."

"Yeah... Does your mom let you drink coffee?" Jake said as he hobbled to the kitchenette.

"Please. I'm seventeen. I drink worse things than coffee."

Jake laughed. "I'll pretend you didn't say that."

The conversation fell into a comfortable silence as Jake went to work making coffee. Macy moved to the couch that Jake had vacated and sat sideways so that she could still see him. Shandi must have still been asleep, which came as no surprise to Jake.

After she didn't answer his text, Jake had assumed Shandi had just gone to bed. For the second time in two days, Jake had been pulled from slumber to someone banging on his door. Once the girls had huddled in the safety of his living room, they'd used Jake's cell phone to call the sheriff and Wes Morris.

As the coffee brewed, Jake moved on to the laundry. He transferred the clothes from the washer to dryer, both of which shared a home with the kitchen area. It had been a long time since his laundry had included female clothing. Shandi insisted that he didn't need to wash them, but Jake did it anyway once she and Macy changed into some of his old t-shirts. He questioned whether surreptitiously cleaning clothes could be described as normal, but he felt compelled nonetheless.

"Do you think that thing targeted us specifically?" Macy wondered aloud.

Jake started the dryer and moved towards the cupboard to fetch some coffee mugs. "I doubt it. I think it just acts on instinct."

A voice came from behind: "*He*. He acts on instinct."

Jake turned to see Shandi standing in the doorway to his bedroom. She looked adorable in his oversized t-shirt, her frizzy hair flying out in a million different directions. He did not—could not—argue with her.

"Sorry," Jake acquiesced. "He. Still trying to adjust to the idea that it's human. It just doesn't seem right."

Shandi walked over to the couch and sat down next to Macy, who laid her head on Shandi's shoulder. Shandi immediately started stroking her hair. Jake now bustled to pour three cups of coffee.

"Do you two take anything in your coffee?"

Macy pushed herself up from the couch. "I'll do it. It's a very exacting process. You'll just mess it up."

Jake took his cup, threw up his free hand, and laughed. "Fair enough. Sugar and cream's right there."

Shandi looked at him. She looked worn out. Tired. Beautiful.

"So, you struck out with Deirdre?" Shandi asked, smirking.

Jake blushed. He didn't really want to talk about it with her; certainly not with Macy in the room. "I guess you could say that. I don't think there was any attraction..."

Shandi looked dubious. Jake didn't like it, so he added, "From either side. Did you hear back from Cam?"

He could tell that she noticed his intentional change of subject, but she didn't call him on it. "Yeah. He called back late last night. Or early this morning, I guess. He and one of the deputies checked out the house. Back door was smashed in, but that was it. Didn't look like he came back."

Jake sipped his coffee, enjoying the warmth in his hands and throat. "That's a relief. More evidence that it—sorry, he—wasn't targeting you."

Macy returned to the couch with two mugs of coffee. She handed one to Shandi. Macy's was khaki-colored with lots of cream and sugar. Shandi took hers black. Shandi smiled at Macy and took a sip. Macy seemed to smile directly at her coffee before taking a long drink.

"Yeah. I think you're probably right. I still don't know if I feel comfortable staying there. We'll probably go stay with my mom."

Like most generational residents of Rose Valley, Shandi's mom lived in town. Why she hadn't gone there after the attack, Jake had no idea. He delighted in the knowledge that she had come to him, and he knew he didn't want her to leave. He wondered if he would actually be able to protect her, but he wanted to be close enough to try.

"You can stay here as long as you want. Seriously. Steve has a guest room over in the main house. I can stay there."

"You sure you don't mind?"

Her response surprised him. "Definitely not. This is a safe place to be. I'm here. Steve's here. Steve's a crack-shot with a rifle. He's a good person to have around."

Shandi sipped her coffee as she considered the offer. She glanced at Macy who focused more on her sugary concoction than the conversation.

After a few minutes of silence and sipping, Shandi looked back up at him and smiled. "Okay. We'll stay here until we can get the door fixed. Only under one condition, though."

"Name it."

"You stay here. Not at Steve's. We can get an air mattress or something. I can sleep out here with Macy. It's not fair for us to kick you out of your house."

"Deal."

Shandi nodded thoughtfully and sipped her coffee some more. "Hey, baby."

Macy looked up. "Yeah?"

"Is that okay with you? Would you rather stay with your dad?"

Shandi pushed Macy's hair back behind one of her ears as her daughter thought for a moment. "I think I should stay here. Dad's away from the house a lot, and I don't want to be alone—especially at night. Can we get my cell phone, though?"

"Of course. We'll need more than our cell phones. We should go to the house and pack some bags. And pick up Macy's car so she can drive herself to school tomorrow." Shandi glanced up at Jake. "Mind accompanying us?"

"Yeah. No problem. I can drive. We can take the truck." He set about grabbing his keys and slipping on his shoes.

"Woah. Slow down there, Maurice. We gotta wait for our clothes to dry."

Jake laughed at her reference to one of their favorite childhood movies. "Oh. Right. Guess you don't want to go out like that."

"Hey now. We look fabulous!" Shandi teased. "I just don't think the outside world could handle all this beauty."

"You're probably right. The house can barely contain it."

Shandi nodded defiantly. "Exactly."

It felt right to slip back into the old banter with Shandi, helping to wash away the guilt of Deirdre and the horror of Shandi's encounter with the beast. Jake then considered that out of courtesy he should let Steve know about the situation.

"I'm going to hop over real quick and tell Steve about all this. You girls relax, have some more coffee. I'll be back in a few minutes."

Shandi forced a smile, but Jake could still see the fatigue of the previous night behind it. She nodded. "Ok. See if he has an air mattress."

CHAPTER 21

Saturday had been a mad rush of conflicting information, but Monday was eerily quiet. The videos had all made it out into the internet over the weekend, and all the wild hearsay naturally died down. Most of the video had been blurry, but it was enough to solidify the picture of the beast in the public consciousness. The opinions of exactly what the beast was varied, but now they all circled around what Shandi had already known—the beast was a man. Or at least, something very closely related to a man. Some said crazy. Others, feral. A few cried Bigfoot. Even with the data collated together to put him in sharp focus, confusion still swirled.

Shandi felt energized to tackle the world's problems again. Sunday had been a slog, and Dan had picked up most of the slack. Both had agreed that he should write the article about the beast attacking her house.

It felt good to be back in her office. Macy had returned to school, which seemed like it would provide maximum protection for her with the increased police presence. She actually felt calm. Serene. Almost convinced that the insanity that had descended on Rose Valley came only from a fleeting nightmare. She knew the reality of the situation, but now she could believe that the beast would eventually be caught. And perhaps, there would even be an upside...

Her mind drifted to Jake. She felt silly for even thinking about him with a monster roaming the town, but Jake kept prying his way in, vying for the attention she couldn't really afford. She liked the distraction that he provided her right now, though. The Beast had become so overwhelming. In between the fear and the worry, she welcomed the image of Jake that night -- alone, in an adorably sleepy stupor, with no Deirdre in sight.

Cam had been furious, of course, that she hadn't gone to him. He'd hidden the anger under the guise of his superior ability to protect them from danger, but Shandi could see through that. She suspected that jealousy might surface whenever she started dating again. Cam didn't want her anymore, but he didn't want anyone else to have her, either.

The one good thing about Cam being upset: he'd used his considerable clout to make sure Shandi's door got replaced as quickly as possible. By the time they'd finished, her door would be indestructible. She thought it a bit overkill considering the beast could just smash any other window. Or door. Or wall. But she knew better than to fight him on it. It made Cam feel better to know that he could do something to protect his little girl. And maybe a little bit because he knew it would get them out of Jake's house.

Enough daydreaming, Shandi! Before the world went crazy on Friday night, the plan had been to go through the archives to see how many times the beast had stalked Rose Valley over the years. With no new reports other than her own from Saturday night, it still seemed like a good place to go next. Maybe the old papers hid information that could be the key to discovering the beast's identity—where he came from. How to stop him.

Shandi stood up from her desk, slipped her cell phone into her back pocket and stepped out into the hallway. She could hear Geneva talking. Then a man's voice that she didn't recognize. He sounded upset. Shandi decided to change course to the front desk in case Geneva needed some back up dealing with an unruly customer.

As she walked into the reception area, she saw a caricature of a man, dressed all in khaki. Behind him stood three young adults—one girl, two boys—none of whom looked particularly happy to be there. They looked tired and frightened. The young girl gave Shandi a pleading, embarrassed look. Shandi took it as an attempt at an apology.

"Do you know who I am?" said the man, his handlebar mustache bouncing up and down like some angry muppet's. "I am Skylar Brooks. World-renowned cryptozoologist. I am here to help. And to do that, I need access to everything you have on this beast!"

"You have mentioned your name already, sir. Unfortunately, it is our policy not to release information to private citizens outside of what we publish in the paper." Geneva remained remarkably calm. Shandi had been there for mere seconds and already she felt her blood pressure rising.

Skylar Brooks harrumphed. "I am not a private citizen. I am Skylar Brooks. I am a credentialed cryptozoologist."

Geneva would not give up the fight. "I have no doubt, sir. Were you hired by the county? Or the city? Or the Sheriff's Department?"

Skylar did not have an immediate answer. He looked towards Shandi, as if he had noticed her for the first time. His bluster dissolved. He flashed her a slimy and unwelcoming smile. Shandi had taken a long, hot shower before coming into work that morning, but she suddenly felt like she could use another. Skylar snapped his fingers, and the mousy girl handed him a book that Shandi hadn't even noticed that she had been holding.

He addressed Shandi. "Hello! I am Skylar Brooks. World-renowned cryptozoologist. Have a signed copy of my book."

Shandi took it without thought, immediately regretting the obvious boost to his ego. She looked down at it. Large block letters screamed the title, *Adventures in Cryptozoology*, but the cover failed to mirror the contents, having only a picture of the very same man standing before her. The photo showed him with a smarmy smile, not unlike the one he'd flashed her moments earlier. She briefly wondered whether Jake owned this book.

"Your colleague here doesn't seem to understand the gravity of the situation. I am not trying to be difficult. I just want to help. You have a cryptid running amok in your town and that is my specialty." He said the last word with too many vowels and syllables.

Shandi considered the possible replies. She would have liked nothing more than to turn him away. Geneva spoke accurately when she said that they couldn't release unpublished information, but the archives existed to serve the public and provide outreach for the paper. Shandi found herself torn. On the one hand, she instinctively hated this man with every fiber of her being. On the other, she needed to go through the archives herself, and it would go much faster with more people looking for the same information.

She opted to be diplomatic, a wholly unfamiliar tone for her. "I appreciate your concern for our town, Mr. Brooks. Unfortunately, Geneva is correct. It is our policy not to release unpublished information to the public. We do, however, have our archives. They stretch back for over a hundred years. Perhaps you can find something useful there?"

Skylar Brooks harrumphed yet again. He remained quiet for a few seconds, looking back at his colleagues. Assistants? Slaves? Their relationship to Skylar seemed ambiguous. None of them spoke, or even met his gaze. They all looked at the ground and fidgeted with their fingers. All except the third assistant, who held a copy of the book. Shandi hadn't noticed, but she assumed Geneva had already received a copy.

"Very well. My assistants will stay behind and look through the archives. I will find someone who will appreciate what I'm trying to do here. The mayor? Or the sheriff? Is that who holds the power in these parts?"

Perhaps Shandi felt particularly mean on this day, but unleashing this boor on Cam thrilled her. "Yes, sir. You should go down to the Sheriff's Department and ask for Sheriff Cam Donner. I'm sure he would be happy to hear what you have to say."

This time, Skylar gave her a genuine smile. Geneva tried to hide a snicker. He mistook Shandi's deviousness for helpfulness, no doubt elated to discover that Shandi finally recognized his greatness. She hoped that she did not regret that decision, because she in no way wanted him to think of her as an ally. She wanted to apprehend the beast as much as the next person, but dealing with the mass hysteria of the beast sounded preferable to dealing with this guy.

He walked out of the building without talking to his assistants. Yet they remained. Neatly lined up, as if Skylar meant to auction them off to the highest bidder. Shandi supposed that she had inherited these kids now. Hopefully they proved more useful than they seemed.

"Right this way," she said, motioning towards the archives.

The three assistants followed her, no longer frightened little field mice. Now they walked like normal people. Eyes up. Shoulders back. One of them even smiled. The boy with the book sat it down on the reception desk as he walked by. Shandi wondered if leaving such a valuable commodity behind constituted a punishable offense in the Skylar Brooks organization.

When they entered the archives, the three looked around with excitement.

"So, these are the archives," Shandi said. "I can tell you right now that the first sighting that we know of was in 1942. October. It's possible that there were earlier. No one has had the time to check. Local lore suggests there were certainly later sightings, though, so going forward from 1942 probably makes the most sense. You can take pictures, but try not to rip any of the pages."

The mousy girl looked at her, started to speak, thought better of it, then found the courage again. "I'm so sorry for my father. He's not all bad. He is a really good cryptozoologist and a great man. He just..."

The girl trailed off with no clear intention to finish her sentence. Shandi supposed calling one's own father a boorish asshat would prove difficult, even if objectively true.

"Don't worry about it. In this business, we've seen it all. I'm Shandi." She extended her hand while considering that she had lied. Shandi's vast experience covered a lot, but Skylar Brooks was a special snowflake of a man.

The girl took her hand and gave it a limp, awkward shake. "Miriam. This is my brother, Cornelius. And my cousin, Tanner."

Shandi looked at each as the girl introduced them, noticing the youth of their faces, older than Macy, but surely not college graduates. No matter. They would expedite her research quite nicely. She originally intended to go through the archives with them, but decided that letting them do the work for her might provide the better option. As much as her inner control freak wanted to direct the entire operation, she reluctantly admitted to herself that she needed a break. She would just need to butter them up first to make sure they'd go it alone.

"It's very nice to meet all of you," she said. "I really do hope you find what you're looking for. Is there anything I can get you? I can have Geneva order takeout if you'd like. My treat."

For delivery in Rose Valley, Mikey's Burger Shack cornered the market. They didn't have a dedicated delivery person, instead opting to send one of the waiters or cooks, even if that meant delaying other orders in the process. None of the customers seemed to mind. Most of the regulars at Mikey's only drank coffee, played games, and swapped tall tales.

The boys lit up at her offer. Miriam looked at them for a few moments without exchanging any words or nods, then answered for them all. "That would be great! We're not picky. We'll eat anything."

The grins on the boys' faces lit up the room with mouth-watering excitement. It had been a very long time since Shandi had been that enthused about

Mikey's burgers. She wondered whether anyone had ever been nice to them before. She also wondered whether they possessed psychic abilities, because the boys hadn't said a word. Only Miriam appeared to have a voice.

"Okay. I'll let Geneva know," Shandi said as she thought of another olive branch she could offer. "We can get you some more chairs. Probably some folding tables. That should make it easier."

Miriam shook her head. "Oh no. That's not necessary, Ms. Shandi. We can sit on the floor. We don't mind at all. We prefer it."

Shandi didn't know what to say to that. These people might carry the label of research assistants, but they were only trained monkeys. She bristled at the thought of what Skylar Brooks must have done to these kids.

These kids had fought their way to adulthood, though, and worrying about their upbringing wouldn't help them now. "Okay. If you say so. Um. Listen. If you don't mind. Could you give me a copy of whatever you find?"

Miriam looked back at the boys. Shandi hoped that it would be an easy decision, but it required a meeting of the hive mind, likely hinging on how willing Skylar might be on sharing his data.

Miriam's face twisted up in consternation when she turned back to Shandi, but she gave a curt nod. "Yes, ma'am, Ms. Shandi. We will make sure you get our findings. Just, uh..."

Shandi knew the question without Miriam having to verbalize it. "I won't tell Mr. Brooks. Don't worry."

Miriam looked relieved.

CHAPTER 22

Jake sat at his small kitchen table when Shandi dropped the book down in front of him. From the cover, Skylar Brooks' remarkably punchable face stared back at him. He read the title. Opened it. Studied the inky black signature.

Had Shandi gotten him a gift? He did like cryptozoology, so it wouldn't be terribly out of line for her to think that he might like this. He warmed inside at the thought of her carefully choosing it from a giant shelf of volumes. He pictured her lovingly picking up each book and reading the back, trying to find something that would endear her to him.

"So, *this* jerk showed up at the paper today," Shandi said sharply, gesturing to the book in front of Jake.

Okay. So not a gift. Good to know.

Having received no correspondence from Skylar Brooks, he was shocked the man had shown up in Rose Valley. "Really? That's crazy. I guess he got my email."

Shandi helped herself to a bottle of water from the refrigerator and sat across from him. She took a swig, then gave Jake a disappointed look. "Oh... my... God. Did you invite this guy to Rose Valley, Jake?"

She didn't look angry, exactly. More like exasperated. He took it from her earlier description of him that the man lacked certain social charms. At that moment, Jake regretted that he had mentioned the email, and he certainly didn't want to admit culpability in the potential invitation of Skyler Brooks to Rose Valley.

"Um. I... No, of course not." Jake tried to sound confident, but failed miserably. "I mean. I didn't invite him, no. I did email him. At the beginning of all this. After the sheep, here. I thought he might be able to help."

"Well. I don't know if he'll be able to help, but he certainly thinks he can," Shandi said, taking another swallow of water.

"That bad, huh?"

"Yeah. He's got these three... assistants, I guess. They claim to be family, but they act like work horses. Like literally. Trained horses. They're scared to death of him. This is not a good man."

"So, what did you do?"

Shandi turned her lips up in a huge devious smile. Her eyes glimmered as she laughed. "I sent him to find Cam."

Jake burst out laughing. It took him a few beats to find his voice. "Oh boy. I hope Cam doesn't shoot him."

"I dunno. I kinda hope he does."

Jake hadn't met Skylar Brooks yet, and he trusted Shandi that Skylar's personality might not have been on point, but he couldn't help wondering whether he might still be useful. Skylar's experience and knowledge stretched far beyond what they knew. If he could bring the beast down, surely it would be worth tolerating him.

Jake wanted to bring it up. Suggest that they should work with Skylar. But he also valued where he was with Shandi. It felt right. The subtle shift in their relationship felt genuine and real. And new. He didn't want to jeopardize it in that moment. She wouldn't stay at his place forever. Probably just another night or two.

"Anyway. The hive mind—" Shandi started.

"Wait. What? What's the 'hive mind'?"

Shandi chuckled. "Oh right. So, his assistants. There's two boys. One girl. Um... Miriam's the girl and the boys are Tanner and... I can't remember. It's a weird name. The name of the prospector guy in Rudolph."

"Yukon Cornelius?" Jake said, without even having to think about it.

"Yeah. That's it. Cornelius. Not the Yukon part. Your recall with movie facts is scary." There was a teasing glint in her eye.

"What can I say? The skills of a misspent youth."

He rattled off another movie reference, but Shandi didn't get that one.

"Yes," she said. "You were quite the rebel."

"I was! I watched R-rated movies when I was like 10."

Shandi laughed. Jake loved when she laughed, enjoying the free and honest mirth of it. To be able to elicit that sort of reaction from her made him feel important.

"Hide your daughters, ladies! Jake Rollins watched R-rated movies when he was 10!" She looked around the room.

Jake brought her back down. "Anyway. You were saying. About the hive mind?"

"Oh right," Shandi said, still smiling. "I think of them as the hive mind. This is the first time I've said it out loud. I guess it sounds silly. But they don't talk to each other. Only Miriam talks. The boys didn't talk the entire time they were there. But they communicate somehow. It's creepy.

"Skylar left them behind," she continued. "when he left to go ask Cam on a man-date. They went through the archives. All of them. Impressively fast. So, I've got a lot of information about the other sightings of the beast over the years."

Jake perked up. He'd almost forgotten that he'd asked Shandi to look through the other archives. So much other, more important stuff had happened since then.

Shandi pulled a piece of copy paper from her back pocket and unfolded it. Beautifully penned words covered the page. Definitely not Shandi's handwriting, which tended towards more of a scrawl. Jake couldn't quite read it from his vantage point.

Shandi looked directly into Jake's eyes. "Ready?"

Jake nodded. She had his full attention. "After 1942, there are reports again in 1951. Not as widespread. Just a few unexplained mutilations. No sightings.

"Then another break," she went on. "Until 1967. Again, nothing like the mass mutilations of '42. Just a few mutilations. There was one sighting reported. Similar description to what we're seeing now. And one unexplained death that year. It could have been unrelated, but the hive mind thought it was worth noting. The guy had been decapitated and they never figured out how.

"After that, nothing. If we're to believe the hive mind—and I do, because they're weird, creepy robots—then this thing showed up maybe three times in the history of Rose Valley."

"What about before 1942?" Jake asked.

"Yeah. They went through that, too. Nothing before 1942."

Jake's mind tried to put the pieces together, searching for a pattern that he couldn't find. Nine years. Then sixteen. Then fifty. One creature could have done the first three, but not the current one. The beast would be far too old. And if a family of beasts existed out there, then why the big gap?

Shandi looked up, an intensity in her eyes. "Ready for the good part?"

Jake nodded. "Definitely."

"Every single report in the paper related to this stuff—including the decapitation—had a quote from someone at Arrowhead Research. Could be a coincidence. Maybe they were just the go-to quote engine for The Reporter back then.

"But it wasn't just that they were quoted in every one of them. It's what they said and who said it. It was always Dr. Cordova, and he consistently, over the course of sixteen years, insisted that each and every incident was isolated and atypical and would soon come to an end."

"How would they know that? That it would come to an end. And a better question, I guess, is—did it?" Jake asked.

"Generally, yeah. Even when there were multiple reports, they were always within a very short time period. Within a week or two."

Jake rubbed his temples. He needed to stand. He couldn't think sitting down. He stood up and started pacing. Shandi turned in her chair to face him but didn't rise.

"What are you telling me, here? That Arrowhead Research is involved somehow?" He asked, not stopping to look at her.

"I don't know if I'm saying that for certain. I'm saying it's a possibility. It's a commonality, at least, and that has to mean something."

Jake continued to pace. Shandi stopped talking. Perhaps because she wanted to let him think. Perhaps because she busied herself with her own thinking. Jake didn't pay much attention. He just paced and thought.

If Arrowhead Research tied into all of this, how did that relate to the here and now? They hadn't gotten involved with any of the recent incidents. Everything that had happened recently seemed far more serious than anything reported in the past. There had never been a mass sighting. The beast was going after more than just livestock. It had maimed a guy. It could have killed Shandi and Macy. If Arrowhead shared responsibility for the existence of the beast, wouldn't they have come forward by now? Or were they so involved that they couldn't afford to admit culpability?

Jake felt Shandi's hand on his. She gripped it. He stopped. She stood up and grabbed his other hand, forcing him to face her.

"Stop for a minute," she said, looking up into his eyes. She didn't let go of his hands.

"When's the next time you're due for an appointment at Arrowhead?"

"Wednesday. Why?"

She squeezed his hands. Pleaded with her eyes. She spoke softer. "Think about this before you react. I know you're going to want to say no."

Jake considered the possibilities of the questions she might ask. Surely, she wouldn't suggest that he steal information from Arrowhead. That would never work. The outbuilding stood nowhere near any data of interest.

Or maybe she meant to persuade him to talk Deirdre out of some information. That was more feasible, but the thought didn't sit well. With Shandi standing in front of him, his hands in hers, the very thought of Deirdre turned his stomach.

"Take me with you."

No. Definitely not. He could think of nothing more awkward and terrifying than putting Deirdre and Shandi together. The fact that he had to see Deirdre again at all made him nervous enough. She had a way of confusing him. Of making him think things he didn't want to think. He couldn't go through that with Shandi there.

Shandi seemed to sense Jake's reaction. She shifted her hands, interlocked her fingers with his, instantly creating more intimacy. He swallowed hard.

"I'll drop you off at the clinic," she said. "Then I'll go to the main campus. I'll sweet talk the receptionist. Or find a clerk. Someone in there has access to information that might help us, and I'll find it. I need *you* to get me through the front gate."

Jake relaxed a little. Her plan didn't involve Deirdre and Shandi sharing the same space, and that seemed strangely important. If that could be guaranteed, Jake felt far less wary of Shandi's plan.

Jake became hyper-aware of how close Shandi now stood. He could feel the heat from her body. Her warm, soft hands softly entwined with his. He fought back certain thoughts, forcing himself to focus on the beast.

"Do you think that will work? Security does seem pretty loose around there, but surely they lock up the good stuff."

"Why, sir," Shandi said as she batted her eyelids. "I think you may have forgotten who you were talking to. Sure, I may report on Wes Morris' completion percentage by day, but by night I'm an investigative journalist. I will use my mad journalist skills to blow this story wide open."

Her confidence intoxicated him. Shandi Mason could get anything she wanted when she set her mind to it.

He nodded. "Okay. Sure. My appointment is at one. I can pick you up at The Reporter after I get done with—dammit!"

Shandi's face changed to confusion. "What?"

"Nothing. I just... With you and Macy here this morning, I forgot to go down to Mikey's. Bernard's going to be pissed."

She didn't let go of his hands when she laughed. "He'll get over it. He's a big boy."

"Yeah. It'll be fine. It's not the first time. It just seems to matter so much to him," Jake said. "Anyway. Yeah. I'll pick you up at 12:30 on Wednesday. At the Reporter. Then we'll head over to Arrowhead."

The conversation went silent. Their eyes lingered on one another briefly. Then she looked down. Jake looked down. Her grip loosened, as if the interlace of their hands surprised her. He didn't want to, but Jake let their hands fall away from each other.

They stood across from each other now. Not touching. Their eyes met again. Jake's heart raced. He didn't want to presume too much. She had let go of his hands. Perhaps she had taken them involuntarily. Her way of getting his attention. But there was something more. Something they both needed from each other. Was it just safety? A mutual place to escape from the fear and confusion surrounding Rose Valley?

The door swung open with a thud and a backpack hit the floor. Macy started talking before she even closed the door. "School is nuts right now. All anyone wants to talk about is the beast."

Jake and Shandi turned away from each other. Jake tried desperately not to look guilty, but he couldn't control the instinctual reaction. Shandi stepped past Jake and towards Macy, her arm touching up against him as she went. His skin tingled. Had she brushed up against him on purpose?

Macy shut the door and looked up at them. Her eyes went back and forth between them. Jake walked to the kitchen sink and started wetting down a rag, intending to wipe down the counters. They didn't really need it, but the act gave him a purpose. He could feel Macy's gaze on him. The room filled with painful, awkward silence.

Until Macy broke it. "Ew. Gross."

CHAPTER 23

Shandi climbed up into the old truck, smiled at Jake, and buckled her seatbelt. "Hey."

"Hey," he said.

Jake looked concerned, but returned her smile. She worried that his concern had been caused by her, even though she couldn't think of a reason why. Since the moment they shared two days earlier, there had been no other indication that their friendship might be turning into something more. She wondered whether she had imagined it.

She knew she could make the next move. She wanted to, but she hesitated. Things had moved fast, but when she distanced herself from her feelings, she couldn't shake the thought that it had only been a few days since Jake seemed to want to be with Deirdre. Shandi needed a stronger sign from Jake.

Tuesday evening had been great. To her relief, Shandi had come home late to find Jake helping Macy with her calculus homework—she was little help in that realm. After dinner, the three of them played games together at Jake's tiny kitchen table. It had been a nice, comfortable evening, but there had been nothing definitive to indicate that Jake had feelings for her.

Shandi focused in on the road as they left the square and headed up the hill to the only stoplight in town.

"How's Bernard?" she asked, breaking the silence.

Jake's concern intensified. "He wasn't there today. Second day in a row. Mikey says he hasn't seen him either."

"Weird."

"Yeah. He's missed his fair share of days. It's not like our games are set in stone. But two days in a row? I think I'm going to drive out and check on him after the appointment today." He seemed to relax just having said it out loud. Shandi realized that his anxiety came from his concern for Bernard, not from anything she'd done.

"Sounds like a plan. I'm sure he'd love the company."

Jake nodded as he navigated his way to Arrowhead Research. Shandi wondered if apprehension clouded Jake's mind. It would be the first time he and Deirdre had spent time together since their date. Non-date? Whatever it is they had shared, she thought it best not to bring it up.

The conversation fell into silence as Shandi watched the town scroll by. As they passed one house, Shandi noticed a man outside his window with a hammer, affixing boards to the frame. Shandi knew from experience that the reinforcements would hardly provide any protection, but she could understand the desire for safety. Was boarding up windows really any different than planning an infiltration of Arrowhead Research? Just a different way to deal with the reality of a monster rampaging through town.

"How's work so far?" Jake asked.

"Good, I guess. This town has a strange memory. They remember Starla Batson's top coming off at the tenth-grade pool party with vivid clarity, but the beast disappears for a few days, and they're over it."

Jake grinned. "I remember that party. Best day ever."

Shandi punched him on the arm, harder than she meant to. He immediately grabbed his bicep and feigned pain.

"Ouch! What? I love swimming."

Shandi shook her head.

"Heard anything from Skylar Brooks?" Jake asked.

"Nah, nothing. Not from the hive mind either. They're still in town, though, so Cam didn't run 'em off like I'd hoped."

Jake nodded as he came to a stop at the red light. Once it turned green, it would just be highway until they got to Arrowhead Research.

While they waited for the light to change, Jake glanced over at her, really looking at her for the first time since she had gotten in the truck. "You look nice."

Knowing she would soon have to convince some reluctant people to give up information, Shandi had put a little extra effort into her appearance. Her hair was bunched up into a ponytail like normal, but she wore dark eye makeup and a bold shade of lipstick. The jeans she'd wriggled into were a touch uncomfortable, but they accentuated her curves in a flattering way.

She smiled flirtatiously. "Why, thank you. Rule number one of being a super sleuth. Always look good."

"Aww. And here I thought you got dolled up just for me."

"Don't flatter yourself, Jake Rollins."

He laughed his easy, casual laugh, as if the joke didn't consume him as much as it just comfortably sat with his soul. She enjoyed partaking in his quiet confidence.

"Any word on the door repairs?"

Shandi panicked as she considered whether he meant to kick her out. Did he not like having her at his place? Or maybe he only wanted to keep the conversation moving. She supposed it must have been annoying to have two women taking up half of his house.

"Oh yeah," he said. "They should finish today. Fun fact: Your door being shattered by a giant monster-man is considered an act of God by insurance companies."

He laughed again. "I did not know that. I'm surprised *they* knew that."

"Yeah. Insurance companies have contingency plans for everything, apparently."

The conversation went silent. He didn't ask when she would be moving out. She took that as a good sign, but felt obligated to offer up the information anyway.

"So, yeah. Macy and I will be out of your hair tonight. Finally, you'll get some peace and quiet again."

He didn't answer right away. Shandi studied his face, looking for some evidence of how he felt about her leaving. Eventually, he replied, "I don't really miss the peace and quiet as much as I thought I would. It might be hard to adjust back."

Shandi smiled to no one in particular as she answered, "Well, given that I have a grown-up's kitchen, maybe we'll have you over for dinner sometime."

"Ouch! You didn't like my toaster oven garlic bread and Velveeta Shells & Cheese?"

She took a fake solemn expression. "Oh no. It was wonderful. A gourmet experience. Just seems like I should return the favor."

Jake nodded, his voice imperceptibly softer when he answered. "Yeah. I'd like that."

He turned the corner and pulled up to the guard gate at the perimeter of the Arrowhead campus. Given that the truck didn't have a working air conditioner, the windows were already rolled down. Shandi braced herself to provide a reasonable excuse as to why she accompanied Jake. She had considered a few possibilities in advance just in case the guard interrogated her.

The guard stepped out of his shack and walked up to the driver's side window. He looked at Jake, then at Shandi. She flashed him her best smile before he turned back to Jake.

"Hey, Jake," said the guard. "Here for a checkup with Dr. Valentine?"

"That's right. My last one, she says."

"No kiddin'? That's great, man. You've come a long way."

Jake nodded. "Yeah. I'm happy to be able to put all of this behind me."

"I hear that," the guard said. "Hey. Were you guys at the game on Friday? I about crapped my pants, man. That's some scary shit."

"Yeah. Pretty insane," Jake curtly responded.

The guard took a beat, letting the silence hang, as if he hoped that one of them would continue the conversation. When neither Jake nor Shandi offered anything more, he tapped the window sill twice and said, "All right. Y'all be careful, now."

"You, too," Jake said as he pulled the truck forward. Shandi gasped for air, realizing that she had been holding her breath.

"Well, that was easy," she said.

"I wasn't worried. I'm a regular," Jake said. "Besides, it's not like this place is Fort Knox. They take visitors all the time. The only guard I've ever seen is there at the front gate."

Jake pulled the truck up to the outbuilding where he had his appointments. Shandi had never seen it before. The tiny, portable building seemed like it would be too heavy to sit so comfortably atop the gray cinderblocks underneath. A few small windows dotted the corrugated metal of the outside walls, but none low enough or large enough to provide a view into the building. A set of metal rollaway stairs led up to the door. It didn't look like a place to get adequate medical treatment.

"All right," Jake said as he popped open his door and pointed towards the main campus. "Main campus is about half a mile that way. I have no idea what's what up there."

Shandi studied the campus from afar. Strangely, no previous story had ever sent her to Arrowhead Research. The times she'd needed to talk to them, they had always sent someone into town to meet her.

Buildings snaked throughout the campus, most of them one-story, all of them seemingly built on a whim. She had been there as a kid many times, but she couldn't quite remember where they had gone on the field trips. She had a vague notion that there had been ample signage describing each building. That would have to be enough.

"Don't worry about me, chief. I can take care of myself," she said, as he slid out of the truck. She unbuckled her seatbelt and scooted herself into the driver's seat.

Jake shut the door and put his hands on the window sill, looking up towards Shandi. "Oh, I'm not worried.

Not for you. Maybe for them. Someone is going to get in *so* much trouble after you're done with them."

She smiled. "Damn right. Your appointment is thirty minutes?"

"Thereabouts, yeah. I can text you when I'm done."

"Okay. Sounds good."

Shandi looked down at the steering column. She had ridden in this truck dozens—if not hundreds—of times, but this would be the first time she had driven it. She quickly figured out how to put it in reverse and did so, her foot still on the brake.

"Good luck," Jake said.

She tried not to think about the fact that Deirdre waited for him in that building. She tried to focus on the fact that Deirdre and Jake shared only a doctor-patient relationship. She couldn't be concerning herself with her insecurities, anyway. She had important things to do. She needed all her wits to get to the bottom of the beast mystery.

Without thinking, she put one of her hands over Jake's.

"Thanks," she said. "You too."

CHAPTER 24

Uncomfortable silence filled the clinic from the moment he stepped through the door. Deirdre seemed nervous, moving more quickly than normal and never meeting his gaze. Nights earlier, he felt like she'd stalked him. That she would pounce on him. The more intense version of Deirdre shared the room with him today, with none of the sexual undertones of that night. His attempts at small talk—even about the beast—were met with icy silence. Jake didn't know how to process it or what it meant.

Arrowhead had already started renovations on the clinic. None of the equipment that he expected to see filled the room anymore. The built-in counters still lined the wall, but the only furniture in the room consisted of a hospital gurney and the metal folding chair in which he sat. The gurney seemed particularly odd.

At the moment, Deirdre stood at the counter with her back to him. He felt safer when her eyes averted, but her back also gave him a sense of dread, wondering what came next. She didn't have the clipboard today. The refrigerator that held the serum no longer held a place in the room. On the counter sat two bags—Deirdre's purse and a backpack.

Without turning, she spoke. "I'm going to need you to get undressed and lay on the gurney, please."

This seemed like an odd request. She had checked the healing of his scars before, but he had never needed to lay down for that. In fact, lying down seemed like it would be counter to the cause. Jake just wanted it all to be over with, though, so he complied. He stripped down to his boxers and left his clothes on the chair.

Deirdre turned around and looked at him coolly. She wore no makeup today. Jake couldn't recall seeing her delicate face without makeup since high school. She looked older than he remembered from a few days ago, and she carried a sense of foreboding with her that unsettled him.

"On the gurney, please," she said.

He froze at the request. His mind swam in an attempt to discern her goal, wondering if she intended some twisted sex thing. Regardless, Jake felt strongly that he should not comply.

"I... I don't really feel comfortable with that. We can just do it standing up, like always," he said as confidently as he could, which turned out to not be very confident at all.

Deirdre sighed and turned back to the counter. "Oh, Jake. I don't want this to be hard for you. Why can't you just do what I ask?"

She didn't want *what* to be hard for him? What did she intend to do to him? His discomfort grew exponentially, as did a cold sense of dread. The situation escalated beyond Deirdre just being weird. Something sinister came for him now.

She turned around and lifted something towards him. With his eyes focused elsewhere, he only saw a glint of something out of the corner of his eye. He threw his hands up once he understood what was happening.

He had never had a gun pointed at him before, and the sheer, adrenal terror of it made him instantly queasy.

"Jesus, Deirdre! What the hell are you doing?"

Jake tried to understand. Had he hurt her feelings? Had texting Shandi that night caused her to go into a jealous rage? It seemed impossible and surreal. This sort of thing happened in movies, but not in real life. Real people just sulked when their feelings got hurt. They didn't point guns at people.

Deirdre remained remarkably calm. She spoke slowly, as if Jake had just misunderstood her before. "Lay down on the gurney."

He couldn't believe that she would shoot him, so he didn't immediately follow her direction. He could surely talk his way out of this. He had known Deirdre for years.

"Listen," he said. "I'm sorry about the other night. You're great. You're beautiful. It just didn't work out. It's nothing personal. It's me. Last year, I went through a div—"

Deirdre interrupted him with a cold, taunting laugh. Jake realized in that moment that whatever her intentions, they had nothing to do with their "date."

"Get on the bed. I don't want to shoot you, Jake, but I will if I have to." She took a step towards him.

With no other remaining options, Jake climbed onto the gurney, the frame rattling and the wheels screeching across the floor as he got himself situated. He heard Deirdre's heels click as she approached, the gun still trained on him. Fear stopped him from looking up to watch her. He focused on breathing, still not convinced that she would shoot him, but also too terrified to test her.

She motioned towards the other side of the gurney. "Give me that. The strap."

He looked towards the side. The gurney had three straps along the side, meant for strapping patients down for transport. She wanted to strap him down. Once she did that, he would have no hope of fighting back. But if he tried to fight back now, she might shoot him.

If someone would have asked Jake how he would have reacted in a situation like this, he would have said that he would fight. That he would die if he had to. Now a gun threatened to end his life, though, and his instinct for survival won out.

He handed her the strap.

She expertly kept the gun on him while she latched the strap to the other side with one hand. She seemed ominously practiced.

Deirdre motioned to the middle strap that would tie around his waist. "Now that one."

Again, Jake complied. Before she latched it, she commanded him again. "Put your arms down. At your side."

Jake did not immediately move his arms. Once she bound his hands, he would have no hope of getting away. Still, she hadn't shot him immediately. That gave him some hope that she didn't want to kill him. He struggled to understand what she *did* want to do to him, but if he did what she said, maybe he would walk away from this. He put his arms down.

She tied off the second strap, painfully tight against his body. He lightly tried to pull his arms up and couldn't. He had no weapons now. She seemed to relax once she had completed this task. She walked a few steps away and put the gun on the counter, immediately returning to Jake. She reached across his body to grab the last strap herself, the scent of her shampoo assaulting Jake's nose and creating a strange dissonance between the situation at hand and the woman he had known her as before.

All three straps secure, Deirdre returned to her bags. With the gun out of her hand, Jake felt like he had a chance to talk to her. "Dee. If you let me go, I won't tell anyone. We can just pretend like this never happened."

She spoke without turning around. "Don't call me Dee."

"Okay. I'm sorry. Deirdre. I'm confused. There must be a misunderstanding." He tried to act calm, despite not being so at all. It still seemed like a bad dream.

"It's not a misunderstanding, Jake. It's necessary. I have no choice." She turned around as she spoke and approached the gurney. When she got there, she leaned over and peered directly into his eyes. "I like you, Jake. You were a good friend."

"Then let me go."

"This is my fault, Jake. I shouldn't have done this to you." She stood up as she spoke, but didn't leave his side. Her voice cracked. Her beautiful blue eyes moistened.

"Tie me up? Then let me go. You don't have to do this to me."

She ignored his pleas. "I just wanted to save you. You have to understand. You would've died if I hadn't done what I did. You were Jake Rollins. No one was ever as devoted to me as you were. You were the most loyal friend I ever had. I couldn't let you die. Not when I had the means to save you."

Jake swallowed hard, not knowing how to interpret her words. "But you did save me. I'm here right now. I'm alive. I'm strong. I'm healthy. We can still be friends."

She sniffled and let out a throaty laugh. "Oh, Jake. We haven't been friends for twenty years. I haven't had *any* friends for twenty years."

"It's not too late. We're both in Rose Valley again."

She regained some of her composure. "No, Jake. It's too late for that. This isn't about friendship. I don't need friends."

"Then what do you want? I'll do anything. Just let me go."

She walked back to the counter and turned her back to him. He struggled against the straps, taking care to do so as quietly as possible. She didn't have the gun in her hand, but she would be able to get to it faster than he would. Even if he broke out of the straps, he would be dead in a matter of seconds. He had to wait for her guard to be down. For her to be farther from the gun.

"There's nothing you can do, Jake. They tried to create an anti-serum. For years. It can't be done. Better doctors than me have tried. It so irrevocably changes you. It can't be fixed."

Jake's face flushed with frustration, annoyed with the vagueness of her explanations. "What can't be fixed? I don't understand, Deirdre. Help me understand."

"You can't control it, Jake. You might think you can. You'll hold it off for a while. The goodness in you might keep it at bay a while longer. But you'll lose. They all lost. And when you lose, people will die."

"What are you talking about?"

"The beast, Jake. That's what they're calling it, right?"

Jake went limp with shock. He didn't understand, but on some weird primal level it also made sense. Could it be possible that he shared bodies with the beast? He had never seen it. It had always attacked when he had been alone, maybe even while he had been asleep. Had Deirdre turned him into a monster? No. That couldn't be right. Jake had seen the video footage. The beast stood taller than him, with muscles far larger than any Jake could even hope to have. It possessed strength greater than any man.

"I'm not the beast, Deirdre. You're confused."

She turned around with a syringe in her hand, filled with something. She sighed. "Of course you aren't the beast, Jake. You're the seeker. The beast can't be killed. I tried to do this the other night, but this way will be easier for you."

So she did mean to kill him. Likely, with the drug in that syringe. The straps on the gurney prevented him from mounting any sort of fight. He couldn't prevent her from injecting him. For the first time since he had entered the clinic that day, Jake confronted the fact that this would be the last day of his life. With no out, and no weapons left at his disposal, Jake did the only thing he could think of.

He screamed. For help. For anyone. As loudly as he could. He fought against the straps, rocking the gurney back and forth. Shandi wouldn't be nearby. No one would be nearby. Logically, he knew that screaming could not save him now, but he did it anyway as Deirdre descended upon him.

Deirdre took his hand, the cold of her fingers shooting through Jake's arm. She turned it over and brushed over the back of his hand to find a vein. His screaming didn't seem to faze her. She held his hand tight. He stopped rocking. He stopped fighting. Tears started forming at the corners of his eyes. Deirdre looked at him. Tears flowed from her eyes as well.

Through sobbing, he pleaded, "Please, Deirdre. Don't do this."

She didn't answer. She inserted the needle into his hand and pushed the plunger. He felt it a strange cold sensation flow through his veins. He didn't know what strange concoction worked its way through his system, or how long it would take before he died, but his death was imminent now.

Deirdre removed the needle, set it on the counter, and stroked his hair. She gazed into his eyes. Though she clearly had gone crazy, and even tried to kill him, if the last thing he saw before he died were those eyes, at least he would die beholding beauty...

He thought it strange that he would think that. He wondered if the drug in his veins clouded his thoughts, making him think strange things.

"I'm just putting things back to how they were supposed to be, Jake."

He wanted to answer, but sleep started to overcome his consciousness. He struggled to remain focused and alert. Deirdre continued stroking his hair. She didn't say anything. She held his hand as if she had nothing to do with his imminent demise. She sat there as a dear friend coping with the inevitable loss of a loved one. It provided a strange sense of comfort, but he held on to the alarming incongruence of it as well. Could she be right? Would his death save the town?

He didn't fully understand his relationship to the beast. He didn't understand how his own death could save the lives of others. But Deirdre's intellect exceeded that of anyone he had ever known. She would not take a rash action. She would not resort to murder if she could devise another solution.

Jake thought of Shandi. Wondered how she would react. Would she be devastated? He didn't want her to be unhappy, but he hoped that she would cry for him.

Attend his funeral. Dream of a life they never had together. He regretted only just now allowing himself to think of Shandi in that way. As someone he wanted to spend his life with. He loved Shandi. Maybe he always had. Since before an age where he could really even understand love, Jake and Shandi had been bonded. He just wished he could have told Shandi that he loved her. Just one time. She needed to know. He wanted her to know.

He thought it ironic that he would have this moment of clarity just as the world drifted away from him. He would have thought that his imminent death would have brought panic, but he found himself calm. Peaceful. He appreciated that Deirdre spared him pain.

A loud noise echoed through the room, but Jake didn't have the strength to react. Deirdre moved away quickly. He immediately missed the comfort of her hand.

He vaguely heard voices, but they sounded as if they came from another room far away.

And then... a gunshot, maybe?

He tried to hold on. He tried to make sense of the commotion around him, but he couldn't.

His breathing slowed, and though it seemed impossible, he felt his heart slowing as well, relinquishing control to the drugs flowing through him. He closed his eyes. He stopped trying to make sense of the world around him. It didn't matter anymore.

His chest inflated. It fell. It did not rise again.

CHAPTER 25

The screams pierced the walls of the outbuilding and straight into Shandi's soul, where she sat in the truck, uncomfortable with the idea of encountering Deirdre. She knew in an instant that they had come from Jake, and before she knew it she was bounding across the parking lot.

Something stopped her at the door, however. She didn't know what she'd find, but good sense prodded her into making sure someone would be on the way to help. She jerked her phone out of her pocket and called Cam.

"Sheriff Donner here," his voice said.

"Come quick! To the first outbuilding at Arrowhead!" she rasped in a whisper, louder than she intended.

"What's going on?" he asked, not as urgently as Shandi preferred.

"I don't know. But it's important." She ended the call and crammed the phone back into her pocket.

Shandi took a deep breath. The screaming had stopped and she worried that she hadn't acted quickly enough. She jumped the stairs in one huge step and jerked open the door, instantly buffeted by the scene before her. Jake lay strapped to a gurney with Deirdre beside him, stroking his hair. What the hell was she even looking at?

Once Deirdre registered Shandi's presence, she moved from Jake's side and reached for something on the counter. Without consciously knowing what would come next, Shandi sprang to her right as the echo of a gunshot rang in her chest.

Deirdre had *shot* at her.

Shandi lunged for Dierdre, who steadied her arm and squeezed off another wild round, Shandi easily evading it. The impact of Shandi's head against Deirdre's small, bony chest felt like it should be hard enough to break her ribs. Deirdre flew backwards into the counter, her head turning as she bobbled the gun, trying desperately to hold on, but it came lose and clattered across the floor.

Shandi wrapped her arms around Deirdre's slight waist and dragged her to the ground, causing Deirdre to finally fight, flailing her arms against Shandi's back. Shandi barely felt it. They tumbled to the ground together and seemed to roll forever before Shandi finally got the upper hand and managed to straddle Deirdre against the floor. Instinctively, Shandi slammed her first into the side of Deirdre's face. It felt good.

Sharp pain shot into Shandi's skull and neck as Dierdre wrenched her hair back. The bitch wasn't very strong, but those arms were ridiculously long. Shandi punched her again. Deirdre pulled harder and bucked with her hips, causing Shandi to lose her balance and fall to the ground. Deirdre flipped the script and straddled Shandi now, but she didn't punch. She wrapped her hands around Shandi's neck and squeezed.

Shandi gasped for air, kicking and reaching for anything that could help her but her arms lacked the reach of Deirdre's and she felt like a cartoon character being held back by a huge powerful hand. Shandi grabbed Deirdre's wrists and pulled as hard as she could to pry them away. Her vision started to narrow and her windpipe ached but she channeled the pain into pulling even harder until she could feel the grip loosening, and then Shandi held Deirdre's wrists apart, with Deirdre unable to push back against the adrenaline-fueled grip of a very angry Shandi Mason.

It seemed that they were at an impasse. In this brief respite, Shandi looked at Deirdre's face and could barely make out any humanity. Deirdre's blue eyes might as well have been red for the fire burning in them.

In one smooth motion, Shandi forced all her strength into her right hand and bent Deirdre's left wrist back further than it wanted to go, not quite far enough to cause an audible crack of the bones, but far enough that Deidre yelped in pain. Shandi took advantage of the distraction, twisted her left hip and threw Deirdre off, immediately scrambling back on top where her right knee rested on Deirdre's throat.

Deirdre clawed and slapped at Shandi's calf, but Shandi only pressed down harder. Deirdre sputtered and gasped, begging with her eyes for Shandi to let her go. For the briefest moment, Shandi wanted to push harder, to choke the life out of this freak, but she couldn't bring herself to do it. Instead, she let up enough for Deirdre to draw a ragged breath.

Then, in an instant, the room filled with uniformed police officers, Cam among them, with his gun drawn. He crossed the room and grabbed Shandi by the upper arm. Shandi did not protest. She stood up beside Cam, and for the first time since it all started, acknowledged the fear surging through her veins.

"Jake. She did something to Jake!" Shandi pointed off towards the gurney, but there were already

Arrowhead Research paramedics at his side, one of them studying an empty vial.

Cam patted her back. "Don't worry. I called for medical, too. Just in case."

Despite her better judgement, Shandi buried her face into Cam's chest. Tears burst from her eyes. She vaguely registered the sounds behind her: a defibrillator, calls for "clear". It went on for too long. Jake wouldn't survive. She shouldn't have hesitated.

Then, a paramedic hollered over to Cam. "We've got him back. The poison did a number on him, but I think he's going to be okay. Might be a while before he wakes up. We need to get him to the hospital."

Shandi peeled herself from Cam's chest and marched over to the gurney. "I'm going with you."

Cam grabbed her by the shoulder, and gently turned her around. "I need you here, Shandi. I need to know what happened."

Shandi's face grew hot. "Screw you!"

He sighed with obvious displeasure. "You're not even related to him. You really should—"

Cam backed off at this, though he expressed his displeasure by stomping around the room and loudly talking to his deputies about piecing the crime scene back together. Shandi didn't care. In a matter of minutes, she found herself crammed into the back of an ambulance, anxiously watching the little line that represented Jake's pulse.

***

She tried to stop her hands from shaking as the ambulance pulled up to the Rose Valley Hospital. Her time with Jake would soon come to an end. She couldn't claim to be his wife. Not even his girlfriend. It would be difficult for her to coax information out of the doctors, but she knew the important stuff. The paramedics knew what poison Deirdre had used, and they'd managed to bring him back from death.

So did you, she told herself. She didn't need adulation, though. Worrying over the details would be useless. Deirdre sat in the county jail and Jake's pulse pattered steadily. Nothing else mattered.

They rolled Jake out of the ambulance and into the hospital. As they approached the doors going back into the ER, one of the EMTs held a hand out in front of her. "I'm sorry, Shandi. You can't follow him in here. I'll do my best to get you information. I promise."

Yet another high-school acquaintance. She trusted that he would try, but also knew that he didn't have much power over what happened to Jake from this point forward. She mumbled a *thank you* to him and turned back to the waiting room.

In the lobby, she sunk down into the first chair she came to, alone. With such a small population, the Rose Valley ER was generally quiet. She needed to calm down and figure out the next move. Deirdre tried to kill Jake. More accurately, Deirdre killed Jake. Shandi wanted to know why. That felt like the most important thing.

Deirdre had spent a year rehabilitating him. Why would she kill him after all the work she had put into his health and wellbeing? She couldn't shake the worry that her staying with Jake had somehow triggered this crazy outburst. Maybe the night hadn't gone how Jake had described. Maybe this was jealousy.

Even if Deirdre and Jake had slept together that night, it didn't explain her behavior, even if she thought Jake had spurned her. There had to be more to it. Shandi felt certain that a piece of the puzzle hovered just beyond her grasp.

Did all of this relate to the beast? Shandi couldn't come up with any plausible connection, but the coincidence was odd—the town gained a beast just as Dierdre lost her sanity.

Jake might have the missing piece of the puzzle. He would know more when he woke up. Shandi desperately hoped that he would. The thought of him dying terrified her.

To get information, she would need someone that the doctors would talk to about Jake's case. He didn't have immediate family in town. His single mother had packed up and moved away from Rose Valley years ago. Would they talk to Steve? Jake lived on his property. Maybe they would give him information.

Shandi pulled her phone out of her back pocket and found Steve's name in her contacts. He answered after a few rings. She prepared to tell him everything, but when she heard his voice, all the adrenaline that had kept her going came crashing down, and she didn't say anything. She just cried.

CHAPTER 26

Machete in hand, Miriam hacked swiftly through the underbrush. She had done this kind of work for years. She came across as timid and unassuming, but only because she had grown up in the shadow of a man who took up enough space for them both. In truth, her father's enterprise would fail without her, though she would never say that out loud. The arrangement worked better this way.

Skylar Brooks stayed back, busying himself with glad-handing every person in Rose Valley that would listen. He played his role. Miriam did not envy it. She did not care for people, or for social graces. The fewer people she had to deal with, the better. She had built a comfortable relationship with her brother, Cornelius, and her cousin, Tanner. Virtually anyone else in her life only served as a distraction.

She did quite like the reporter she had met, though. People rarely treated them that nicely, even though Miriam knew that the reporter mostly just wanted to exploit their research. She much preferred being used graciously to being abused by her overbearing father. Maybe Shandi could be an ally in things her father wouldn't touch.

For days the three of them searched the landscape surrounding Rose Valley. They found all manner of interesting things. Caves and rivers. Waterfalls and old campsites. Burnt out cabins in the woods. Abandoned cars. The occasional hunter, camper, or skinny-dipper. The outskirts of Rose Valley overflowed with intrigue and wonder, but the three of them sought only one particular wonder.

She chopped through more shrubbery, following the sound of water. She heard it some feet away, and could always rely on water as an interesting place to explore. Every animal needed water—even people.

Tanner followed closely behind her with his rifle. His aim impressed the most accomplished of marksman, and Miriam admired him for it. Cornelius trailed further behind. She loved him dearly, but he too often reminded her of their father, taking notes and documenting their discoveries.

They finally came to a clearing, where a creek meandered through the grass. They hadn't seen it walking in; it came at a strange angle. Across the small creek stood an imposing limestone rock face, the bedrock of Rose Valley: a town sturdily built on nothing but the dependable hardness of limestone.

Miriam looked back and saw Tanner motioning to his right. He shifted his weight subtly, and she heard a quiet click of his rifle. She learned to recognize these things from Tanner. And from Cornelius. They found talking both wasteful and costly. When dealing with Skylar Brooks, remaining silent proved to be the better path.

She looked to the right as Tanner directed and saw a cave. Caves had not been uncommon thus far. Most sat empty, or far too small to be of interest. Occasionally garbage littered the floors. One cave had phallic symbols etched into the walls. Cornelius laughed, but Miriam found such displays of graffiti childish and uncouth.

Along with Tanner, she moved towards the cave. She sloshed through the creek without hesitation. The trickling stream wasn't very deep, and her waterproof boots kept the water at bay. As they approached, she could tell this cave would be bigger than most of the ones they had encountered.

She slid her machete into the specially-made sheath attached to her belt and removed a flash light from a pouch on the other side. She clicked it on and shined it into the mouth of the cave. Wherever she pointed the beam of light, Tanner's rifle followed. She waited patiently for Cornelius to catch up.

With all three of them together, Miriam took the first step into the cave, immediately noticing the refreshingly cool air. She looked around. Something reflected the light back to her eyes. All three approached the bauble.

As they walked into the cave, Miriam realized that it stretched back farther than she had first thought. Another antechamber laid in front of them, around the corner from what initially looked like it would be the back of the cave. Her interest was piqued.

She shone the flashlight down across the ground of the antechamber, sweeping it across the floor to catch the bauble again. Nothing immediately reflected, but Miriam's patience and determination could not so easily be deterred. Tanner and Cornelius did so with her, fast enough that she did not fall over them.

Her eye finally found it. A small metal thing. Perhaps just a soda tab. They had seen a number of those, along with beer caps. The residents of Rose Valley did not respect the environment in a way that Miriam found suitable.

She slowly approached it, bent down and picked it up, excited to find not a soda tab, but military dog tags with a chain attached. Scrutinizing the tags, she could see the tarnished, brown metal struggling to maintain its integrity. It felt brittle in her fingers.

Her brothers crowded around her as she aimed the flash light directly at the tags. The words were shadowed, but sharp eyes ran in the family. With some shifting and focus, Miriam had no doubt as to the name—William P. Hargrove. Following that came a social security number and an address in Mississippi. Miriam had studied maps extensively. She recalled that Mississippi sat roughly five hundred miles to the East. These dog tags had come a long way from home, both in time and space.

She removed a Ziplock bag from one of the pockets on her shorts and dropped the dog tags in, returning it to her pocket once she'd preserved it to her satisfaction. This find certainly intrigued her, but she hoped that the more interesting find lay around the corner in the antechamber.

Shining the light forward again, Miriam stepped forward. Cornelius and Tanner did not step with her. They moved on her second step, creating a V formation. It had never been necessary for their survival that they form up in any particular configuration, but Miriam felt strongly that this configuration would provide maximum security—in case of an attack.

A number of things lined the ground in the antechamber. Unlike the other caves, however, she wouldn't classify this stuff as garbage. It looked more like a haphazard home. The middle of the floor lacked any debris at all, the dirt almost entirely dug away from the limestone flooring. The walls bore no drawings or writing. Only things on the floor. Things that did not go together and did not make sense.

When Miriam decided an attack unlikely in this small room, the three fanned out. The room provided little space to fan, but they managed to spread out enough so that they could each study a different wall of the room without touching one another. They had been in much tighter spaces together. To have a fear of confined spaces would have been counter to their profession.

Miriam studied the ground along her chosen wall, silently counting the strange tchotchkes. Some of them looked recent, while others looked very old. The oldest seemed to be a Superman doll that looked like it was made in the 1940s. Cornelius interrupted her search by offering up one of his finds to the group. She turned to look at it.

Cornelius held a relatively new stuffed animal. No more than a few years old, but it looked better cared for than the other items in this room. It had not been in this cave for very long. It's stuffing oozed out of one of the seams, making it hard to identify, but it appeared to be a cartoon potato. Miriam found that amusing. Cornelius' find did seem important, and focusing on it seemed the right call. The newness of it meant that the inhabitant of this cave had been here recently.

Miriam realized that it also meant that no animal lived in this cave. Perhaps it served as shelter for a homeless person, but Miriam didn't think so. The cave lay too far off the beaten path. It would not serve to have a house so far from town if one's livelihood centered on the goodwill of people. Furthermore, Miriam had seen no vagrants in Rose Valley. With a town of its size, a large homeless population seemed incredibly unlikely.

Chances were good that this cave might belong to their cryptid. Knowing nothing about it, she found it feasible that it might choose to collect such odds and ends. Perhaps it liked the smell, or the bright colors. She began to get excited.

With no words, Miriam and Tanner backed out of the small antechamber so that Cornelius could photograph the relics inside. They did not have enough bags to properly remove all the things in here. They would have to take pictures and return another day for a proper excavation.

As Cornelius took his photos, Miriam heard a sound behind her that didn't come from Tanner. Nor Cornelius. Without taking the time to think of what it might be, she casually looked towards the mouth of the cave to see a lithe silhouette. Tanner noticed it as well. Cornelius sensed that Miriam and Tanner's focus had shifted, stopped taking pictures, and joined them in looking at the thing before them.

In their days in Rose Valley, they had encountered most of the wildlife, and this creature didn't have the dog-like form of a coyote, or the stout, short-legged body of a wild boar. Though it clearly came from the feline family, the long elegant legs and tail ruled out a common bobcat. Miriam thought it seemed quite impossible, but the shape in the cave mouth could be nothing other than a cheetah.

Normally, Miriam would have taken this as a good sign. More often than not, their hunts for cryptids ended with the discovery of a perfectly well-known animal. If Rose Valley's beast had just been a cheetah, then the expedition would be over and they could catalog yet another success. But she had seen the beast in the videos, and knew full well that the creature that stalked the town bore no relation to the cheetah.

The three of them huddled together, trapped by the predator. The cheetah did not move. It stood at the mouth of the cave, as if contemplating whether it could trust them, or perhaps whether it could eat them.

Tanner knew exactly what to do, though. He did exactly what Miriam would have told him to do if they had needed to waste time discussing it. He raised his rifle, aimed it squarely at the heart of the cheetah and fired. The cheetah collapsed almost immediately, with a strange chirping sound that made her feel instantly guilty.

After the cheetah fell, Miriam saw another silhouette, smaller and adorable. Tanner had just killed this poor cub's mother. Miriam felt bad, no doubt, but they had certainly killed many animals in their adventures. She would take it back if she could, but although the three of them were experts in a great variety of topics, the resurrection of cheetahs did not make that list. They would just have to take the cub back to town and make sure to find it a caretaker.

The three of them walked to the mouth of the cave. The cub did not run from them, which Miriam found surprising. Perhaps the cub had been around humans before.

Miriam reached down and let it sniff her hands. Tanner handed her some jerky from his pack, and she offered it to the cub which devoured it quickly. Miriam could tell that the two of them would be fast friends. She scooped up the cub. It seemed heavier than reasonable for its small size, but the strength-training that Miriam did every other day made the cub's weight bearable enough.

Shadows stretched across the trees. Though their training prepared them to forage in the dark, it was best that they headed into to town. The others agreed, and they began the trek back.

Per usual, Miriam took up the lead with Tanner in the middle. Cornelius had less to document, so he managed to keep the pace. After a few feet across the creek, the foliage rustled behind them. Miriam stopped, pulse increasing. Something large. Larger than Cornelius. And Tanner. Even a full-grown cheetah.

Miriam had a knack for distinguishing things by sound, and she had an immediate and distinct impression that the thing behind them presented a clear and present danger. She turned to look, only to find the very thing they had been searching for. Upon seeing the imposing figure before them, she felt no elation at the discovery.

She ran. Tanner ran after her. Cornelius brought up the rear. The beast did not immediately give chase, giving Miriam a glimmer of hope that perhaps the beast did not find them interesting.

The cub writhed in her arms, making it difficult for her to maintain her balance through the rough terrain. But she persisted and ran as fast as she could. She heard Tanner's rifle go off, using the boom to determine he was still close behind her, firing on the run.

She could hear Cornelius tearing through the brush behind Tanner, but she worried that his slower speed would make him easy prey. The beast would surely catch him first if it gave chase. But maybe it wouldn't. They made good ground and had a healthy lead.

As soon as she allowed for the possibility that the beast wouldn't chase them, her hopes shattered as she heard the branches and trees explode as the beast moved through them, lumbering and loud. It was gaining ground with every loping step. Tanner's rifle fired some more, this time farther away from her. He must have stopped to get a good aim.

Miriam could not leave them behind. She rounded back to survey the scene. Tanner crouched behind a rock, firing his rifle as often as he could. His aim impressed as always. Multiple shots hit the beast. In the chest. In the legs. It stumbled and slowed.

Cornelius caught up. He passed Tanner and approached Miriam. Tanner fired some more. The beast kept coming. The rifle's stopping power paled in comparison to the resilience of this thing. They should have carried larger firearms.

Tanner stood up. He had also given up on his rifle. He looked to his belt, pulled a canister from it and jerked a metal pull tab from the top. It spewed a fine white mist. Tanner coughed and lobbed it towards the beast. He blinked furiously. The pepper spray had gotten into his eyes and he couldn't see. Neither Miriam nor Cornelius would be able to carry Tanner.

He ran towards them without his sight. She started running as well. Cornelius slowed, unable to keep up, feeling the effects of study instead of exercise. Tanner miraculously followed the sound of her footsteps, she assumed. Or perhaps he could see just well enough to make out the path.

Miriam stopped in her tracks when she heard a blood-curdling scream, not from the beast, but from Cornelius. Tanner ran past her, grabbing her arm as he went. She ran again. Tanner let go of her arm. She realized that he needed her to run in front of him so that he could find his way. She felt sickened at the thought that they may have lost Cornelius, but she knew that she had to save Tanner and herself if she could.

She had never run this fast or this long. She didn't hear the beast behind them anymore, but kept running.

Tanner kept pace behind her. The cheetah cub had gone catatonic. It must have sensed the urgency of the situation. It needed Miriam to survive and must have known as much on some intuitive level.

They ran at full speed until they got to the jeep. Miriam turned and looked behind her. She did not see Cornelius. She could not hear him. The tears fought to break free from her resolve, but she pushed them back. This eventuality always loomed on the horizon. The beast had killed Cornelius. She could not mourn now when she could save herself and Tanner.

Miriam put the cheetah cub into the back seat and went to the cargo area of the jeep. She opened it, slid a large box to the back of the cargo area and popped open the top, hefting the elephant gun free from its case. She walked back to the front of the Jeep, laid on the ground, resting the gun on its stand, sighting it in the direction they'd just come from. She willed herself to be very still, all but stopping her breathing. She listened.

The .585 Gehringer elephant gun packed the most powerful punch in their arsenal. If the beast emerged from the woods, she would not hesitate to use it, but she could hear nothing. The beast gave up the chase. She shook in anger, desperate to shoot something. Tanner arrived beside her, knelt down, and put his hand on her shoulder.

Miriam understood his meaning. This moment could not be about revenge. The beast might come back. This moment had to be for running. She packed up the gun and climbed into the driver's seat, with Tanner already inside and buckled in. She started the Jeep, willed away her tears, and drove as fast as she could to Rose Valley.

CHAPTER 27

The sheriff said to sit. Deirdre sat.

He didn't need to provide direction for the next part. She put her hands on the table and the sheriff handcuffed both of her hands to the loops bolted to the table. Through the one-way mirror, Dub could tell that Deirdre was uncomfortable, which boded well for how quickly she might talk.

Cam rounded the table and sat across from her. He took off his hat and sat it on the table. "Why did you do it, Dr. Valentine?"

Deirdre didn't answer. She stared straight at the sheriff. Through him, really. Dub didn't expect her to cooperate easily, so her flat, stoic expression hardly surprised him. They could fluster her into omission if they could just delay her asking for a lawyer. That would give them more time to try to get her to screw up and let something slip. Dub liked their chances. The brighter ones always believed they could outsmart the cops.

Cam's voice echoed through the speakers: "From my understanding, you've spent a year making sure Jake Rollins survived his accident. So why kill him?"

Again, she offered no answer. Dub knew from experience that she wondered whether she could win the battle of wills by making Cam lose his temper. She would hope to trick them into committing some breach of protocol that she would eventually be able to use to go free on a technicality. Given the bruises that Shandi had left on her face, Deirdre would likely be willing to accept a few blows from the sheriff if it meant she walked.

Normally, Dub would have no qualms about Cam's ability to keep his wits about him, but the sheriff looked incredibly tired. Dark circles lined his reddened eyes. Dub doubted that Cam had slept the night before, given the murder of Cornelius Brooks.

Cam spoke frankly. "Look. I know Jake was always obsessed with you in high school. Maybe he got that way again? Is that it? Did he cross a line? Did he do something to you?"

Deirdre looked for a second as if she might laugh out loud. The sheriff leaned back and folded his arms across his chest. Cam's patience was wearing thin.

Dub considered interrupting and trying to take over, but imagining the ass-chewing that came with that made the prospect unappealing. Cam proved difficult enough to deal with on a full tank. Dub estimated it better to let the sheriff do what he wanted, and hope that he recognized when he hit his limit. At least Dub could avoid the blame if Cam didn't.

"Do you realize how serious of a predicament you're in, Dr. Valentine? Getting convicted of first-degree attempted homicide is likely to carry a life sentence. Do you want to spend the rest of your life in prison?"

Dammit. She didn't know that Jake had survived yet. Cam had just given her too much information. She clearly wanted Jake dead, and her believing that she accomplished her mission provided leverage.

Dub studied Deirdre's face as she raced to process the sheriff's slip up and saw the exact moment it dawned on her that the medics had found the vial, knew exactly how to respond, and had undone all her hard work. She slumped down, took a deep breath, and tried to shake off the blow. The sheriff's mistake might yield fruit, after all.

Deirdre leaned forward, regaining her composure, unable to resist asking for clarification. "Sorry. Did you say *attempted* homicide?"

Cam perked up. He looked contemplative, confused, then guilty. The sheriff didn't answer Deirdre. Instead, he put his hat back on his head, stood up, and left the room. Dub breathed a sigh of a relief.

As Cam slipped through the door, Dub spoke first: "Don't worry about it, sheriff."

Cam rubbed his temples. "I'm just so damned tired, Dub. It's bad enough that we've got a monster on the loose, but now a murderer?"

Dub nodded, sympathetic. "Well, at least she's not on the loose anymore. Let's just give her a few minutes. Let her stew on it. You changed the game on her by letting her know that Jake's still alive. That might rattle something loose."

Cam grunted. "I need some coffee. Can you take over?"

"Sure. No problem." Dub delighted in the challenge.

Intent on leaving her with her silence, Dub stared at Deirdre through the mirror. Like many of the boys in their class, he once lusted after her back in high school. He'd asked her to dance once at their freshman homecoming party, and she'd promised him that she would during the next slow song. Like an idiot, he asked her again and again, and she always replied the same, even when the DJ announced the last song. The lusting had petered out after that night.

When Deirdre began to look sufficiently annoyed, Dub walked into the interrogation room, still finding it awkward to turn a door handle with his non-dominant hand. Deirdre immediately started studying his face.

He sat across from her as she looked directly into his eyes. Dub lacked the stature of Cam Donner, coming off as far less intimidating, but he hoped that this seeming weakness might throw her off.

"I know it can be hard to confront an assault," Dub began. "If that's what happened here, just tell us. We only want to help. If Jake hurt you in some way, then your actions will be viewed more favorably by a jury. We just want to help you."

Cam had already tried this tactic, but Dub had a different aim. He let the question hang. Dub didn't believe for a second that Jake had assaulted her, but the implication of weakness might annoy her.

"Jake didn't rape me, if that's what you're implying," she said.

Dub nodded. "Okay. That's good. That's very good. Did he hurt you in some other way?"

He could see the frustration sneaking across her face. "No. I'm not a helpless little girl, Deputy."

"No, no. Of course not. You have a very impressive body of work. You're very accomplished."

She sat in confident silence, looking strangely proud, as if her career could somehow exonerate her from attempted murder.

When she didn't respond, Dub continued, "It was an accident, then? Maybe you didn't know what the drug that you gave him would do to him?"

She glared at him. "I have two PhDs. I've worked in medical research my whole career. I'm the most accomplished medical professional in Rose Valley. What do you think?"

Dub had her now. "So you're saying that you knew that injecting Jake Rollins with that drug would kill him, then?"

Her face went pale. As Dub had hoped, Deirdre had lost herself to pride. She didn't answer, but Dub could see it from the flush on her cheeks, and the tightening of her muscles. Anger burned in her eyes.

He gave her time to answer, but when she didn't, Dub carried on. "To make sure that I am 100% clear on this. Jake Rollins did not rape you. Jake Rollins did not hurt you in any way. Yet you gave him a drug that you *knew* would kill him. You had a gun that you fired at Shandi Mason. Is that how you got Jake to cooperate with you?"

Deirdre exploded, "None of that matters!"

Dub let her outburst dangle in the quiet air of the interrogation room. She hadn't really given him any more information, but she'd lost control of her emotions. He studied her face.

"Thirsty, Dr. Valentine? Can I get you something to drink?"

She didn't answer. She refused to look at him.

"How about a coke? Or a diet coke? Yeah. You look like you probably drink diet coke."

She mumbled, "Dr. Pepper. Diet Coke is worse for you."

"Dr. Pepper. You got it, Dr. Valentine. Just sit tight." With a grin, he added. "And don't go anywhere."

Cam stood outside the door by the time Dub exited the interrogation room, sipping black coffee from a mug with "World's Greatest Sheriff" painted on the side in puffy, colorful letters.

"Good job, Higgins," Cam said between sips.

"Thanks, sheriff."

"We should have a plan of attack when we go back in."

Dub nodded. "Sure. Sounds like you're coming in too then, next time? A little good cop, bad cop?"

Cam laughed. "Something like that. I'm pretty sure she thinks we're both bad cops. Arrogant little bitch."

"Yeah. But arrogance works to our advantage. She knows Jake's alive now. For all she knows, he's awake and he's told us everything. The evidence is overwhelming. She's too flustered to ask for a lawyer. I think we broke her." Dub pointed to Deirdre through the glass. "You can see her working it out in her head now."

Occasionally, an emotion would manically flash across Deirdre's face, as she shuffled in seconds between looks of fear, confidence, and amusement. Though she would deny it with her last breath, Dub would bet his job on the fact that she belonged in a looney bin. How she got to be that way, he'd never know, but as much as he didn't like her, a small part of him still felt bad for her.

After Dub returned with the Dr. Pepper, Deirdre looked serene and resolute, as if she had reached the solution to all of her problems. To most people, all of that would be undetectable, but Dub possessed an uncanny ability to read the smallest of micro-expressions. Words were often the smallest part of communication.

Dub nodded, and Cam cracked open the door, immediately going to the corner to stand, while Dub took the seat across from Deirdre. She looked back and forth between the two of them, a vague mix of fear and defiance mixed in her eyes.

Dub slid a Dr. Pepper towards her. It had a straw so she could drink it without the use of her hands. She ignored it and spoke before either of them had a chance. "Okay. I tried to kill Jake. You know that already. There's no reason for me to be coy about it. I did it willingly and knowingly. He needs to die."

Dub looked at the sheriff. Dub had been certain that they had broken her, but he didn't expect this. Cam looked equally shocked.

"And why does he need to die, Dr. Valentine?" Dub asked.

"Because as long as he's alive, that thing—the beast—will wreak havoc on Rose Valley. It started with livestock." She motioned towards Dub's hand with the limited movement of her wrist. "And self-defense. But it will progress past that. Soon it will start killing people."

Dub glanced at Cam again. Though Deirdre didn't know it yet, it had already moved past self-defense. The gory pieces of Cornelius Brooks attested to that. This had started with Deirdre attempting murder, but had transitioned into something else entirely.

Cam stepped forward from the corner. "What does that have to do with Jake?"

Deirdre ran her big eyes to Dub, then to Cam, making sure both were focused on her before she started. "One year ago, Jake almost died when that truck smashed his car. I saved him with an experimental serum developed by Arrowhead Research in the 1940s."

Cam's weight shifted. Dub was enthralled.

"The beast escaped from Arrowhead Research over seventy years ago," Deirdre continued. "It's like a blank canvas. It doesn't think for itself. It only kills. Its instinct is to kill anything and everything that crosses its path, but it's influenced by the seeker. The other seekers were all killed to stop the beast in the past, but now Jake is the seeker."

Dub leaned forward. "The seeker?"

"That's what Dr. Cordova called it. The one you call the beast, Dr. Cordova would have called the spear.

"I'll make this as simple as I can for you," she said. "One subject was basically given a lobotomy and a serum that increased aggression and testosterone. He was already large. But this serum made him even larger. It made him resilient to pain and enabled him to heal far quicker than a normal human. It was like steroids on, well... steroids.

"Then another subject was given the complementary serum," she continued. "Also intended to boost physical attributes, but focused more on healing ability. The idea was that the seeker didn't need to be strong. It just needed to survive so that it could direct the spear. The serum I gave Jake mutated his neural pathways, linking him to the spear in a psychic connection of sorts. It's all very complicated."

It sounded far-fetched and impossible, but maybe the truth hid somewhere in this story. Dub asked, "But why? What was this even for?"

Deirdre did her best to shrug while still attached to the table. "I don't know. Crazy scientists with infinite government money trying to beat the Nazis, I guess. Originally, they just wanted to find a way to create telepathic links for faster battlefield communication, but that didn't work, so Cordova started carving away at the spear's brain until there was nothing left, convinced that the telepathy would work if his brain wasn't so independent."

"Who would volunteer for something like that?" Cam asked.

"How the hell would I know? It was war. Might have volunteered. Might have been assigned."

Deirdre was getting impatient, and Dub worried that if they didn't get back on track, she'd clam up. "So, you're telling us that Jake is controlling the beast?"

Deirdre nodded. "Sort of. Yeah. Not exactly, but that's the easiest way to think of it."

"So, Jake is an accessory to murder, then?" Cam suggested.

Deirdre shook her head "No. I wouldn't say that. He doesn't know that he's even doing it. His brainwaves activate the spear, but it's failed telepathy. Jake's thoughts and feelings might influence the spear, but they don't control it. They just... enable it."

Now Deirdre used the silence of the room for effect. Dub looked at Cam and could see that he also struggled to process the new information. Time to regroup. But Dub still wanted to understand why the solution to this problem involved murdering Jake.

Deirdre broke the silence. "I didn't think the spear was still alive. It had been dormant for fifty years. It seemed like an acceptable risk. Giving Jake the seeker serum should have had no affect because there would be no spear for him to activate.

"But it wasn't dead. It was alive. Dormant somewhere in Rose Valley. I injected Jake with that serum every week for a year. At this point, even stopping his treatments won't revert the changes."

She turned her attention solely to Cam, clearly wanting him in particular to understand. "Listen, sheriff. I've run all the permutations. I've looked at all the research. We can't undo this. As long as Jake is alive, so is your beast. The spear might as well be indestructible while it's active. Killable in theory but you won't get anywhere near it without a lot of people dying. And you'd need way bigger guns than you've got."

Bigger guns, huh? The sort of guns the blowhard from Missouri had offered might do the trick, but Dub didn't like the prospect of siding with Skylar Brooks. Giving a man like that power could only lead to bad things.

Deirdre rattled on, "They tried to stop this thing in the past with all of the traditional means that you'll throw at it, but they won't work. They always had to kill the seeker. Jake is vulnerable. He has slightly elevated healing capabilities, sure, but those won't stop a bullet. Or poison. Or deadly drugs.

"It's like Jake's brain is the power," she continued. "Unplug Jake and the spear is out of juice. The spear goes dormant and you can scour Rose Valley until you find it and destroy it."

Deirdre leaned forward in her chair briefly, then relaxed and leaned back casually, mimicking a lawyer resting her case to the jury. She clearly wanted them to reach the same conclusion as she: that killing Jake provided the only solution to their problem. Dub wasn't sure about that, but he did feel confident that this woman lacked a few crucial cards in her deck.

Cam walked towards the door. "Dub will put you back in the cell."

Cam left, and Dub unlocked her handcuffs, awkwardly and slowly with only his one good hand. She stood up and looked at her Dr. Pepper. "Can I take that with me?"

Dub shrugged. "Sure."

It seemed the least he could do for a madwoman likely to spend the rest of her life in prison.

CHAPTER 28

Macy felt the heat rising to her cheeks, certain that red splotches rose through her porcelain skin and betrayed her emotions to the shirtless man in the doorway. Chiseled and tan, with sharp features, dreamy eyes, and close-cropped blonde hair, the man before her commanded her attention. Wes worked hard for his muscles, but the college-aged kid in front of her boasted the body of a man. O.M.G. Was she cheating on Wes?

"Um. Hi. You must be, um... Tanner?" she asked.

A perfect smile spread across his face, cordial and welcoming even as sadness tinged his eyes. Macy expected there would be. When her mom asked her to deliver food to the survivors of an attack, she resisted at first, but she was starting to see an upside to this visit.

"That's me," he said. "And you are?"

He could talk? Her mom had made it very clear that only the girl spoke. Evidently, Macy could expect a different level of interaction. "Oh. Right. I'm Macy. Macy Donner. You met my mom, Shandi. She wanted me to bring you her condolences. And some burgers. She would have come herself, but she's in the hospital with her new boyfriend right now."

Tanner's smile somehow got even bigger as the sadness briefly melted away. "Mikey's?"

She thrust the greasy bag toward him. "Yeah. It's kind of the only choice around here."

"Awesome."

He took the bag and disappeared into the motel room, leaving the door wide open. Macy felt uncertain as to whether he meant to invite her in, or if he just loved Mikey's burgers that much. She stood in the doorway, not quite sure what to do, until a plain, brown-haired girl came around the corner. The girl's watery, bloodshot eyes surveyed Macy from head to toe, then relaxed.

"Don't mind Tanner. Sometimes he thinks with his stomach." She threw a brief glance at Tanner. "I'm Miriam. Come on in."

Macy stepped cautiously into the room until she could see the entirety of it. Despite living her whole life in town, she had never had an occasion to visit the Rose Valley Motor Inn. The shabby room sagged under the weight of age, just like she would have expected. Tanner dumped the contents of the bag onto one of the two queen-sized beds, then quickly got to work on his greasy double-meat burger.

Covered in a collection of knives and guns, Miriam's bed had no room for food. Sudden panic surged in Macy, and she froze.

Miriam sensed the unease. "Oh. This must look strange. I'm just cataloging my equipment. Nothing to worry about. Just part of the job."

That must have been some crazy job. Macy had the vague notion that Miriam and Tanner traveled around looking for monsters, so it kind of made sense that they would have weapons. But seeing such a variety invoked an overwhelming sense of discomfort. Some of Macy's friends took a passing interest in firearms, but the topic seemed more dangerous than exciting to her.

Macy decided to try and make small-talk. "So, are you guys in college?"

Tanner spoke through a mouthful of tater tots. "Yep. Good ol' Mizzou."

Macy had never heard of it before. "Oh. Where is that?"

Miriam laughed gently as she picked a knife up and polished it with a nearby cloth. "Mizzou is the colloquial term for The University of Missouri."

Colloquial. Macy played with the word in her mind, deciding that it must be a fancy college word meaning nickname. Her decision on a university hung over her as an important To-Do item. "Is it a good school?"

"Well, it's the best in Missouri. Not sure if that makes it good or not. Missouri isn't the most metropolitan place. But we like it well enough. It's in the SEC, so that means it has a respected football team. Does anything else matter?" Miriam said with a hint of sarcasm.

"Oh. Like Texas A&M," Macy commented.

Tanner swallowed a bite of burger. "Yep. Except Mizzou is in the east, so they don't have to play Alabama all the time."

Macy beamed with pride that her forced knowledge of football matters would serve her well even outside of her courtship with Wes. "That must be nice. Alabama is unstoppable."

Tanner smiled with a wink and a nod before taking another bite. He still didn't have a shirt on, which Macy found incredibly distracting. What red-blooded American girl could be expected to carry on a conversation with his rippling biceps stealing her attention?

Miriam brought Macy back to the conversation. "You're in high school, I presume? What year?"

"Senior."

"Ah. So, time to find a college, huh? I don't know if my advice is worth anything, but get as far away from here as you can. If you stay close by, you'll never escape. Trust me on that." Miriam's voice was clear with conviction.

To attend any university, she would have to leave Rose Valley behind, but she hadn't really considered looking out of state. Perhaps going so far away would provide some benefit. Macy felt the weight of Rose Valley pressing down on her every day. She would miss her parents, but getting far away from her insular, tiny life sounded wonderful.

Macy suddenly heard the voice of her mom reverberate through her brain, reminding her she had been sent on a mission of emotional support. "Sorry about your brother. If there's anything we can do for you, just let us know."

Tanner's chewing slowed, and Miriam paused her cleaning before answering. Her voice lowered. "Thanks. We really appreciate Ms. Shandi. You have a good mom."

Macy nodded. "Yeah. She's pretty great."

"Sometimes bad things happen." Tanner remarked from the bed. "We just have to be strong. Carry on, ya know?"

"Or get revenge," Miriam said softly while staring at one of her guns.

Tanner put his burger down, stood up next to Miriam and began rubbing her back. "Only if we can't save him, though, right?"

Miriam looked up at Tanner, taking a few beats to answer. "Right. Of course. Just so long as *he* doesn't turn him into a carnival sideshow."

Macy felt uncomfortable in the tenseness of the moment. Her parent's divorce certainly stung, but that seemed inconsequential next to the loss of a brother. Though she had no siblings, Macy could imagine how terrible Miriam must have felt, and she worried that all of the weapons and training might lead to something dangerous.

Tanner turned towards Macy and flashed her his gorgeous smile. "Thanks for the burgers, Macy Donner."

"Uh. Sure thing." She started towards the door. "Oh, let me give you my number. In case you need something."

Her cheeks flush again as she realized what she had just done. *Smooth, Macy. Very smooth.*

Tanner walked across the room, fetched a phone from the small table in the corner, and tossed it at her. She thankfully caught it and started punching in her number. She typed her name into the contact entry, vaguely aware of him crossing over to her to stand by her side. Her pulse increased, and she forced herself to think of Wes.

Tanner leaned over. "You can just put Cutie in there for the name."

"Tanner, behave," Miriam said from deeper within the room.

Macy couldn't take any further embarrassment. She just awkwardly handed him his phone without finishing her name, muttered a good night, and disappeared into the warm Rose Valley air.

CHAPTER 29

As Shandi stood in a throng of other professional reporters, she felt acutely inadequate. Rose Valley had never had a true press conference. There had never been a reason. Most of the journalists hailed from stations near Rose Valley, as far away as Austin. Some traveled from national outlets. Shandi wished she could have the same cool detachment as the rest of the reporters, filled with wonder and excitement as they waited for Cam to take the podium.

Pulling herself away from the hospital had been hard, but Dan insisted that his "best" journalist be in attendance. She lacked the strength to protest, and reluctantly accepted that it might be good for her. Her journalistic toolbox provided no help to Jake in his current state, and Deirdre sat (and would hopefully rot) in jail. At least here, Shandi could do something to make her feel like she hadn't strapped in to the world's worst rollercoaster.

The makeshift risers in front of the Sheriff's Department had come from the high school choir. A tangle of wires and cables all led up to a podium. Shandi had always just used a handheld recorder, and lately, her cell phone; she had no idea how to tap into the microphone system that all the different outlets had set up. The stage had a few chairs on it. The mayor sat in one already. Shandi could only guess at who would sit in the other chairs.

Like most press conferences, the event lacked any sense of mystery. The news had been in the wild for hours: Cornelius Brooks had been killed by the beast. Violently. The Sheriff's Department could easily ignore sightings and dead sheep, but when people started dying, they could no longer turn a blind eye.

A hush fell on the crowd as people entered onstage. Dub Higgins took a seat. Then Skylar Brooks, followed by Miriam and Tanner. Shandi reflected on what Macy had told her about them, and she found her heart aching for their loss. They seemed good kids, despite their oddities.

The high school principal took the last chair, an old man who'd held his position for decades. He had been there so long that Shandi remembered him serving as her principal, though her memory painted him with lush, dark hair instead of the graying and thinning pate he sported now. It seemed strange for him to be in on stage.

Cam stumbled onto the stage last, immediately approaching the bank of microphones in the center. He was crisply dressed. The cowboy hat on his head looked new, in contrast to his usual dirty, grimy one. The same care hadn't been afforded to his facial hair, though. His mustache almost disappeared within a full beard. His countenance showed defeat. He had never weathered a storm this violent in Rose Valley, and the toll it took showed in his entire body.

He pulled a folded-up piece of paper from his breast pocket and cleared his throat. "I'd like to thank the mayor for being here, as well as Principal Steele. They are both pillars of our community and share my condolences for all of those affected by recent events.

"At approximately 8:15pm," he continued. "central standard time yesterday evening, Cornelius Brooks of Missouri was murdered by what the media has dubbed The Beast of Rose Valley. Earlier yesterday, the Sheriff's Department also discovered the body of Bernard Jones on his property, where it appeared that another attack from the beast had occurred."

Bernard? The rumor mill had missed that one. Jake would be devastated. Since Bernard had no family in town, she presumed that the principal served as a stand-in. Bernard had loved nothing more than coaching at Rose Valley High.

Cam continued, "The Sheriff's Department is working tirelessly to get to the bottom of these murders and to apprehend this creature. Photographs and video have been distributed to the media to help educate citizens of Rose Valley. If you see this creature, please immediately report it to the Sheriff's Department. Do not engage. Do not try to capture or otherwise harm it. Though not armed, it is highly dangerous.

"Due to the seriousness of this situation, we are instituting a curfew here in Rose Valley. All residents are expected to be in their homes no later than eight PM. The Sheriff's Department will strictly enforce this curfew. Citations will be issued for any person out past this time without express permission from the department."

It was about time. A curfew probably would have made more sense after the football game, but leave it to Cam to ignore a problem until it had spiraled completely out of control. Seriously, did it take a death before he was willing to admit that he was in way over his head?

"If you are watching this broadcast from outside of Rose Valley, *please* do not come here. The Sheriff's

Department will be putting up checkpoints at all major entrances into Rose Valley to dissuade visitors.

"In order to apprehend this criminal as quickly as possible, we are seeking volunteers to participate in a county wide manhunt. A meeting will be held at the First United Methodist Church of Rose Valley, tomorrow, on Saturday afternoon at two PM. All able-bodied citizens who are willing are invited to attend."

Cam paused for the first time and looked at the crowd. He looked scared, briefly, before regaining his composure, his loss of nerve perceptible to only to those who knew him as well as Shandi. It terrified her to see Cam so out of his depth. It made him seem more vulnerable and invited memories of the man that she married. If Cam didn't know how to save them, then all seemed lost, and that thought frightened Shandi more than the beast.

"Though these are trying times for Rose Valley," Cam said. "we will persevere and capture this creature. Rose Valley will be a safe place again. At this time, I will take questions from the media."

The crowd exploded with murmurs and hand waves. Shandi couldn't make out any one question, and found herself so overtaken by the loudness that she did not attempt to ask any herself. She supposed that whatever she wrote in the Rose Valley Reporter would be unimportant compared to the live news segments that would be airing across Texas, and possibly even the country. She felt small and unimportant.

The Sheriff looked overwhelmed at first, but finally pointed at a young man in a tan suit, who immediately launched into his question: "In what way was Mr. Brooks killed?"

Cam shifted uncomfortably. "Much like the livestock victims of the beast. Next question."

Shandi felt her stomach churn as her mind immediately tried to construct a picture of a mutilated kid. She pushed it back as far as she could, but still struggled to maintain her composure. Shandi searched the faces of Miriam and Tanner for any reaction, but both remained remarkably stoic.

A small blonde woman in a pencil skirt spoke next. "Based on the video from the football game, this creature does not seem to be affected by guns. What steps are being taken to prepare for this?"

"The Sheriff's Department is working with partners to obtain higher grade munitions and other weaponry appropriate for hunting large game. Though it was able to shrug off bullets from a handgun, we believe that larger rounds will prove more effective. Next question."

Another reporter. "Have you made any progress in identifying what exactly this thing is?"

"Negative. At this time, we are approaching the beast as if it is a wild animal of unknown origins. We have partnered with Skylar Brooks, father of Cornelius Brooks. Mr. Brooks specializes in hunting monsters just like this." Cam motioned towards Skylar. "The department will use his expertise in devising a plan to bring this thing to justice. Next question."

Shandi's face tingled. She would never have expected Cam to team up with Skylar Brooks. Surely Cam could see through that huckster. A wave of guilt crept through her as she realized that she'd indirectly introduced the two of them. No good could come of the alliance.

"Was Mr. Jones also murdered in a similar way to Mr. Brooks?" another reporter asked.

"Though no one was present, the current theory is that Mr. Jones went into cardiac arrest upon seeing the beast in person. His shotgun was broken in half, which is comparable behavior to that displayed at the football game. His chickens were also mutilated in a similar method as the earlier livestock. Next question."

Shandi found her mind wandering. She had a hard time caring about the beast with Jake in the hospital, and though she tried to focus on the beast, her mind drifted instead to other criminal activity. The fact that Jake had almost been murdered seemed to be at least as important.

She put up her hand.

Cam pointed at her. "Ms. Mason."

"Sheriff. Why have there been no charges pressed against Deirdre Valentine for the attempted murder of Jake Rollins?"

The crowd fell eerily quiet. Did they not know of what had happened to Jake? Cam's nose flared and his face reddened.

"That line of questioning is not related to the purpose of this press conference. No further questions."

Cam stormed off the stage. Shandi peered through the crowd, desperately trying to keep her eyes trained on Cam's trajectory. She wouldn't be surprised if he headed for her, but then she also felt a sense of safety in the crowd of people. He wouldn't get too irate with her with an audience. Thankfully, he did not approach her.

The others streamed off the stage. Shandi lost track of them. Reporters yelled more questions, trying to get anyone to answer them. A spry journalist waylaid the Principal and peppered the old man with questions. Skylar Brooks fell to another reporter. Dub stayed on the stage, his eyes surveying the crowd, as if expecting trouble.

Shandi had no interest in trying to wade through the chaos to get any statements. It didn't feel as important to her as it should have. She just wanted to get back to the hospital. Jake might wake at any moment and she had an overwhelming need to be there when he did. She certainly didn't have the requisite skillset to stop the beast, anyway.

As she turned to go, she felt a hand on her shoulder. She turned, and saw Miriam's red, puffy face.

"Hey, Miriam. I'm so sorry—" Shandi started.

Miriam embraced her in hug, catching Shandi off guard, but Shandi instinctively returned the embrace by wrapping her arms tightly around Miriam.

Miriam whispered, "It's not an animal."

When Miriam released, she grabbed Shandi's hands. Shandi felt a plastic bag in her palm, and looked down at it as Miriam disappeared into the crowd without another word.

Confused, Shandi looked down at what Miriam had given her. It looked like dog tags. Old ones. What Miriam had said provided nothing new; Shandi had been certain for quite some time that the beast shared more with man than any animal. Had he been a soldier?

Realizing that Miriam had likely given her something that neither Cam nor Skylar knew about, she furtively slipped it into the front pocket of her jeans. She would need to study it in private. Everyone focused on stopping the beast. Killing him. No one seemed to be worried about the person underneath or whether they could help him. Perhaps this small trinket promised a new direction.

Her head pounded in the loudness of the crowd. She needed to get away. To a quiet place. To Jake.

CHAPTER 30

At some point, he became aware that he still clung to life. His mind danced between deep sleep and a lighter slumber. He could hear things. Smell things. He thought he might wake, but would then slip back into unconsciousness. He couldn't make sense of what he heard. Not yet.

Jake found himself unable to tell the difference between his memories and his dreams. The dreams came frequently, and his tendency to float near wakefulness caused him to recognize and to remember them.

***

A wedding. His own wedding? No, but at the same venue. He sat in the audience. The bride entered to the sound of No Sleep Till Brooklyn by The Beastie Boys. It felt wrong somehow, but he accepted it as normal. Her face hid behind some kind of fog.

He looked around him and saw familiar faces. Steve. Liz. Bernard. His mother. Directly next to him sat Macy, dressed in a hideous orange dress. It looked like a bridesmaid dress. Macy stood and walked to the front, taking her place as the Maid of Honor.

The groom stood there now, though he hadn't been there before. Cam Donner looked respectable in a khaki tux with his badge on the lapel instead of flowers. Despite being indoors, he wore his aviators. No officiator. Only Cam and Macy stood at the front.

Steve suddenly appeared next to Jake. He had been sitting farther away before. He wore his usual outfit, not at all appropriate for a wedding. He looked at Jake, frowned, and shook his head, as if mourning for some lost thing. Jake did not understand what had been lost.

Jake looked back towards the bride. The fog lifted to reveal Shandi, beautiful in a shoulderless white gown. She seemed to glide rather than walk as she went down the aisle. Cam and Macy beamed with pride and excitement as she approached.

Steve put his arm around Jake. To console him. For what? For losing Shandi to Cam? He searched for a feeling of regret that he didn't feel, then became overwhelmed with all-consuming sadness.

His eyes focused back to Shandi. He needed to see her again, glowing and ethereal. Only this time, she did not glide down the aisle. In her place floated a coffin, being carried by unrecognizable men. Macy's and Cam's excitement vanished, replaced with inconsolable tears.

The wedding now became a funeral. Shandi's funeral. Jake began to weep. Steve held him tighter. The tears became more powerful, swallowing him, filling the room with water. He couldn't breathe. Steve disappeared, following by everyone else in the congregation. Jake gasped for air, alone and abandoned.

***

Jake felt certain that he had woken with a start, but he couldn't be sure. No, wakefulness still eluded him. He wanted to conquer sleep. He needed to know without reservation that Shandi was alive. Some deep part of him had an overwhelming fear that she had died. Because of him, perhaps. That felt right. It had been her voice he'd heard, before falling unconscious. She fought with Deirdre. There had been a gunshot?

Now he fought to wake up. He felt himself drifting off again. He tried desperately to stop it, and forced his attention back to Shandi. He saw her for a split second, in jeans and a tank top, her phone in front of her, interrogating him about something. Then she vanished again.

***

He thought of Brooklyn. He had never been to Brooklyn. He told himself that he should not sleep until he got there. He wondered if Shandi had been there. Did people visit there often? He realized that he knew very little about Brooklyn.

A chessboard materialized in front of him, but no opponent sat on the other side. The white pieces moved on their own. He answered with nonsensical plays. The white king fell over. Jake won, but had done nothing to earn him that victory.

A creeping terror rose up from behind him. From inside of him. He recognized it, shuddering under the primal, relentless force. He felt it fill him from head to toe, conquering every inch of his body until he became unrecognizable. He transformed into something else. Something bigger.

He whisked away back to high school. In band, where he played the trumpet. The trumpet felt tiny in his hands, his monstrous fingers far too large to properly push the valves. He put the trumpet to his mouth to play, but he accidentally crushed it. It made him angry.

He heard a saxophone, playing random jazz music. He looked up and saw Cam, playing the saxophone as he had in high school, not as teenager Cam but as Sheriff Cam.

Still angry from crushing his trumpet, Jake stood up and howled, shocked by the chilling noise that issued forth from his throat. He waded through the chairs and music stands, throwing them from side to side. Straight towards Cam. He realized as he approached that he meant to kill Cam.

Cam did not stop playing the saxophone as Jake began ripping him apart. First his legs. Then his arms. The music became discordant as one hand stopped pressing the keys. Then the other, leaving only a throaty, reedy cacophony of noise. Cam continued to blow. It made Jake even angrier.

Though it seemed impossible, Jake ripped Cam's head off. The saxophone dropped to the ground. Jake held Cam's head in his hands. Someone screamed.

Deirdre glared at him. And Shandi. And Liz. All three of them. He had not gone to high school with Liz, but it seemed natural that she stood among them. Deirdre held up a gun and pointed it at him. His anger gave way to overwhelming fear.

She pulled the trigger, and a loud bang echoed through Jake's head. He felt the bullet hit him in slow motion. He could feel it rip through his intestines little by little, blood spewing in every direction. He dropped Cam's head and fell backwards into chairs and music stands, sheet music filling the air like snow. Shandi and Liz laughed. Deirdre yelled in triumph.

***

Again, his mind jumped awake. He couldn't trust the reality of it, but a new brightness filled his vision. He blinked over and over, attempting to get a handle on what he saw, scared that it would be some horror scene. As his eyes adjusted however, he realized he was staring at a blank white ceiling.

Jake could feel the bed beneath him. He could hear the buzzing of the lights overhead. He moved his toes and his fingers. They all worked. This seemed more real than the dreams before. Though he couldn't tell from within the dreams, he felt certain from outside them that he'd finally conquered sleep.

He looked around the room, recognizing a hospital room. Near the foot of the bed there sat a chair filled with Steve. His baseball cap covered his eyes, and his worn cowboy boots comfortably rested on the end of the bed. He wore a *Class of '97* shirt that seemed impossibly old. Jake smiled. No more nightmares.

For now.

Jake suddenly felt very hungry and very thirsty. He searched for a call button, knowing that every hotel bed hid one somewhere. Though he felt alert, his groggy state made the task difficult.

He kicked the bottom of Steve's boot. Steve roused, slipped up his cap and gazed at him, smiling.

"Mornin', Jake."

Jake looked out the window at the bright light. "Is it morning?"

Steve looked at his Timex. "No, I guess not. It's afternoon."

"How long was I out?"

Steve rose. "Almost two days. The doctors didn't know how long it would take. I should get someone."

Jake nodded. Within minutes, nurses busied themselves with his care. They adjusted his bed to a sitting position. They brought him food and drink. He ate quickly at first, but realized that it would make him sick if he continued. Steve sat there all the while, not interrupting. He seemed to understand that Jake needed to meet his basic needs first.

After he'd eaten and drank, Steve helped him up so he could freshen up in the restroom. He found it easier than he expected. Unlike the car accident, it seemed that he had immediate control of his body and most of his strength. He splashed water on his swollen face and brushed his teeth with the cheap, plastic toothbrush provided by the hospital. He studied his face in the mirror. He looked more rested now than he had for days.

Once Jake returned to the bed, he forced himself to confront reality. He needed to ask a very important question, but the answer terrified him.

"Is... did she?" he asked. "Is she okay?"

Steve leaned forward in his chair with a grin. "Shandi? She's fine. She saved your ass. She beat Deirdre half to death the way she tells it."

Overwhelming relief washed over him. In his half-asleep state, he had convinced himself that Deirdre had shot Shandi. Assuming this, he'd feared waking up at all.

"And Deirdre?"

"Cam arrested her. She's in jail. Hopefully forever, but they hadn't pressed charges as of the last I'd heard. That really chaps Shandi's hide."

Fragments of memory started coming back to Jake, piecing together the strange things that Deirdre had said. She'd implied that he controlled the beast somehow. That her killing him could stop it. The memory felt far away, ambiguous.

"The beast," said Jake. "Deirdre said that I was controlling the beast. That's why she had to kill me."

Steve did not answer right away, most likely trying to determine whether this claim represented the truth or a drug-induced fantasy. He pulled his cell phone from his pocket. "The Sheriff will want to know this, Jake. I should call him. You can tell him."

Jake pleaded, "No. Not yet. Please. Shandi. Call Shandi first."

Steve stopped. He looked at Jake, clearly weighing his options. Jake knew that he needed to talk to Cam. Jake's testimony likely kept charges from being filed against Deirdre. They needed Jake's perspective on the situation. Jake—more than anyone—desperately wanted to see Deirdre punished for what she had done, but Jake had almost died, and his perspective changed.

Steve turned back towards his phone. Jake didn't know if he'd intended to call Cam or Shandi. Steve put the phone to his ear and waited.

Suddenly, the silence of the room broke with a nurse's approach. The person approaching wore hard-soled shoes, frantically clopping forward with hurried purpose. Not quite running, but walking faster than normal. It couldn't be a nurse.

As the steps grew closer, music began to accompany them. Not music. A ringtone. Steve smiled and put down his phone.

Shandi appeared in the room. She looked at Steve. Looked at Jake. Her eyes glistened. She dropped her purse on the floor, moved across the room in minimal steps and took Jake in her arms.

Jake reciprocated as tightly as he could. They held the embrace for what seemed like an eternity. Steve mentioned something about getting coffee and Jake heard him leave the room. Jake's face burrowed against Shandi, eager to never let her go. She smelled wonderful; partly feminine and partly earthen.

When she finally let him go, she stayed near him. She looked at his face. She said nothing. She just sat on the edge of the bed, holding his hand, light tears occasionally running down her face. The happiness and relief that she was alright continued to overwhelm him. He began to cry as well. He wanted to say so many things, but didn't know how to verbalize them all.

So, they sat. In silence. Together.

CHAPTER 31

To Shandi, it no longer mattered whether Jake gave her any indication of his feelings. The threat of losing him made it clear she needed him. She could not wait for him to make moves, or wonder about his motivations. She could only expose her heart to him and hope that he reciprocated. As she held his hand in the hospital bed, though, she felt certain their feelings were mutual.

She needed to catch Jake up. He needed to know about Bernard. And Cornelius. He needed to know about William P. Hargrove, even though she herself didn't know much about him yet. She needed to tell him that Cam had teamed up with Skylar to lead a manhunt against the beast. She relied on him as a partner in this and needed his guidance again. But all of that could wait.

She leaned towards him. He understood her goal, hopefully because he wanted the same, and immediately leaned towards her as well. Their lips met, and Shandi instantaneously warmed. He let go of her hand and cupped her face in his hands. They held the kiss. It felt real and raw. It felt right, like she had always imagined.

Shandi didn't want it to end, but she needed to breathe. And they needed to talk. She backed away, and took his hand again. He smiled. She smiled back.

"How did you know I was awake?" Jake broke the silence.

Shandi twisted her mouth up. "I didn't. Not really. I just knew I needed to get back. I've spent a lot of time here over the last couple of days."

"I suppose that's a lame way to start the conversation after all of this," he said. "Let me start over."

She giggled lightly. "It was a good question. But okay. You can start over."

"I love you."

Shandi's heart stopped. Or skipped. She tried to control the quickening of her breath, as her head felt suddenly light and airy. If not for his hand holding her down, she worried that she might float away.

She suppressed the millions of nuances and intricacies that they would have to navigate from this point forward. They would have to deal with Macy. And Cam. The town, in general. Both had failed at marriage once before. She forced herself to slow down. Marriage took it too far. Jake just stated a feeling. All the ramifications of that could be saved for another day. Another time.

She wrapped both of her hands around his. She wanted him to feel the honesty and rawness in her response. She stared directly into his dark brown eyes. She didn't want him to doubt it. "I love you, too, Jake."

Silence overtook them again, but their eyes stayed locked on one another. Their hands remained intertwined. Her mind raced. She wanted her head clear so that she could focus on this moment.

Jake broke the silence again, this time with a huge smile. "Okay. Good. With that out of the way, we can get to work."

Shandi laughed. "Just like that, huh?"

He pulled her down and kissed her gently. "Yep. Just like that."

There would be time to explore this later, Shandi told herself. When Jake escaped from this hospital bed, and when the town conquered the beast. When Deirdre had been charged and convicted. When Rose Valley returned to normalcy, *then* they could define what they felt. They could make plans together. They could tell Macy.

Shandi suddenly remembered Bernard. It would destroy the moment they shared, but she knew she couldn't keep it from him any longer.

"Um. There's something terrible I need to tell you, Jake."

He frowned. "Okay. That sounds ominous."

"Bernard is dead. He had a heart attack when the beast showed up at his ranch."

Shandi watched as Jake's face dropped. Perhaps his eyes contained no more tears, because no new ones came. He just looked quietly stunned. She squeezed his hand.

"It was my fault," he said, staring off blankly.

Shandi didn't understand. "What do you mean?"

"Deirdre. She said that I... couldn't control him. That I could try, but I would fail. I think maybe the beast acts based on me? I was worried about Bernard. I missed a game with him. The beast went there because I was dwelling on it, I think."

Shandi struggled to process the new information, feeling as if it had literally hit her in the chest. It made sense that Deirdre's actions were somehow related to the beast, but Shandi couldn't have predicted this. She didn't know what to say, or how to react.

Jake continued, despite Shandi's shock. "She said that the only way to stop it was to kill me. That's why she tried to murder me."

"I don't understand, Jake. *How* did she do that?"

He shook his head, still staring off into the distance. "I don't know. The drugs she gave me after the accident caused it somehow."

"So, you and the beast have a telepathic link? You can see what he sees?"

He finally looked at her again. His eyes no longer held the loving warmth from before, but rather pure fear and confusion. "No. Maybe. I'm not sure. I don't think so. Maybe it's the other way around. That he sees what I see? Or maybe he sees what I think?"

Shandi started putting the pieces together, trying to recall all the times the beast had shown up in Rose Valley. Firstly, the mutilations. She couldn't account for the goat, but the sheep had been killed at Watermelon Ranch where Jake had lived. He surely would have thought about those sheep on occasion.

Then the cheetahs. She had mentioned they might be the culprit the day that the sheep had been killed. She had planted the idea in Jake's head. The beast had then showed up at the cheetah pens, killed a cub, and accidentally released the others. Shandi refused to keep following that path of thought, but Jake did it for her.

"I fell asleep thinking about the football game, and then he attacked." Jake's face went pale as fear crept into his eyes. "And then your house. I was thinking about you. The texts. And I..."

As Jake trailed off, Shandi saw the pain in his eyes. Jake had sent that thing to attack her house? No. He couldn't have done that. Not on purpose.

"I-I'm sorry, Shandi," Jake stammered. "I didn't mean to. I didn't know."

She stroked his hair, trying to comfort him while also wrestling with the concept that Jake might be dangerous—intentionally or not.

"But surely you weren't thinking negative things about those people?" she asked.

Jake shook his head. "No. I just thought about them. In general. Deirdre said something about my goodness stopping it from killing. That I wouldn't be able to do it forever."

Certainly, the science of it all eluded her, but she also didn't understand the link between Jake and the beast. Why would such a link be created? What purpose would it serve?

War, she thought. It could be used in war.

Shandi rubbed her hand along her pocket, feeling the outline of the dog tags that Miriam had given her.

The beast wasn't a monster. He was a soldier.

Shandi fished the plastic bag out of her front pocket and held it up in front of Jake. She watched his eyes study it, trying to focus on the corroded indentations that made up the words on the dog tags.

"Miriam found these in a cave. Right before the beast killed her brother."

Jake had never met the hive mind. He did not react with sadness, but with concern about what it meant. "It's started, then. The beast is killing people."

Shandi continued, "I haven't had time to run it down. I'll save your eyes the trouble, though. It says William P. Hargrove. There's a social security number, and an address in Mississippi."

"Any relation to Karen?"

Karen. Of course. Shandi hadn't made the connection yet with all the chaos in her life. Karen Phillips, formerly Hargrove, lived in Rose Valley. She had graduated a few years before them. Could she possibly be a relative of the beast?

"I hadn't thought of that. Maybe there's a connection if her family came from Mississippi originally. She may not have any idea, though. It would have to be at least two generations back."

Jake nodded. "Worth a shot. Maybe she has old documents or family stories that could shed light on things."

Shandi liked his line of thinking. As the evidence mounted for the beast being a man instead of Bigfoot, Shandi found herself more and more inclined to try to help him. She could only presume that Arrowhead Research had created him somehow. If they could turn him into this monster, then maybe they could turn him back.

Shandi remembered the last important thing she needed to tell Jake. "Skylar and Cam teamed up."

"For serious?"

"Yep. Seriously. They're organizing a manhunt. They're going to try to hunt him down. There's a town meeting tomorrow afternoon," Shandi said.

"What's today? Friday? I should be out of here by then, right? We should go."

"You haven't seen what the beast can do, Jake, but I have. I don't want to be anywhere near that thing. Hunting it is crazy. People are going to die."

"I know. But... I might be able to control it."

Shandi rolled her eyes without meaning to. "But how, Jake? You didn't even know you could until now."

Jake shrugged and peered off into the distance again. "I don't know, Shandi. Maybe it won't help. But the more information I have about what they're trying to do, the better. He came to the ranch after the football game. Maybe he stays near me. Maybe I have to be near him to control him. I don't know how any of this works.

"Deirdre wanted to kill me. She thought it was the only way to stop him. But what if I can control him? Direct him? What if I can lead him into a trap."

Shandi doubted it would work. He made reasonable points, but it terrified her to think of putting Jake in danger. Still, in a sea of bad choices, this seemed the best so far.

She nodded, reached up to his chin, and guided his face back towards hers. Their eyes locked again. It still felt amazing, like she could see directly into his soul. She marveled at the exhilaration and the comfort that filled her body. She leaned over to kiss him. He kissed her back. The spark ignited easily again. Focusing on more immediate concerns would not take the relationship away from them as she feared.

"Okay. We can go. But we need to focus on you first. We need to get you out of here."

"Don't worry about me. I feel fine. I feel better than fine. This is almost over. I know it. We can stop this. *I* can stop this."

Shandi laughed. "You're remarkably confident for someone who died two days ago."

"Wait, what? I died?"

Shandi's cheeks flushed. Of course, Jake would have no idea that his heart had actually stopped for a brief moment. It seemed like fairly important information that he might take as frightening. But she refused to let him dwell on it. He lived now. Awake. Energetic. She had him and would never let him go.

No more frightening information for today.

She leaned over and kissed him. He did not protest.

CHAPTER 32

The old rock house stood as sturdy now as it ever had, looking exactly as powerful as the first day Shandi saw it as a kid. Locals called it the old schoolhouse, but it had been a home far longer than it had ever served as a place of education. She wondered when those stones first came together to form a house, and took a mental note to look it up when she got back to the office. Her parents hadn't gone to school there and her grandparents had died before Shandi shed the immature bonds of adolescence and grown to care about their remarkable history. She wished she'd turned her journalistic talents towards documenting her own family.

The owner of those rocks had changed many times over the years. She vaguely remembered that Jake's grandparents owned it in the sixties. His grandparents had left their mark on a great many things in Rose Valley. The immediately previous tenants had been the Hargrove family, but now it belonged to the Phillips family. Karen's father had deeded it to her after her mother passed away. Now she lived there with her family and her ailing father. It seemed like a lot of mundane detail to know about a person that she barely knew, but Rose Valley held so few secrets.

Jake desperately wanted to go with her on this visit, but she insisted that he stay behind. Though he seemed like his old self again, she couldn't help but believe that the effects of the drugs still made him weak. Shandi fought the doctor's decision to release him so soon after he awoke, but she also understood her own overprotective streak.

She walked up the stone steps to the front porch, impressed by their sturdiness. She wondered if they had been an original part of the house, or if they had been built some time later.

The screen door squealed as she opened it. With no doorbell, she knocked, instead.

"Coming!" she heard inside.

It felt like minutes before the door cracked open. Karen Phillips stood in the doorway. She exceeded Shandi's age by almost ten years. Her brown hair struggled against faint streaks of gray that looked more dignified than old. Her face still shone with a smooth freshness, and her alert light brown eyes danced with excitement. Though larger than some, Karen still boasted a shapely and appealing figure.

"Shandi? To what do I owe the pleasure?" she said with a smile.

Shandi extended a hand. Karen shook it dutifully before Shandi answered, "This is going to sound really strange, but are you related to someone named William P. Hargrove?"

Karen nodded almost immediately, clearly recognizing the name. "Yeah. I never met him, but he was my grandfather."

Shandi dropped her shoulders. "Would you mind if I come in and ask you a few questions about him?"

Karen motioned inside. "I don't know how much I'll be able to help, but sure."

Shandi found herself in the living room of the old house, impressed by its nice appointments and surprised to find the insides much more modern than she expected. The air smelled vaguely of cinnamon. She took a seat in a recliner next to the couch.

Karen did not sit. "I'll be right back. I'm just going to get us a little snack and something to drink."

Karen disappeared into the kitchen before Shandi could tell her she wasn't hungry. As a journalist, Shandi had learned long ago that going along with someone proved to be the most reliable way to put them at ease. The more comfortable she could make them, the more information they might share.

Shandi suddenly became aware of someone watching her. She looked towards a hallway to her right and saw an old man in a wheelchair. She awkwardly smiled at him and managed a small gesture that vaguely resembled a wave. He stared and said nothing. Shandi couldn't bring herself to look away, as if turning her back to him would cause him to get up from the chair and devour her.

"Here we go. I made this fresh this morning. It's my grandfather's recipe." Karen floated into the room. Shandi found a sweet potato pie in her hands and a glass of milk on the coffee table in front of her. Clearly, the cinnamon smell had come from the baking.

Shandi motioned towards the man in the wheelchair. "Is that your father?"

Karen nodded. "Yes, ma'am. He's pretty despondent these days. I apologize if he was staring at you. I don't think he knows what he's doing anymore. He just roams around the house. He just celebrated his 78th birthday last week."

Shandi made an effort to meet his gaze. "Happy Birthday, Mr. Hargrove!"

He did not respond. Shandi took a bite of pie so that she had something to do to fill the awkward silence. She immediately forgot about all of that, though, when the pie hit her tongue in a euphoric explosion of sugar.

After savoring a couple of bites, Shandi decided to get down to business. She took out her cell phone. "Do you mind if I record this?"

"Oh no. Not at all."

She seemed to have no reservations about sharing her family history, which relieved Shandi. Too often, getting information from people proved difficult.

"So, what can you tell me about your grandfather?"

Karen looked towards the ceiling, as if trying hard to remember obscure facts. "He was in the army. I think he was a Major, maybe? He died in the war in 1942 when my dad was only three. He didn't go by William. Everyone called him Billy."

"Did he live here in Rose Valley?"

"He grew up in Mississippi, I'm pretty sure. But they moved to Rose Valley in 1940, I think." She looked over at her father. "Is that right, daddy?"

The man offered no answer. Karen waved her hand at him in minor annoyance before continuing. "I think he was assigned here. To help with some sort of research, maybe? I guess at Arrowhead. I don't know where else it would have been. But then they shipped him overseas and he died somewhere in France, I think."

Shandi contemplated how best to navigate the next part. She didn't want to alarm Karen, but she also felt obligated to tell Karen what she knew. She decided that leading with a prop might be easiest, so she pulled the dog tags out of her pocket and handed them over to Karen.

"These were found here in Rose Valley," Shandi said. "In a cave."

Karen's eyes lit up as she processed the meaning of the thin metal offering. "This is neat! I wonder how they got there. Can I have them? I'd love to add them to my scrapbook."

Shandi hadn't anticipated that, but it made sense that Karen would want them. She hoped that Karen would trust her enough to let her hold on to them. "Um, sure. But would you mind if I held on to them a while longer? I'm working on a story and I might need these still."

Karen didn't answer immediately, warily looking between Shandi and the dog tags. With a sigh, she finally replied, "Of course. I know where to find you if you don't bring them back."

Shandi smiled. "So are you sure that William—sorry, Billy—died in France?"

"That's what my mom always told me, yeah. Daddy didn't like to talk about it much. It was hard for him growing up back then without a father." Karen cheeks flushed suddenly. "Oh, I'm so sorry. I don't mean that it's bad. You're a wonderful mother, Shandi. It was just harder back then, you know?"

Shandi took no offense. Though she hardly could claim mother of the year, she delighted in the woman that Macy seemed destined to become. "Don't worry about it. I understand what you mean."

Karen's father mumbled something. Shandi couldn't make it out. She looked towards him, as Karen stood up and crossed the living room to his side. "What was that, daddy?"

He spoke louder this time. "Never sent home his body. Mama cried for days."

No body. Perhaps he had never gone to France at all. Perhaps he never left Rose Valley, now inexplicably old and tragically altered. Shandi wrestled with whether or not she should share her suspicions with Karen, especially with her father nearby. She decided not to. She couldn't be sure that Billy Hargrove had become the beast.

"I didn't know that, daddy," Karen said, tenderly stroking the few tendrils of gray that clung to his pate. "Thank you for sharing that."

He spoke again. "Mama saw him after he died."

"Like she saw his spirit, you mean, daddy?" Karen asked.

The old man shook his head, jerky and labored. He took a deep breath. "No. He came to visit one night. She saw him in the yard. I remember looking through the window. He got stronger while he was in France."

He took another strenuous breath. Shandi thought for sure that he lacked the strength to go on, but he did. "Mama cried again that night. Like she had when she learned he died. She didn't know I saw. He never came back after that."

A chill ran down Shandi's spine. The beast had come to see his wife. Some part of his humanity must have remained back then, and maybe some part of it existed even now. Did he know his son was nearby?

None of this information provided definitive proof. This all could just have easily been a coincidence and the overactive imagination of a young child who had lost his father. It seemed impossible to believe that he would remember something like that from the age of three. Though maybe this memory sprung from an event from much later than 1942.

Clearly, the beast had been in Rose Valley for many years.

Something turned Shandi's mind to the night the beast had attacked her house. He had taken one of Macy's stuffed animals; a cartoon potato that they called Scallops. Had held onto it even while he chased them. It hadn't been at the house or on the road when Cam had gone back, so perhaps he had taken it with him. Had it reminded him of something from his previous life?

Shandi thought of another question. "Back before the war, what did Billy do for a living?"

Karen looked at her father, frowning when she realized his focus was wandering. "He was a farmer in Mississippi. I remember because of his amazing pie recipe. He grew sweet potatoes."

Shandi blanched as she remembered Macy's stuffed animal. Her doubts about the relationship between Billy Hargrove and the beast evaporated. The beast and Billy Hargrove inhabited the same body. And more importantly, he knew it.

CHAPTER 33

The First United Methodist Church of Rose Valley overflowed its fire marshal mandated capacity. Sunday morning wouldn't come for almost twenty-four hours. Unlike church services, this congregation consisted of more than just Methodists. It contained just as many Baptists, as well as a great number of people who generally professed to believe in God yet couldn't find the time or energy to attend church. There may have been the odd Atheist or Catholic, but unlikely that any other denomination attended. The theological options in Rose Valley were few.

At the front of the church stood not a preacher, pastor, or reverend. The man at the pulpit carried himself with much more confidence and charisma than any of those callings. Like the pastor might have done, though, Skylar Brooks meant to convert people to his cause.

In the front left pew sat a string of unlikely allies, starting with Cory and Steve, neither of which attended church, for obvious reasons. Then Jake and Shandi, followed by Macy and Cam. On the other side of Cam sat Dub Higgins, and then Marie, the only one of them that didn't look uncomfortable. She dressed as if ready to attend church, looking every bit the part of a God-fearing woman.

Cam and Dub both wore their uniforms. Both had their guns; Dub's noticeably shinier since it was brand new. Both even had their hats on. Shandi thought this disrespectful given their location, but The First United Methodist Church of Rose Valley did not serve as a place of worship on this day. It had transformed into something much more sinister.

Skylar Brooks tapped the microphone with his forefinger three times, cleared his throat, and began his sermon. "You're scared. Your town has been beset by evil. You fear for your children. Your livelihoods. You just want it to stop. I can understand that. I sympathize with that. I know you'd like nothing more than to hunt this beast down and shoot it dead.

"But you also have an opportunity. You stand on the precipice of making Rose Valley the most famous small town in America. And it starts by not killing this beast, no. But by capturing it. By putting it on display. By studying it. By proving to the world that Rose Valley will not be controlled by its fear. You can't let this creature torment you, and I will make sure that you don't.

"You've heard of Lake Worth, Texas, I presume," he continued. "I expect your Mighty Jaguars have met them on the gridiron a time or two. Well, in 1969, Lake Worth was in the place you now find yourself. A vicious creature was on the loose. It attacked cars. It threw a tire at some people. They weren't safe. They were scared. Like you are now. My father saved them.

"I was 12 then. It was the first time my dad let me go on a hunt with him. My father may not have captured Lake Worth's Goatman, but he scared it off and it never returned."

Skylar took a long pause. He looked around the room, as if to make eye contact with every single person in the congregation. Shandi didn't care for his intense stare, but she could tell that she sided with the minority. She jotted "Lake Worth Goatman 1969" down on her notepad. The townspeople may have bought into this farce, but Shandi refused. No matter what Skylar said, he was nothing but a snake-oil salesman and, when she had the time, she intended to prove it.

Skylar went on. "The great thing about America is that we don't have to settle for the failures of our fathers. I loved my dear old man, but I can do better than he did. We can all do better. We can capture this animal."

Cornelius certainly had to settle for his father's failures, Shandi thought morbidly. So far, there had been no mention of Cornelius. Skylar's own son had been ripped apart by the beast and yet Skylar still focused on his own fame and fortune.

"And mark my words. It is *just* an animal. It seems more than that right now, but it isn't. It's an animal and it can be stopped. Just like any other animal. Maybe not with your standard issue law enforcement weaponry." Skylar motioned towards Cam and Dub. "Maybe not even with the shotguns that you use to keep coyotes out of your hen house. But it can be stopped. I have the right tools for the job."

Skylar motioned behind him and Miriam stood up from one of the choir chairs. Unlike Skylar, who exuded smarm, Miriam just looked angry. She reached into one of the open black cases and pulled out an enormous weapon, too large for her small frame though she held it with confidence, the butt resting on her hip. Miriam clearly had experience with this weapon.

A murmur went through the crowd. Skylar smiled. "Don't worry. It's not deadly. Not to the beast anyway. It's just a tranquilizer gun. It's used to bring down very large game.

"Certainly, you'll want to be careful. If you shoot yourself with this gun, you may find yourself taking a very long—maybe even permanent—nap. But this is an easy weapon to use. Especially for you. You are not city-folk. You know how to handle your guns."

A few "hear-hears!" broke out in the crowd, along with solemn nods. Shandi began to worry. She exchanged looks with Jake. Though the biggest follower of cryptozoology that she knew, Jake didn't look comfortable with Skylar Brooks' methods, either. Macy, on the other hand, looked completely engrossed, which unnerved Shandi.

Cam didn't look comfortable, but neither did he look appropriately appalled. When she'd learned that he intended to work with Skylar, Shandi assumed that meant that Skylar would advise him, not take over the entire operation. Surely Cam could see that Skylar lacked real credentials. He obviously spent a lot of money on expensive weapons, but that didn't make him proper law enforcement.

Skylar nodded at Miriam and she carefully placed the gun back into its box. Skylar looked back to the congregation. "I'm not here for your money. I will let all able-bodied people borrow one of these guns. If you return it in good shape, then there's no need for payment. The only thing I ask is that I be the first to study this creature. To catalog it. To photograph it. I want to apply the scientific method to this problem. I want to make sure this thing ends up in the biology texts that your kids read at school.

"I cannot do this without your help. We have almost 30 square miles to cover if we're going to flush this thing out. We will need to work together. Leave no stone unturned. No cave unexplored. We will set up traps and cameras. We *will* find your beast."

Shandi startled when cheers broke out. The room bulged with people she had grown up with. Some of them her peers, some her teachers, and some her friends, yet they'd all seemed to have bought into Skylar. She felt surrounded by strangers. She could understand the fear, especially since they'd watched it take down one of the very people who was charged with their protection. Still, this course of action felt wrong, hasty, and a bit too mob-like for her tastes.

The cheers died down and Skylar resumed: "I've been working with your Sheriff to make sure that we are as effective as possible on our hunt. He will now brief you on the particulars."

Cam stood and straightened his khaki button up. Before heading to the pulpit, he briefly glanced at Macy but not Shandi. If he had looked worn out at the press conference, now he bordered on "zombie." Shandi sat close enough to the front to see the blood-red veins of his eyes, to see his face drooped from exhaustion. Concern welled in her. Had he slept at all?

Cam started his portion of the speech. "Starting tomorrow afternoon at two PM, roughly twenty-four hours from now, we will begin a county wide manhunt. We will organize at the Sheriff's Department, where each person will be issued firearms commensurate with their skill level. There will be no need to try out. I know each of you well enough to know what you can handle.

"I have spoken with Principal Steele and the superintendent of schools. We have all agreed that school should be closed until we can bring the beast to justice."

Several of the more rebellious teenagers whooped at this. Under most circumstances, Shandi would have taken the excitement to mean that they wanted to get out of school, but she suspected that in this case they wanted to get their hands on those tranquilizer guns.

She shuddered thinking they might lose teenagers in this manhunt. No. Manhunt afforded this show too much gravitas. They now teetered on the brink of self-destruction.

Cam continued. "Be prepared to stay out overnight. We will brief you with more particulars tomorrow afternoon. If you don't feel up to the task, please stay in your homes. Contact the Sheriff's Department if there are any sightings. Thank you."

Cam stepped down from the pulpit and the crowd erupted into a thousand different conversations. Shandi's row stood almost in unison as Cam approached them. He walked directly to Shandi.

"I talked to mom," said Cam. "She's agreed to let Macy stay with her. Do you mind taking her up there tonight?"

Cam's mom lived fifteen miles away in another town. Shandi expected Cam would try to get Macy somewhere safe, but she suspected Macy might object. And she did.

"What? No. I'm staying here. I want to help. I can hand out water or something. Wes is staying. He's going to get one of those guns and kill the beast!"

Of course Macy already knew Wes' intentions. Maybe from a text, or social media. In this rare instance, Shandi agreed with Cam.

"No," Cam told her. "You're going to grandmom's. End of story. I'll keep Wes safe."

Macy could always be counted on to believe that her father could do no wrong. Shandi had no doubt that a promise of safety from Cam would be effective.

Macy did not look immediately convinced, but she remained quiet. They could hope for no closer to acquiescence.

When Macy didn't answer, Shandi jumped in. "Sure. I'll take her there tonight."

Cam nodded and disappeared into the crowd, not acknowledging Jake or Steve. Neither of them seemed to care, but it irked Shandi. She went out of her way not to show any outward affection toward Jake in public yet. She feared Cam's reaction to their relationship more than anything else, and this type of behavior from him proved exactly why.

Shandi turned to Jake. "Whadya say? Wanna come with me to drop off a wayward teen?"

Macy looked defiant, but confused. "Hey! I'm not wayward."

"I'd love to," Jake said with a smile, as Shandi pulled Macy in for a half-hug.

Macy made a face. "Ew. Are you guys going to make out the whole way?"

Shandi feared the fallout from telling Macy about Jake, but based on Macy's body language she already seemed suspicious. Shandi hadn't really dated since the divorce, and Macy loved Cam so much.

"No," Shandi replied. "Of course not. We're going to make out the entire time you're gone!"

Jake's smile broadened. Macy rolled her eyes.

CHAPTER 34

Jake felt a flutter of anxiety about what the next couple of days would bring. Despite knowing his connection to the beast, he didn't know how to use that connection to benefit himself or Rose Valley. Once the whole town fanned out on the prowl, he feared that more people would die, ensuring an overwhelming amount of pressure to figure out how to communicate with Billy. But where to start?

Macy insisted that they needed air conditioning for such a long ride, so now they rode back towards Rose Valley in Shandi's Camry, Jake's left hand interlaced with hers. It seemed unnecessarily dangerous and juvenile to be holding hands while cruising down the highway at seventy-five miles per hour, but Jake liked it nonetheless.

Saving the beast presented a tall and unfathomable order, even if the order came from Shandi. Jake doubted that they could save this creature, but Shandi once again swayed his confidence in their ability to pull it off. Of course, it would be a lot harder now that the whole town would be out looking for the creature. Though Jake worried that Billy might kill people, he also feared that a few townspeople would accidentally kill each other. Arming a whole town with tranquilizers seemed like a monumentally bad idea.

Shandi glanced over at him. He saw her out of the corner of his eye and turned to meet her gaze but her eyes turned back toward the road. She took a deep breath.

"We're lucky... in a way," said Shandi. "I thought for sure that Cam was aiming to kill Billy. But now we know the goal is to capture him. I don't know if the tranquilizers will work, but at least we'll have a shot even if we aren't the first to find him."

Jake nodded. "Yeah. And we have an advantage. If I can just figure out how to use it. I don't really focus on myself much, so he's never had a reason to come to me."

"Yes, you're very selfless," Shandi teased.

"You know what I mean."

"Yeah. I know. Maybe you don't need to bring him to you, though. Maybe you just need to bring him somewhere you'll both be. Subtle distinction, I know. I was thinking the schoolhouse."

Jake thought about that. It made some amount of sense. Billy Hargrove had never lived at the schoolhouse, but his son and granddaughter lived there. If anything meant anything to Billy anymore, it would be his family. Still, it seemed unsafe.

"It puts people in danger, though. How old did you say his son is? 78? He can't run or protect himself. He'll be a sitting duck if Billy decides to kill him instead of reconnect with him."

"True," she said. "He can't, but we can protect him. We can get Steve. He's a crack shot. You said so yourself."

"That's assuming the tranquilizers work at all," Jake remarked.

"Hmm. Maybe we don't give Steve a tranquilizer gun. Maybe we get him something stronger. Something that might even kill the beast. I know that's not our goal, but we need to cover our bases."

"Okay. Yeah. That could work. Steve could even stay away, so that he wasn't in immediate danger. He could shoot Billy before he even knew that Steve was there... if it comes to that, of course."

Shandi didn't immediately answer, but she did nod before drifting back into thought. Jake assumed she was thinking about the same thing he was. The best plan in the world would be useless if he couldn't make the beast come to them.

After another mile of silence, Jake asked, "Do you think Karen will go along with it? You haven't even told her that the beast might be her grandfather."

Shandi twisted her mouth up in thought before answering. "Yeah. Good point. I guess I don't know. She was very willing to share information, but I don't suppose she's going to be keen on putting her father at risk."

"I guess all we can do is ask. Maybe we should have a backup plan."

"I think Steve has to be our backup plan. We can take a tranquilizer gun and try that first, I guess, but I'm not very hopeful."

Jake relaxed when she said this. He harbored his own reservations as to whether a tranquilizer would work. He needed to know that Shandi would be willing to kill Billy if they had to. After what Deirdre told him, he prepared for the possibility that either he or Billy would have to die.

"This is insane, Shandi. Insane. Is this really happening?"

She squeezed his hand and took the time to really look at him. "Yeah. It's really happening. But some good came of it. You got me out of the deal. A fine catch, if I do say so myself."

Jake laughed. "Yeah, I suppose you're a pretty good prize. Though I did have to die to get you, remember."

"Oh right. About that..."

Jake waved his free hand. "Nah. I get it. There's nothing else to tell. I died. Not a big deal, right? Is it really death if you come back to life?"

"Medically? Yes. It absolutely is."

"Well, I guess that just makes me special then."

Shandi smiled. "I'm not sure that's what makes you special, but something does."

"Macy would hate this so much right now."

"Yeah. She would. But she isn't here right now. It's just us."

Jake stopped on that statement. There had been so much to worry and think about that he considered for the first time that they would be together. Alone. Without Macy. Without any responsibilities until tomorrow afternoon. He suddenly got the very strong urge to ensure that he did not go home alone.

He looked at her. She radiated so much more beauty than he'd ever realized. Not from her hair, or her eyes, or her smile, or even her perfect tiny body. Now he saw something more than that—her essence. The way that she embraced life and never wavered from a fight.

"So, my house is kind of a disaster," he said. "I had these crazy houseguests for a few days, and then some crazy lady killed me. It's been a rough week."

Shandi laughed. "Poor baby. Does Steve provide housekeeping services?"

"If he does, I've been missing out."

She turned off on the main highway through Rose Valley. It wouldn't be long now until she would drop him off at Steve's. He had spent his entire life without Shandi, but now the thought of going another night without her seemed like it would be impossible to survive.

He told himself to man up and stop being a chicken. He should have just outright suggested that he stay over at her place. Something held him back. He worried that he might lead the beast to her again, that he wouldn't be able to stop her from getting killed.

As she turned into the gates of Watermelon Ranch, she let go of his hand. The car rumbled over the cattle guard, as the rocks ricocheted loudly off the undercarriage of the car, creating an awful racket. Shandi pulled up in front of the guest house, put the car in park, and turned to him. He didn't say anything or make a move to get out.

She laughed. "Get going, boy. Pack a bag and get back out here. We've got a lot of work to do."

Jake's face turned up in a silly grin. Perhaps that's how a good relationship worked. Perhaps this presented the beginnings of their own hive mind.

"Yes, ma'am!" he said as he hopped out of the car.

He ran inside and threw a smattering of clothes into a backpack. He tried to go through the list of what he would need to lure the beast and decided that he only needed his mind and the knowledge of how to use it to lure the thing. Hopefully he could find the latter when it really mattered.

After gathering all the essentials, he ran back to the car and dropped in next to her with his backpack in his lap. Shandi put the car in reverse and headed back down the long, rocky road to the highway.

Tomorrow would be a huge day. People would likely die. Maybe even him. Or Shandi. Deirdre said he had to die to stop the beast. But he couldn't accept that. Not now.

As they made their way to her house, Jake wanted to wrap his arms around Shandi. To fall into bed with her. To laugh. To love. To feel alive. He didn't plan for it to be their last and only night together, but just in case, he wanted to make it as memorable as possible.

She caught him staring at her.

"Whoa there, chief. First things first. We still have some planning to do."

CHAPTER 35

Sitting in a cell at the county jail, Deirdre desperately wished she had studied law instead. She had wanted to cooperate, to turn the Sheriff to her cause. That plan was thus far not working out like she'd hoped. The days blurred together. Surely, they meant to either charge her with something or release her soon.

The Rose Valley Sheriff's Department had two jail cells that served as mirrors to one another across a narrow hallway. One end of the hallway ended in what Deirdre assumed was a very thick brick wall. The other led out into the main area of the department, separated by a door that no one had bothered to close. Dub had told her that if she needed anything, she could always "holler," but she didn't think she needed to resort to that just yet.

She decided that the next time an officer checked on her, she would request a lawyer. She should have already done it. She chalked it up to one more thing that she avoided because of pride. In her career, she had learned early on that confidence was important. A woman would not be taken seriously, otherwise. But now her hubris betrayed her at every turn.

She had received the occasional roommate over the last couple of days. Mostly drunk teenagers. The Sheriff had no qualms about sticking men in the cell with her. It seemed inappropriate, but none of them had caused any trouble.

Currently, there was no one in her cell, or the sister one across the hall. She had enjoyed the silence at first, but now it was gnawing at her nerves. She had learned from the last drunkard that the beast had killed a college kid from Missouri. The one before had mentioned that the beast had killed Bernard Jones as well, but the latter said that he had just died of a heart attack. Deirdre didn't know which one was true, but if the beast had killed even one of them, that meant that the carnage would only ramp up from there.

Deirdre didn't know for certain how the beast would react as long as Jake was in a drug-induced coma, but she suspected that the beast would remain active. Jake would dream and his mind would meander. It might confuse the beast, cause him to do strange things or to become easily distracted. But it wouldn't shut him down. He was out there somewhere, ready to prey further on the residents of Rose Valley.

She stretched out on the bench and stared at the ceiling, drifting in and out of a fitful half-sleep until she jolted awake from shouts and scrambling elsewhere in the building. Probably some belligerent drunk. Who could blame someone for throwing a few back when their hometown was under siege by a monster?

When the shouting didn't die down immediately, she began to wonder whether it was more than that.

Then the first gunshot left little doubt.

They sounded like muffled pops from within her cell, but there was no mistaking the sounds. She lost count of how many shots were fired. Dozens, at least.

Something bigger than a handgun fired, echoing down the narrow hallway. Whatever was happening had moved closer to her cell. Closer, panicked shouting ricocheted back to her, as gunsmoke drifted in.

Through the shouting came growling, followed by a scream that tore through all of Deirdre's resolve. She craned her neck to see deputies running past the hallway opening, shouting orders to each other. She couldn't make out all of them, but she didn't need to. She knew what was coming.

She needed to hide. Maybe find a weapon of some sort. She realized that jail cells were not designed to provide either of those things, and settled for crouching in the back corner closest to the hallway entrance.

"Fall back!" she heard a shout, unmistakably from Sheriff Donner.

Deirdre heard a door open. She presumed it was the back entrance to the department. They were running. They were going to leave the beast alone with her. Her heart jumped, and she tried to make herself even smaller, knowing that it was futile. This was not something she could reason her way out of. The bars didn't look so strong now. She was going to die.

She could tell when the beast had stopped at the entrance to the hallway. Maybe it was his breathing, or his labored steps on the concrete floor. He moved towards her at an agonizingly slow pace. She held her breath.

She jumped when she saw it standing outside of the door to her cell. She had never been able to study it in person before. Regardless of what he had been before, he was a monster now. Paradoxically, Deirdre distracted herself from imminent death by admiring this amazing creation. He was so strong and resilient and fast. He seemed to have an unnaturally long lifespan. Maybe he was even immortal.

She didn't create him, but she had studied the serum that had. With the money from her grant and a few more years of research, she might have perfected it. She could have created real-life superheroes. Not mindless monsters like this one, but truly enhanced humans.

She knew he had no functional brain. Not really. She knew that as he stared at her, he wasn't pondering whether he wanted to kill her. The thoughts that he received from Jake were surely so muddled and confusing. It was a wonder he could make sense of it at all. And that's why the experiment had always failed. Eventually, the voices in his head were too overwhelming, and he reverted to his base state of aggression.

She watched as he reached up and wrapped both of his massive hands around two bars in the cell door. She winced when the steel hinges creaked, then eventually popped. He pulled the door towards himself and dropped it on the floor like it was made of paper.

He only loomed in the doorway, not entering. Was he toying with her? No. She was only projecting. He had no way to process such emotions. Jake, on the other hand, surely wanted her to suffer. The evidence did not support the theory that Jake could directly control The Beast like that, but Deirdre couldn't help but wonder.

As he moved to take a step into her cell, a gunshot rang down the hallway and the beast reeled backward. It wasn't a handgun. It sounded much larger than that. The beast started towards the sound of the shot, away from Deirdre. Another shot rang out and the beast stumbled, backed up, and dropped to his knees. This gun wasn't going to kill him, but it was pushing him back.

"Dr. Valentine. Come here. Now!" the Sheriff yelled.

She needed no further invitation. She scrambled on all fours towards the cell door and stood up to run as she reached the entrance. The beast grabbed at her, latched on to her ankle and caused her to fall hard on her chest. She kicked with her other foot. He grabbed that one too. She tried desperately to find something to hold onto in the smooth concrete floor, but there was nothing to stop her from moving backwards.

Another shot rang through the air, the bullet whizzing above her head. The Beast howled in rage and loosened his grip on her ankles. She got to her knees and crawled a yard away before getting back to her feet. Her ankles hurt, but they weren't broken. She ran as fast as she could towards the Sheriff, too scared to look back at how close the beast might be. Her body blocked the path now. The Sheriff wouldn't be able to fire again until she cleared the hallway.

She was moving too slow. The Beast would catch her at this rate. She willed her legs to move faster, ignoring the pain and the fear.

To her surprise, the beast did not catch her. She squeezed past the Sheriff and he immediately fired another round. She stood in the hallway now, unable to see the beast. The Sheriff crouched on one knee, aiming the rifle. He dropped the muzzle of the gun, and stood up.

"Let's get out of here," he said to her.

He sprinted towards the back of the hallway to the rear entrance of the department. She should have followed, but she saw another path. If she followed Cam, she would still be in his custody. But if she ran the other direction, she might escape. Without weighing the pros and cons, she ran away from the Sheriff towards the front doors of the department.

"Stop right there, Doc!" she heard him cry.

She didn't stop. He wouldn't shoot her. Not when his ammo was so precious. He needed to keep his gun ready for when the beast regained the strength to walk out of the cellblock. He wasn't going to waste it on her tiny, fragile body. She felt her feet slip out from under her as she hit a wet patch of blood, causing her to fall to one knee. Her stomach lurched as her eyes scanned over two halves of a dead body, but she suppressed the bile in her throat, pushed herself up and lunged forward.

She heard the beast growl behind her as she crashed into the door and out into the warm night's air. It was dark, with no one in sight. It must have been late. She took off in a dead run across the highway, into a field, and then into a grove of trees.

She stopped to catch her breath as another shot rang out. They wouldn't be chasing her right now. They couldn't afford to. She was a tiny little girl, not an immortal monster.

After catching her breath for as long as she dared, Deirdre walked deeper into the woods away from the department. She didn't know where she was going just yet, but she knew she needed to clear as much ground as possible before the beast vanished and left the deputies with nothing to do but hunt her down.

The Sheriff could have shot her, but he hadn't, and Deirdre took that as a sign. Cam couldn't kill Jake. But she could. And Cam wanted her to. She understood, of course, that such an unholy alliance could never be verbalized, but he had forged one with her on this night when he let her go.

Yes. There could be no doubt. Sheriff Donner counted on her to kill Jake and save Rose Valley.

CHAPTER 36

Jake fought to flex his fingers, shooting fire up his arm as his mind groggily pushed away nightmares of Deirdre bearing down on him. With his watch pinned, he couldn't tell how long they'd been asleep, but based on the lack of circulation in his arm, it had been a few hours at least. He didn't want to move. Her body against his felt heavenly, energizing him with her every shallow breath. But he also didn't want to have a non-functional arm, so he slowly shimmied his arm out from under her and rolled over on his back. She protested a little with soft murmurs but otherwise remained asleep.

The moment his skin left contact with hers, he regretted it, so he lightly reached out and laid his hand on her hip, causing her to sigh. Darkness enveloped the room, but his eyes could make out shapes here and there, adding to the odd sensation of being in someone else's bedroom. The clock read 1:24am. He pondered on the weird juxtaposition of emotions coursing through his body. Dread of the manhunt mixed with an overwhelming sense of happiness and contentment.

As he lay there trying to fall back asleep, he felt a light buzzing in his wrist, followed by his phone ringing from the nightstand. The screen showed a Rose Valley number, but not one that came from his address book. It could have been a wrong number, he supposed, but that seemed especially odd since his cell phone didn't have a local number. Jake avoided answering his phone in any case, especially at night, and tonight provided the best excuse of all to do so. It eventually went silent.

Almost immediately, it rang again. Shandi stirred and mumbled, "Who is it?"

"I don't recognize the number."

"Read it to me," she said, her voice hoarse from sleep.

He read her the number to appease her.

"That's Cam."

Jake blinked. "Should I answer it?"

Shandi nodded and sunk back into the pillows. She didn't seem terribly concerned.

Jake answered on speakerphone so that Shandi could hear. "Hello?"

"Jake. This is Sheriff Donner."

"Hi, sheriff, what's---"

Cam interrupted the pleasantries. "Listen. I'm really sorry about calling you in the middle of the night like this. I just. I should have pulled the trigger. But I didn't. I just wanted to tell you as soon as possible."

Jake glanced at Shandi.

Cam continued before Jake said anything. "The beast attacked the jail earlier tonight. We lost a good officer. But also..."

He trailed off. Jake's mind followed the sheriff's train of thought as fast as he spoke, his blood going cold the moment the sheriff uttered his next words.

"Deirdre escaped."

Shandi audibly gasped and immediately got out of bed. She turned on a lamp and searched around the room for her clothes. Jake sat up in bed in a panic, trying to process the news. Cam continued, thankfully oblivious to the fact that his ex-wife rushed around the room naked.

"It's probably not a big deal. If she's smart, she skipped town. But just to be safe, I'm going to send a deputy out to your place. Just to keep an eye on things."

Deirdre's zealotry had led her to attempt to murder him once, and Jake had a hard time believing that she would have walked away from her mission. Regardless of Cam's promises of safety, Jake suspected that Deirdre lurked in the shadows of Rose Valley along with the beast now.

Shandi pulled on the last of her clothes, and moved towards him, having put together the implications of the conversation faster than him. Given his current location, sending a deputy out to Watermelon Ranch served no discernible purpose. Before Jake could react, Shandi began talking into the microphone.

"Cam? Don't be mad, okay?"

"Shandi?" his voice cracked with surprise.

She gave Jake a strained look before answering, "Yeah. We can talk about this later, but right now I need you to know that Jake isn't at his house."

"Then where the hell is he?" Cam said, the volume of his voice escalating.

"He's at mine," Shandi said, closing her eyes to prepare for Cam's reaction.

The line went silent. Shandi looked worried. Jake didn't know what to do. He wanted to comfort her, but touching her under the circumstances felt exceptionally inappropriate.

Shandi couldn't take the silence. "Don't be mad, Cam. There's not time for that. I promise that we can sit down, just the two of us, and have a sane discussion about this. But right now, we need to make sure Deirdre doesn't get to Jake, right?"

The room fell agonizingly silent once again for what seemed like an eternity before Cam finally answered, "I'm on my way."

The line went dead. "Oh, that's not good," Jake said.

Shandi sighed. "That's not exactly how I wanted him to find out about us. But what's done is done. The good news is that he'll be here if Deirdre shows up."

Jake half-joked, "Yeah, but the bad news is that he might kill me first."

Shandi made a show of pulling him down to her for a kiss before responding. "No. He'll be fine. He just needs some time to process it. You're not his favorite person."

She walked towards the bedroom door, glancing over her shoulder as she went. "It'll probably be better for you if you have clothes on when he gets here, though."

Jake looked down and surprised himself, somehow having forgotten that he didn't have any clothes on. He found his garments strewn around the room, slipped them on as fast as he could and joined Shandi in the kitchen, where she busied herself making coffee. Though adrenaline served just fine as a wake-up call, the aroma of the coffee enticed him.

"Could you make sure the door is locked?" Shandi asked him.

Surely, they had locked the door, right? Who would leave the door unlocked when a monster roamed the streets? Jake rewound his memory to the previous night, dwelling on the sensations of them devouring one another, while Shandi haphazardly tried to get her key into the lock. Perhaps such a distraction had kept them from locking the door, after all.

Being unfamiliar with Shandi's house, Jake couldn't tell what the direction of the lock meant. He reached for the handle so that he could turn it to find out, but when he gripped it, he felt it turn from the other side. He jumped back. The door opened and there was a gun pointed at his face. He followed the muzzle down a rail thin arm and into the blue ocean of Deirdre's eyes.

"Back up!" she yelled at him.

Jake backed up. Shandi rushed to his side and grabbed his hand, as Deirdre stepped inside without closing the door. She kept the gun level with Jake's face, hovering only a few feet away. Even she wouldn't miss at that range.

Deirdre's eyes flicked down to their hands. "Isn't that so sweet."

Jake dropped Shandi's hand. "Deirdre. Don't do this. We know who the beast is. You don't have to kill me."

"The man that was the beast is long gone, Jake. You're not going to get him back. And you're not going to be able to kill him either. Don't kid yourself." Her eyes filled with a rage that Jake had never seen.

"How do you know, though? Can't we at least try? You don't want to kill me, Deirdre. We've been friends for a long time."

"It's the only way they've ever been able to stop him. The doctors killed three seekers to keep him dormant. The difference was that they knew what they signed up for. They knew the risks. I know you didn't ask for this, Jake, but there's no other option."

Out of the corner of his eye, Jake sensed an imperceptible tensing of Shandi's muscles. Having overpowered Deirdre once before, Jake feared that Shandi would try it again. Before he could stop it, Shandi lunged, and Jake instinctively stepped in front of her. Deirdre fired.

He screamed as pain roared through his right arm. He grabbed it with his left hand, feeling the warm sticky goo of his own blood ooze between his fingers. Shandi screamed his name. With his back to Deirdre, Jake fell forward into Shandi's arms. She gingerly lowered him to the ground, then ripped her shirt off in one smooth jerk.

Jake winced as Shandi wrapped her shirt tight around the wound. He felt queasy. It looked like a serious wound, but he wasn't losing consciousness or anything. Not yet.

He forced himself to look up at Deirdre, desperate to know where she stood and what her next move might be. She looked stunned, with the gun still out in front of her; the muzzle drifting with him towards the ground. But she looked less resolute now, her anger losing out to fear.

Once Shandi seemed satisfied with her triage work, she stood slowly, keeping her hands up where Deirdre could see them. Jake hoped that Deirdre's willingness to fire had scared Shandi away from trying anything else stupid. Once Shandi stretched to her full height, Deirdre shifted the gun to Shandi's face.

"Don't move, you little bitch."

Jake wanted to end it somehow. He couldn't bear the thought of Shandi getting shot. He spent so much time worrying about whether the beast might come for her that he'd never considered that Deirdre might also want her dead. Jake would have bet on Shandi for any number of things, but not hostage negotiations.

"Listen, Deirdre. Just let me talk, ok?" Shandi said with remarkable calmness.

Deirdre didn't answer, but neither did she fire her gun or make any move indicating she would. Jake took that as a good sign. Shandi did as well.

"His name is Billy Hargrove. He was a major in the army. He was assigned to Arrowhead Research. They did this to him. You can undo it."

Deirdre shook her head. "No, I can't. No one can. Billy Hargrove is dead! We can kill Jake, and then that thing will go dormant. We can kill it then, maybe. Cut off its head or something."

Jake interjected, "Why didn't they do that the last three times, then?"

Deirdre glanced down, seemingly contemplating the shaking that flowed through her entire body. She flinched as if she would point the gun towards Jake, but then thought better of it and kept it aimed at Shandi. Jake didn't like it.

"I... don't know. Maybe they didn't know how to find him?"

Shandi jumped back in. "Or maybe they didn't want to kill him. Maybe they knew they could save him eventually."

Deirdre shook her head. Jake saw Shandi tense up. *Please, Shandi, don't do anything stupid.*

Deirdre locked her elbows. The gun rattled as she decisively pointed it at Shandi again before answering, "You're not going to confuse me. I know what I have to do. I know more about this than you could ever hope to. Killing the seeker is the only way!"

The intensity of the moment overwhelmed him, adrenaline surging as the pain in his arm throbbed in rhythm with his heart. The baby blue of Shandi's shirt turned redder with every pulse.

Shandi gently kicked Jake's foot and spoke again, "Right. Because the seeker is the one that controls the beast, right? He can make him do what he wants."

"We have to do this, Shandi," tears started forming in Deirdre's eyes. "I don't need to kill you, but we have to kill Jake."

Jake pondered Shandi's meaning. She wanted him to summon the beast. But he didn't know how. Where would he even start?

Given that he didn't see any other options, Jake closed his eyes and focused. He focused on Deirdre. He pictured her in his head. Her blonde hair. Her big blue eyes. Her imaginary form took shape in his mind. Worried that just Deirdre wouldn't be enough, he thought about Shandi's house. He described it to himself in vivid detail. He thought of every color, every corner, every material adorning the outside. He thought of her cars in the driveway. He thought of the entry way to the house.

Shandi and Deirdre kept arguing. Jake couldn't pay attention. He had to focus. It took all his concentration. He tried to think of everything that the beast would need to understand his meaning. He thought of the backdoor to the house, where the beast had smashed in the last door. He thought of the stuffed animal Shandi had mentioned. He called the beast's name. *Billy* echoed through his mind. He didn't know if the beast even knew his own name anymore.

Though it was labored and difficult, Jake focused harder on pushing himself into a meditative state. The minutes melted away. Jake lost track of how long he focused on calling Billy. Every time Shandi or Deirdre distracted him, he pushed it away and went over all the details in his mind again. He pleaded for Billy to save him with all his waning strength, but nothing happened.

Jake gave up hope, realizing that his pleading would not save them. His efforts better served them by teaming up with Shandi to overpower Deirdre in some other way. Jake opened his eyes again and looked up at Deirdre. Her fingers tensely curled around the trigger, threatening to shoot Shandi at any moment. He took stock of his strength and wondered if he would be able to get himself over to Deirdre, to at least trip her and knock off her aim.

Though already overflowing with fear, Jake suddenly felt a new wave of it surge through his mind. It felt foreign, not like his own fear, but like an empathetic understanding of someone else's. It took him a few seconds before he found the truth of the situation. The beast had arrived. He knew it. He *felt* it.

When he looked up again, Billy hulked in the doorway behind Deirdre. Jake looked to Shandi, her eyes wide with fear. Yes, the beast was here.

Billy's massive frame surprised Jake, even though he had seen it in videos and pictures. The overwhelming fear made room for a small amount of fascination. He had brought this monster to them. He could direct Billy. He could save them.

Deirdre noticed them both staring at the doorway. At first, she seemed reticent to turn around, clearly wanting to keep the gun on Shandi, but as their eyes got wider, and the fear on their faces became more apparent, she couldn't resist.

Deirdre let her arm fall to her side as she turned, somehow sensing that a gun wouldn't save her. The beast let out an inhuman growl, chilling Jake to his bones. Time seemed to stand still. Jake's heart pounded, and he regretted that he brought Billy here. He didn't want to be responsible for Deirdre's death. She spun back around, took two steps forward, and pulled the gun straight up to Jake's face.

He panicked, pushing away his regret and scrambling to save himself from death. He couldn't stop a bullet, but maybe he could stop Deirdre. He shut his eyes and forced himself to conjure the image of Deirdre in his head again. He tried to imagine her how she appeared right there in that moment, but his mind only presented Dee, from high school, with her effervescent smile and tireless drive.

Jake's eyes snapped open. The beast pounced. The gun fired. Deirdre screamed.

CHAPTER 37

By the time Deirdre pulled the trigger, the beast already reached across his body and grabbed her arm. The bullet missed Jake's head by inches. As Billy spun her around, the gun flew out of her hand and clattered across the floor. Shandi scrambled over to it, scooped it up, and pointed it at the beast. She knew it wouldn't help her, but she felt safer having it in her hands and not Deirdre's.

The beast enshrouded Deirdre's face in his massive hand, muffling her screams. Her body kept twisting, as he continued pulling on her arm with an ungodly force. A horrible, sickening crack echoed through the room, and the screams stopped suddenly. The beast tossed Deirdre aside like a rag-doll, her body crumpling to the floor in an unnatural tangle of limbs.

Shandi forcefully stifled the urge to scream. The beast turned towards her, not immediately descending on her. She suddenly realized that the gun presented a threat to Billy without offering any real protection to her. Pointing it at him would only serve to make her a target. She sat it on the ground next to her and slowly stood with her hands up. She didn't know if he would respond to that body language, but it seemed as reasonable as anything else.

She glanced at Jake, saw his eyes closed and felt her heart thump in fear that he had passed out. His hand twitched, indicating that he still lived, and she suppressed the need to drop down beside him. Maybe he just didn't want to see what had happened to Deirdre and what might happen next.

As Billy took a step toward her, Shandi froze in place, afraid that if she ran, it would trigger a predator instinct in him that he wouldn't be able to ignore. She needed to show him that she did not fear him.

"Billy. It's okay. It's not your fault," she said, her voice far weaker than she had hoped.

He looked deep into her eyes. She could see more there now, recognition at his name, perhaps, though she might've been imagining it. He kept advancing on her. She forced herself to stand her ground, unable to control the forceful shaking of her limbs.

He stood directly over her now. She slowly tilted her head back to look at him, reminding herself that this creature had once been a man. He had done horribly gruesome things, but those atrocities could hardly be blamed solely on him. Arrowhead had done this to him, sentencing him to a life of pain and agony. She could only hope that he could still recognize and appreciate sympathy.

In an instant, he spun and ran out the door, stopping to let out one of his inhuman howls as he crossed the porch. Shandi breathed a sigh of relief and moved back to Jake. His eyes fluttered open now, but he looked drained.

Before she could talk to him, a gunshot rang out. Then more. She heard the beast growl. She jumped back to her feet and ran out onto her porch to see Cam shooting at the beast from the other side of his Suburban.

"Cam. Stop!" she yelled.

It didn't matter to her in that moment that she stood on her front porch in jeans and a bra. Cam looked up at her with surprise, giving the beast time to run. Only once Billy had moved far enough away did Cam scuttle to the front porch and grab Shandi's shoulders.

"Are you okay?"

She pointed towards the door and responded with a single, shaky word. "Deirdre."

Cam rushed inside. Shandi followed. Cam quickly glanced over at Jake, but then went to Deirdre and knelt beside her. As Shandi took in the way that Deirdre's head sat, she knew the beast had killed Deirdre. No one could be twisted up in that way and survive. Cam put two fingers to her throat. The look on his face confirmed it. Deirdre would no longer present a threat.

He looked back at her. "Did the beast do this?"

Again, Shandi nodded. Cam moved to Jake and studied Shandi's blood-soaked shirt wrapped around Jake's arm. He looked into Jake's eyes and patted his cheek. "Stay with me, Jake. You'll be fine."

Cam shouted something into the radio on his shoulder, helped Jake to lay down on his back, then found a footstool in the kitchen that he used to prop up Jake's legs. Shandi felt immediately grateful that Cam had shown up when he had. She found herself unable to act. She wanted to go to Jake, to comfort him and hold his good hand, but instead she just sank to the floor and stared off into the distance. Cam would have to handle it for now.

Soon, EMTs flooded into her house. Most of them went to Jake, some to Deirdre, but one came to Shandi. She felt guilty taking the attention of someone who might be able to help Jake. She felt fine. She just needed to collect herself. She waved the EMT away and got back on her feet. He forced a blanket over her shoulders and she accepted it.

She watched as they gingerly removed her shirt from Jake's arm. She winced at the blood, unsure whether losing that much blood meant a death sentence. She wouldn't be able to get to Jake now. She could barely see him in the sea of medics. She didn't remember what Cam had ordered into his radio, but it seemed to have gotten every EMT in Rose Valley to her house.

One of the medics looked at Cam. "He's going to be fine. It looks bad, but it's mostly superficial."

Cam clapped him on the shoulder. "Thanks, Brian."

That didn't compute to Shandi. Jake looked far too weak for it to just be a superficial wound. Something drained his energy, and if not the gunshot wound, then...

The beast. Jake brought Billy to them, and most likely Jake saved her by sending Billy away. Could that have taken a toll? It seemed reasonable. Shandi felt an overwhelming sense of relief as she started to accept the EMT's promise. Jake would be fine. Only Deirdre would die tonight.

Cam stood up and disappeared into Shandi's house. One of the medics brought in a gurney and started strapping Jake to it. Healthy or not, Jake seemed destined for another visit to the Rose Valley emergency room. She would go with him, of course, and for that she would need a shirt.

She dropped the blanket on the floor and navigated around the hubbub. As she turned the corner to her bedroom, she almost ran directly into Cam's chest.

"Sorry. I didn't mean to scare you. Here," Cam said as he thrust one of her t-shirts towards her. She looked down at the faded green leprechaun on the front, trying to remember the last time she'd wore it. Maybe not since they had been married.

Shandi smiled despite the situation, and replied, "Thanks."

She turned around and slipped the shirt over her head as she walked. Cam followed and patted her on the back in an uncharacteristic show of comfort.

Cam called out, "Brian!"

One of the EMTs walked over. Cam put his hand on the young man's shoulder, stood to full height, then looked him straight in the eyes. "This is Jake's girlfriend. Make sure you keep her in the loop. I don't care what your stupid rules are. You treat her like his family, y'hear me?"

Brian nodded. "Yessir, Sheriff. You got it."

Cam nodded back and smiled. "Good. Thanks, Brian."

She expected Cam's reaction to be much less gracious, especially when he had arrived to her so scantily clad. But that had always been the way with Cam. When you needed him to come through—when it *really* mattered—he would never let you down. She too often forgot that about him.

Brian motioned for her to follow out to the ambulance, where she climbed into the back next to Jake. The back of the ambulance left little room for her to squeeze in, but she didn't mind. It was the least she could do.

As they rushed through the streets of Rose Valley, Shandi felt her wits returning to her. She thought about

Deirdre and expected to feel remorse or horror, but she didn't. She felt anger, then a brief flash of embarrassment, and then the resolute surety that Deirdre deserved what she got. Shandi smiled, content in the fact that Deirdre couldn't hurt Jake anymore, and that she wouldn't be able to convince anyone else that the beast couldn't be saved.

Billy recognized his name. Shandi would have bet her life on it. Their plan would work. They could find the humanity in him. They had to.

CHAPTER 38

The sun dropped low on the horizon, threatening to abandon Rose Valley and offering the last of its rays to illuminate the dying brown fields. Three vehicles pulled up to the schoolhouse, filled with a sheriff, a one-handed deputy, a reporter, a rancher, a quarterback, a cryptozoologist, and Jake. Though he spent the morning in a hospital room, Jake insisted that he be released. The superficial wound already felt better.

Cam shared everything he knew from Deirdre, leaving Jake wondering whether his arm owed its rapid recovery to the serum. He found it strangely unsettling to have an increased healing capacity; he worried that it would mean that he would live longer than those he loved and he would watch them all die. Dying of old age seemed incredibly far away at the moment, but death seemed to be increasingly common in Rose Valley of late.

The manhunt teetered on the edge of becoming a runaway train. Either they found the beast tonight, or someone else in town would. Jake didn't know if he could summon Billy again. The first time had been under duress and desperation in a last-ditch effort to save himself from Deirdre. Now the mission turned to saving Billy from himself. Shandi seemed certain that they could. Jake was doubtful.

The Sheriff had ordered some of his deputies to erect a cage in front of the schoolhouse. Shandi had convinced Karen and her father to act as bait. It seemed a reckless thing to do to Jake, but the cage provided at least some protection. It certainly wouldn't stop the beast, but it might buy them the time they needed to fill him full of tranquilizer darts.

Skylar boasted unearned confidence in his darts, but Miriam disagreed with his assessments of their efficacy. Through few words, it became clear that Miriam and Tanner would rather kill the beast as revenge for Cornelius. Both refused to participate in trying to turn the beast back to humanity without a backup plan of heavy weaponry.

Shandi and Jake insisted that Steve be armed with something more heavy duty than tranquilizers, but Skylar flatly refused. He controlled the good weapons, leaving them little recourse but to obey.

As they stepped out of the yellow jeep, Dub approached Steve and Jake with hushed tones. "Hey. I wanna show you something in the back."

Steve and Jake followed, as Cam insisted that Skylar inspect the workmanship of the cage. Pretending to need Skylar's approval provided a guaranteed way to ensure his cooperation. Jake sensed what Dub intended to show them. When they got to the back of the jeep, Dub opened the back and slid a large wooden crate towards them.

Dub popped the top as he spoke. "This is a CZ-550 with a .585 Gehringer cartridge. It'll shoot through a tank or bring down an elephant. Strongest weapon Mr. Brooks brought as far as I can tell. I don't care what that nutbag says. Take it. Now. Before he comes back."

Steve didn't ask any questions. Jake vaguely knew that Steve possessed no experience with a gun like that. Steve might be unable to hit his mark—especially on the first try. If he missed and riled up the beast, it might do more harm than good. Jake couldn't worry about that, though. His responsibility centered only on getting Billy there.

Steve took the gun and scurried off. Jake didn't know where Steve intended to set up shop, but the plan called for him choosing somewhere far enough away that the beast wouldn't immediately see him. Jake made a point of not paying attention to Steve's direction. The less he knew about Steve's location, the less likely he would be to accidentally draw the beast to Steve.

Dub put the top back on the box and made a show of shoving it into the very back of the cargo area, behind all the tranquilizer guns and other gear. Jake helped. Dub impressively piloted with just one hand, but it also slowed him down.

The two of them managed to get it situated just as Skylar came around the corner, his face beaming with excitement. "Ready to be a part of history? You will only be a footnote next to me, but being a footnote is better than not being part of it at all, right?"

Cam, Wes, and Shandi joined them. It seemed especially silly to bring Wes along, but he hunted Cam down and insisted in a foolish display of chivalry and pride. It displayed a sweet, grand gesture of devotion to Macy, but that didn't make it smart. Wes boasted a strong, able body, though, and he had been toying with guns his whole life. His acumen with a firearm would far out-class Jake's.

Skylar started unloading the tranquilizer guns, and Jake cringed every time he got near the empty rifle box. Even the mere movement of it might have alerted him that the gun no longer lived within. Luckily, Skylar never touched it.

Earlier in the day, Skylar held target practice for the townsfolk. Jake skipped because of his hospital stay, but presumably Dub, Cam, and Wes all took turns firing this weapon. There would be no room for mistakes. If Karen and her father could not calm the beast, the situation might get violent very quickly.

As each person took their weapon, Jake felt a warm brush of Shandi's hand against his. He took it as she leaned her head on his good shoulder. Always so full of confidence and surety, Jake sensed fear behind her bravado now. He admired her insistence that they try to find Billy in that creature.

Skylar asked, "Did the rancher already take his?"

Dub replied coolly, "Steve is his name. And yes. He's already setting up his position. Thought he should get a head start."

Skylar didn't seem to question it or even take a count of the guns that remained. Jake breathed a sigh of relief.

"Comms check. This is Steve," buzzed in Jake's ear. Cam had provided radios for each of them, tuned to a channel specifically for their party. Many of the townsfolk carried radios on various channels across Rose Valley. With any luck, none of them would tune to their channel.

Cam held the button on the black radio attached to his shoulder before speaking. "Coming in loud and clear. Over."

"All righty. I'm in position. Keep me posted," Steve's voice echoed again.

This time Jake smiled and pressed his button. "Ten-four, good buddy."

Cam gave him a stern look as he crossed past them and made his way to the front of the jeep. Shandi let out a soft giggle as she took the last tranquilizer gun from Skylar. Though Cam made it clear that shenanigans would not be tolerated tonight, Jake searched for anything to keep his mind light and loose. He worried that if he couldn't stay calm, he wouldn't be able to deliver.

In front of the jeeps and Suburban sat a single chair. Jake expected makeshift barricades, but none existed. Previous experience suggested they wouldn't stop the beast anyway, so Jake presumed that Cam decided that they would be pointless. It would have made Jake feel better, nonetheless.

To Jake, just sitting there felt cowardly compared to the heroics that the others geared up for, but he understood the importance. He didn't know how to shoot a gun with any accuracy, anyway, and some part of him didn't want to be responsible for hurting Billy. It felt like they barreled towards an incomplete solution. Was there another way?

Jake took his seat. Shandi walked up beside him and surveyed the scene. She waited for Cam to walk away, then leaned over to give Jake a deep, passionate kiss. She looked into his eyes.

"You've got this, Jake. We'll keep you safe." She lifted the gun up on her shoulder as she stood back up. "You've got action Barbie protecting you now."

Jake smiled as Shandi walked away. She laid her gun gently on the ground and walked towards the door of the schoolhouse. It seemed impossibly unlikely that Karen didn't already know of their arrival, but she still hid inside her house. Karen answered the door almost immediately, and though she stood too far away for Jake to see her face, her body language exuded fear.

He hadn't been there when Shandi told them all about Billy Hargrove. He wondered if Karen or her father had cried. He wondered if they even believed it. They must have, he supposed, or they wouldn't have played along. It seemed insane that they would have agreed to participate, but they resolutely strode out of their house anyway. People in Rose Valley tended to trust the sheriff's promises of safety.

Shandi took them to the cage and got them situated within. While Karen looked fearful, Jake noticed that her father did not. He looked proud and resolute.

Shandi returned to the line and picked up her gun again. Skylar and Cam exchanged looks, as a ringtone echoed into the night air. Cam fished his cell phone out of his pocket.

"Sheriff Donner here."

Jake could hear yelling on the other end before Cam responded, "Calm down, Ralph. What?"

Cam went silent for a few seconds, then his eyes went wide. He hung up the phone and turned towards Jake. "One of the teams ran into the beast. You gotta call him here, Jake. Now."

No pressure, though, Jake thought to himself. He closed his eyes and tried to recreate the steps he used at Shandi's house. He thought of the schoolhouse. He had seen it thousands of times in his life. He recalled every corner. Every rock. Every color. He thought of the door and the windows. He thought of the chimney that had once served as a bell tower in a former century.

He felt nothing as he thought about the schoolhouse. He recommitted himself and switched focus. He thought of Karen's kind face. He thought of Cam. Skylar. Wes. Dub. He thought of Shandi. He could picture her most vividly of all. He thought of the cage. Visualized its makeshift strength. He thought of the two yellow jeeps and Cam's ridiculous Suburban.

Still nothing. He turned his focus to Karen's father. He thought of the pride that the old man seemed to have at the prospect of seeing his father again. Jake thought of the emotions that must have been flooding through the old man's body as he waited patiently for a reunion that he thought would never come. Jake had no children, but he thought of his own strange protectiveness that he felt for Macy. He thought of the burgeoning love that he held for Shandi.

Then they hit him. The same gnarly, foreign emotions from before, but this time he expected it.

Billy drew near. Jake felt the overwhelming fear from last time, but the feelings grew into some deeper, more exotic emotion, perhaps one wholly uncommon to the human species. An emotion that could only be felt by someone who had been through the atrocities that Billy had seen.

Jake opened his eyes.

Billy remained silent as he approached. He walked slowly, hunched over and cautious. He glanced towards the five people with guns, but ignored them. He stopped a few feet from the cage and stared into it, clearly assessing the people inside. Jake wondered whether Billy had the wherewithal to detect a trap.

Billy took a few more steps. The old man started to visibly cry, causing Karen to kneel beside him and wrap her arms around his frail frame. Billy stood directly outside of the cage now. The old man pried Karen's arms off. He summoned all the strength left in his 78-year-old body, stood and walked to the side of the cage. He leaned against it opposite the beast, using the crisscrossed steel to support his weight.

"Dad?" he said, his voice labored with heavy breathing.

Billy cocked his head as if trying to understand what he heard. He reached out and brushed his fingers against the old man's, with a lighter touch than Jake would have thought possible. Jake felt Billy's confusion. He felt him trying to solve the enigma before him, trying to make sense of what surely felt impossible to him.

"Jun... ior," Billy forced out strenuously, as if he discovered talking for the first time. Jake heard gasps from the front line.

Shandi whispered, "It's working."

Jake steeled himself, preparing to use his mind to direct the beast away if he had to.

William Hargrove, Jr. sobbed now. Billy seemed confused by it at first, but then forced out, "Don't... cry."

The moment shattered as the beast howled unexpectedly. Jake jumped. Someone had shot the beast. A tranquilizer dart hung loosely in one of Billy's massive arms. Jake surveyed the scene. All eyes trained on Skylar, the idiot who'd pulled the trigger.

Billy charged them, eliciting a flurry of curse words and yelling. Jake closed his eyes and tried to force Billy away, but he could tell immediately that it wouldn't work. For the first time since he learned to feel Billy's emotions, he felt an overwhelming sense of anger. This is what Deirdre warned them about. Jake wouldn't be able to control him in this state.

Tranquilizer darts peppered Billy's chest now. Each shooter fired in turn as quickly as they could. Billy did not falter. He reached Wes first, as Wes scrambled up to run. The beast caught him by back of the shoulder and pushed him to the ground. Wes screamed in pain as he caught his weight with his hands.

Billy stood over Wes, breathing hard, and Cam suddenly appeared, hitting Billy in the neck with the butt of his gun. Billy shrugged it off and hit Cam in the chest hard, sending him flying backward, landing a few feet away with a thud. Miraculously, Cam held on to his gun.

The beast turned his eyes on the next closest target—Deputy Dub Higgins. Dub dropped his firearm. Jake stood as Skylar ran and jumped into the jeep. Shandi sprinted back to Karen and Junior.

Billy bent down and picked up Dub's gun. He snapped it in two, threw each half in a different direction and growled in Dub's face.

"Cam! No!" Jake heard Shandi scream.

Jake looked towards Cam who leveled the tranquilizer gun, prepared to fire again. As Jake's eyes followed the trajectory of the muzzle, however, he realized that the dart wouldn't hit Billy—Cam meant to shoot Jake.

"He can take it, Shandi. It won't kill him."

Shandi took off towards Cam. Jake froze, suddenly very tired. He didn't know what he should be doing or how to defuse the situation. Dub's life hung in imminent danger. Wes laid on the ground in pain. Would Jake being tranquilized have any effect on Billy? Jake decided that he needed to take the risk. In all likelihood, Jake could survive. The serum would provide him the extra boost he would need.

Jake nodded towards Cam. "Do it!"

Cam fired. Jake felt the dart pierce his chest. It stung a little, but the pain proved bearable. The effect of the tranquilizer went to work immediately. Jake dropped down to his knees. Shandi changed directions to intercept him, as Jake struggled to focus. Dub backed up slowly, but the beast did not pursue him.

As Jake fought to keep his eyes open, he witnessed Billy stumbling and scratching at his head. This wouldn't bring him down, but it confused him. Slowed him down. Maybe it would give them the time they needed to get away. Jake could do this last thing to save them.

Jake couldn't distinguish between his own emotions and that of Billy anymore. They became one and the same. He felt an overwhelming love for Junior that he vaguely knew emanated from elsewhere. He felt responsibility for those who would die, and the fear that he would never wake up. That he would never see Shandi again.

She made it to him just before he lost consciousness, tears streaming down her red face. He detected both sadness and anger.

"I'm sorry" was all he could think to say before losing track of everything around him.

CHAPTER 39

Shandi was panicked and exhausted. She didn't try to collect herself or fight. She just held Jake and cried. She blamed herself for the unconscious man in her arms. She focused on this plan so intently that she refused to accept any course of action that might outright kill Billy.

The tranquilizer dart seemed to have worked at least a little. Billy stumbled in a cloud of confusion. At first, he had held his head in his hands, but now he started lurching forward as if he could fight off the disorientation with action.

With the beast stunned, Shandi heard Cam in her ear. "Steve. Take him out."

Whatever unholy weapon Steve wielded boomed in the distance. Shandi didn't know where the bullet ended its trajectory, but Billy remained unscathed. Another shot fired. Another missed.

"Dammit," Steve shouted through the earpiece. "The kickback on this thing."

The gun blasted again, echoed almost immediately by another. A bullet struck Billy in the shoulder. He screamed in rage. Blood gushed out of a gaping hole, pouring down Billy's arm, pooling onto the ground in amounts that Shandi could barely stomach. Perhaps this gun would work.

"Um... That wasn't me that hit him," Steve said in her ear.

Billy fell to his knees and looked directly towards Shandi and Jake. In a surreal moment of clarity, Shandi watched Billy's head nod forward, meeting her eyes with purpose and determination. There was something new in his eyes now. Something resolute, but sorrowful. Did Billy want to die?

She looked around to see if there was anyone else nearby. Dub had cleared the area and taken shelter behind the Jeep. Cam scrambled upright, and ushered Wes to safety. She and Jake shared this moment alone with Billy. Her tears fell faster as she fought the overwhelming feeling of sadness that she felt for both Jake and Billy.

Studying the brutality of the bullet wound, Shandi waffled between hope that the gun might kill him, and fear that he would die before she could save him. His life must have been agonizingly painful. He had subsisted on murder and mayhem. That sort of unending madness would surely leave anyone hoping for an end to it all. She hadn't considered that before this moment. Perhaps more humanity could be found in killing Billy, rather than trying to save him.

"This is for Cornelius, asshole," rang into Shandi's ear, a voice filled with vitriol and hate. Miriam loved her brother, and would be underestimated no longer.

Another shot rang out. This one struck true, perfectly aimed. A huge hole opened up between the beast's eyes as he collapsed to the ground. Shandi watched his face as he went down, unsure whether she only hoped for the slightest hint of a smile that she saw on his face. The night went silent. Shandi strained to see if Billy's chest would rise or fall, but she couldn't tell. It seemed so cruel and unfair. Billy deserved a better outcome than this.

Focusing on Billy's breathing reminded her to also check Jake's. She found his wrist and tried to find a pulse. At first, she panicked. She felt nothing. But after adjusting her fingers, she felt a faint heartbeat. Asleep. But alive.

It seemed like minutes before anyone dared to come back out from the protection they had sought out. Shandi just held Jake and refused to let her eyes leave the beast. She expected Billy to wake up at any moment, unable to believe that he was no longer a threat.

Cam drew up the courage to check first, as always. He approached Billy and put his fingers to his neck. They waited in silence for him to finish. When he stood up, he breathed deeply. It looked as if he might collapse from exhaustion right there.

"I think he might actually be dead," he said.

Shandi sniffled, trying to regain her composure. She felt a strange mix of happiness and sadness. She so desperately wanted all of this to be over.

Shandi startled as Cam pulled his handgun from its holster and yelled, "Stop right there."

In the distance, Miriam and Tanner approached. They both held massive guns. They stopped at the sheriff's insistence and set the guns on the ground. Once they had, Cam relaxed and let his arm fall to his side. Miriam and Tanner continued their approach.

From a different direction came Steve. He also carried a massive gun, but Cam took no action to stop him. Eventually, the three of them convened on the beast with Cam. Miriam kicked Billy's body in the side. Shandi wanted to protest—to defend Billy—but she remained quiet, relinquishing any control she desired to have over the situation.

One of the doors on the jeep opened. Skylar stepped out. He looked calm and collected now, with no hint of the cowardice he'd displayed mere moments ago. He did not approach Billy's body, though, belying the composure he feigned.

"Miriam! How dare you! Do you realize what you've done?"

Miriam's eyes burned as she met Skylar's gaze. "He was your son. And you didn't even care. You just wanted to capture your prize."

In a smooth and quick motion, Miriam snatched the gun out of Steve's hand, braced herself and fired it directly into Billy's back, roughly where his heart would be. Blood flew back up and splattered those nearby. She threw the gun into the hard dirt.

"Enjoy your mountain of flesh," Miriam said as she walked off. Tanner followed.

CHAPTER 40

The crowd buzzed with excitement. New mayors didn't often receive so much fanfare, but this day offered a particularly auspicious occasion. One and a half years had ticked by since the beast tore through Rose Valley, an incident that most residents had been able to put behind them. On the surface, at least. A great number of them seemed to have developed a strange, unexpected pride in having overcome the adversity.

Though he showed no excitement for the inauguration, Jake insisted that they attend anyway. He and Cam would never be friends, but Jake still voted for him when the time came. Shandi agonized in the voting booth forever. Jake never asked who she voted for.

Arrowhead cooperated once Deirdre implicated them. They insisted that she acted alone without authorization to use the seeker serum and assured the Sheriff's Department that all vestiges of the project would be destroyed. Jake harbored doubts.

Billy's remains had been cremated. He would certainly not be coming back now. Since Arrowhead maintained that the serum was a misunderstood drug, Jake didn't know whether there would be any long-term side effects. With Billy dead, though, the nightmares had abated.

The crazy story about the immortal World War II soldier had made the rounds on the internet for a few days, but the pain of it all only lived on in a select few. It was just one more weird government experiment to throw on the pile, ripe for conspiracy theorists to pick apart and blame for other, unrelated things. Jake suspected that there was a lab somewhere looking into it, but the official response insisted that it was a failed experiment that would never be revisited.

Jake and Shandi stood holding hands, waiting for Cam to take the stage in front of the city limit sign. The faded red billboard that previously pictured cheetahs and giraffes now sat shrouded in a large black tarp. Jake felt uneasy at the sorts of things that might adorn the sign now.

Shandi's phone rang. She let go of Jake's hands and answered it.

"It's Macy," she said to Jake as she tapped the answer button. "Hey, baby."

Jake strained to hear Macy's voice on the other end, but only managed to pick up faint murmurs. Any hints as to the conversation only came when Shandi spoke again. "I know, right? The man has good tastes."

Shandi held her left hand out in front of her as she answered. The late autumn sun danced off the diamond on her ring finger.

"No, it's okay. I understand. You're a big college girl now," Shandi said into her phone.

After a moment, she asked, "How're Miriam and Tanner?"

Jake spotted Karen across the crowd. He tapped Shandi on the shoulder and whispered, "I'm going to go say hi to Karen."

Shandi nodded, as Jake snaked his way through the crowd. When Karen saw him, her eyes teared up. She took his hand with both of hers. "Jake. It's good to see you."

Though he found it awkward, Jake pulled her in and wrapped his arms around her in a hug. "I didn't get a chance to talk to you at the funeral. I'm sorry about your father."

Karen backed away from his embrace and dabbed her face with the back of her hand. "Thanks, Jake. He was ready to go. We really appreciate what you did for him. Seeing his father one last time. It meant a lot, regardless of the outcome."

Though he wanted to be sensitive, Jake's curiosity got the better of him. "How's the lawsuit going?"

"Oh, you know lawyers," Karen said with a dismissive wave. "They won't let me talk about it. But there's hope that some good might come out of all this. It's hard to stay strong, though. Some days I just want to give up on all of it."

"Don't give up. Billy. Your dad. Your whole family needs this."

Karen smiled, giving Jake the distinct impression that she was already nearing the end of her rope. He could relate. He'd been talking to a lawyer about a lawsuit of his own, but Arrowhead had worked hard to pin as much blame on Deirdre as they could, and their lawyers had far more resources than he. As indignant as he had been at one time, each day stole away a little more of his resolve.

A hush fell on the crowd as Mayor Cam Donner took the stage. He wore a suit instead of a police uniform. He had abandoned his mustache in favor of a clean shave, his hair exposed without a hat and lightly tousled by the wind. Though no smaller than he had been as Sheriff, he seemed more agile and slippery than before. Jake respected the help that Cam offered when they needed it the most, and he knew that Cam would be inextricably linked to him via Shandi for the rest of his life, but he still found Cam's desire for approval and power unsettling.

Jake said his goodbyes with Karen and made his way back to Shandi's side as Dub Higgins followed Cam onstage. Dub's neatly pressed khakis broadcasted an attention to detail that the previous sheriff lacked. His hand had long been out of the cast, but his fingers still curled up in an unnatural position still. It didn't seem to faze him, and it certainly hadn't stopped him from being elected sheriff after Cam had resigned to run for mayor.

"I gotta go, baby. Your dad's about to give his speech." She paused before continuing, "No. I'm sure he understands. You're far away. You can't come back for every little thing. Okay. I'll call you later. Bye!"

Cam smiled into the crowd, considerably more adept at public speaking than he had been over a year ago. "Citizens of Rose Valley. I am deeply honored to have been elected as your mayor."

The crowd erupted into cheers, claps, and hollers. It was more noise than a crowd that small should have been able to produce. Despite Miriam being the one that had taken down the beast, Cam had received the credit. To the townspeople, he saved Rose Valley from certain destruction.

"We have been through a lot. I know we have. And we stood strong. We were not deterred by our adversity. We grew from it. We are stronger now. We embraced it."

On cue, the black tarp on the sign behind Cam fell away to reveal a new, mostly black sign. Two yellow serpentine eyes floated among a field of stars. A silhouette of the city sat below. Cursive letters adorned the top with *Welcome to Rose Valley,* leading into the bottom block letters spelling out: *Home of the Beast.*

Cheers filled the air again. Jake shuddered. Shandi looked equally horrified. They felt alone in a sea of people. They had both grown up in Rose Valley. Neither of them really wanted to leave, but it seemed inevitable to Jake in that moment that they would have to. The agony of living in a town that glorified his pain would eventually be too much for him to handle.

Jake felt a clap on his back and turned to find Steve next to him. Cory appeared beside Steve and said, "Well, this is crazypants."

Jake just nodded, as Cam continued, "Wes. Come on up."

Wes Morris walked up on the stage sporting an all-black football jersey, the numbers crisp and sharp. Rose Valley lost out on going to state the previous year, primarily because Wes shattered one of his wrists when the beast attacked him. Without football, he'd chosen to skip college entirely and stay in Rose Valley to work on his father's ranch. Macy broke up with him when he gave up on his future.

Cam motioned to Wes. "This is the look of your new football team—The Rose Valley Beasts!"

More cheers. Despite a century of being the Rose Valley Jaguars, now they would play as the Beasts. Just like that, the entire identity of a town had shifted.

"We'll also be renovating the football facilities with state-of-the-art tech. The city council voted unanimously to rename the field to the Bernard Jones Memorial Stadium!"

Cam had really pulled out all the stops to ingrain himself with the townspeople. Jake agreed with this one, though. Bernard would have loved nothing more than to have become synonymous with football in Rose Valley.

"Now a few words from a good friend of Rose Valley—Skylar Brooks!"

Again, more clapping as Skylar took the stage. He looked exactly as before, except Miriam and Tanner didn't flank him this time. He stood alone.

Skylar spoke into the microphone. "Rose Valley inspired me with its bravery. You were all a pleasure to work with. I regret that we weren't able study the beast, but we did the best we could on that fateful night."

Shandi made a face that Jake fully understood the meaning of. Skylar contributed nothing to putting an end to the nightmare except for having sired Miriam. In fact, if not for his zealotry, they might have had a real shot at saving Billy instead of killing him.

Skylar continued, "Today I am proud to announce that next January, I will be opening a new cryptozoology museum in Rose Valley—*The Skylar Brooks Center for Cryptozoological Research.* It will revolutionize the field, and you will all be a part of it!"

After a lifetime of not really finding any monsters, it came as no surprise that Skylar would latch on to the one time he had finally found one. Billy was hardly a cryptozoological discovery, but such details didn't stop Skylar from capitalizing on the horror to further his own fame.

Steve let out a sigh. "Seriously? I don't know if I can take this anymore. I'll catch you guys later."

Steve and Cory disappeared into the crowd, leaving Jake and Shandi suddenly more alone. Jake looked at her and she looked back. Everything drowned away. It didn't matter what Cam or Skylar did. It didn't matter if the Rose Valley mascot changed from jaguars to "beasts." All of that presented only a distraction. He and Shandi would build a beautiful life together, and that's what mattered the most.

Without thinking about it, Jake said, "Let's just go. Let's leave Rose Valley. Let them have their circus."

She looked apprehensive, surely hesitant to leave her home. Jake immediately felt bad for even suggesting it, realizing that he asked an unfair sacrifice of her. "Nevermind. Silly idea."

She took both of his hands, tip-toed up for a kiss, then melted into a hug. Jake felt so happy and so comfortable in that moment. He didn't know what would become of Rose Valley, but at least he had her.

Shandi murmured from his chest, but he couldn't make out what she said. She must have realized it, because she unentangled herself from his grasp, leaned back, looked deep into his eyes, and nodded.

"Yeah. Let's do it."

ACKNOWLEDGEMENTS

Whenever you read this part of the book (for those few who do), it always starts with basically the same sentiment—writing and publishing a book is hard! Way harder than it sounds. I'd like to thank the team at Evolved Publishing for getting this across the finish line. I couldn't have done it without the help of Mike Robinson, Richard Tran, and Dave Lane (aka Lane Diamond).

To my mom, who took up the mantle of my very first champion, even when my stories made no sense.

To my wife, who didn't laugh too hard when I told her I wanted to focus on writing a book. Her support made it all possible.

To my cat, Havok, because he always listened when I read him my rough drafts.

To my grandmother, who always gave me unfettered access to her collection of Time Life's *Mysteries of the Unknown* series, allowing me to warp my mind with modern day fairy tales of scary monsters.

To my high school English teacher, Mrs. Hart. Though I always fancied writing, it was she who convinced me that I could be good at it.

To my beta readers—Allison, Tex, Mistie—thanks for helping me hone in on what the book eventually became.

To all the people who influenced the characters: Steve, Denise, William, Holly, Jason, Dub, Cody. You might not see yourself in these pages, but some kernel of you made it in.

And lastly, to Glen Rose, Texas—the real Rose Valley. Growing up in such a small town is a special gift, and I will always be grateful for all the unique experiences it afforded me.

ABOUT THE AUTHOR

J.P. Barnett grew up in a tiny Texas town where the list of possible vocations failed to include published author. In second grade, he worked harder than any other student to deliver a story about a tiger cub who singlehandedly saved the U.S. Military, earning him a shiny gold star and a lifelong appreciation of telling a good story.

Fast forwarding through decades of schooling and a career as a software engineer, J.P. Barnett stepped away from it all to get back to his first real passion. Years of sitting at a keyboard gifted him with some benefit, though, including blazing fast typing hands and a full tank of creativity.

As a child, J.P. consumed any book he could get his hands on. The likes of Stephen King, Michael Crichton, and Dean Koontz paved the bookshelves of his childhood, providing a plethora of fantastical and terrifying tales that he read way too early in life. Though the effect these books had on his psyche could be called into question, these masters of storytelling managed to warp his mind in just the perfect way to spin a fun yarn or two.

J.P. currently resides in San Antonio with his wife and hellion of a cat, both of whom look at him dubiously with some frequency.

For more, please visit J.P. Barnett online at:
Website: www.JPBarnett.com
Twitter: @JPBarnett
Facebook: JPBarnett.Author
Instagram: JPBarnett.Author

WHAT'S NEXT?

THE KRAKEN OF CAPE MADRE
Lorestalker - 2
by
J.P. Barnett

Spring break will never be the same after a legendary creature rises from the depths.

It's been almost two years, but the nightmares still haunt Miriam Brooks—grisly images of her brother being slaughtered. A relaxing Spring Break at the beach seems like a good way to put some distance between her and the troubling past, but paradise shatters when she saves a tourist from something lurking beneath the waves.

Soon, she's on the trail of a sea creature from the legends of Vikings and Pirates. The fishermen of Cape Madre tell tales for the right price, and Miriam quickly learns of a string of disappearances all related to this mysterious monster.

The cops and the coast guard are meant to handle the crimes of men, but Miriam's been trained to find the creatures of lore—creatures like this. Pulled back into the life she wants to forget, Miriam is the last line of defense between man and myth.

CPSIA information can be obtained
at www.ICGtesting.com
Printed in the USA
LVHW031611200222
711583LV00002B/245